Author Note

For the last four years my youngest son has spent part of his summers volunteering on the Scottish island of Oronsay. The first time he returned home he told me all about the Vikings on the west coast of Scotland, and how the Viking fleet had been based on Colonsay. I was intrigued, and wanted to do some more research. In September 2014 I was lucky enough to spend a week on Islay and Jura as my husband wanted to go whisky-tasting. The weather, contrary to all expectations, was blue skies and sunshine the entire time. I had a thoroughly good time and became more determined than ever to write a Viking romance set on the west coast of Scotland.

It took me a little time to get it right, but here it is.

As ever, I do hope you enjoy reading Sigurd and Liddy's story as much I did writing it.

I love getting comments from readers and can be reached at michelle@michellestyles.co.uk, or through my publisher, or on Facebook or Twitter: @michellelstyles.

SOLD TO THE
VIKING WARRIOR

Michelle Styles

This is a work of fiction. Names, characters, places, locations and
incidents are purely fictional and bear no relationship to any real
life individuals, living or dead, or to any actual places, business
establishments, locations, events or incidents. Any resemblance is
entirely coincidental.

Published in Great Britain 2017
by Mills & Boon, an imprint of HarperCollins*Publishers*
1 London Bridge Street, London, SE1 9GF

© 2017 Michelle Styles

ISBN: 978-0-263-92560-9

Our policy is to use papers that are natural, renewable and
recyclable products and made from wood grown in sustainable
forests. The logging and manufacturing processes conform to the
legal environmental regulations of the country of origin.

Printed and bound in Spain
by CPI, Barcelona

Born and raised near San Francisco, California, **Michelle Styles** currently lives near Hadrian's Wall with her husband, a menagerie of pets and occasionally one of her three university-aged children. An avid reader, she became hooked on historical romance after discovering Georgette Heyer, Anya Seton and Victoria Holt. Her website is michellestyles.co.uk and she's on Twitter and Facebook.

Visit the Author Profile page
at millsandboon.co.uk for more titles.

To my loyal readers,
who asked for more Viking-set romances.

Chapter One

AD 873—Islay, Viking-controlled Alba. Modern-day Scotland.

'No good giving me that reproachful look of yours, Coll. I made a promise, so we have to go, even if I'd rather be anywhere else but there.' Eilidith gathered her thin woollen cloak tighter about her body and tried to ignore the biting cold while her wolfhound padded softly beside her.

In the half-light before dawn, Liddy could make out the Northman stronghold in the distance and, beyond the forbidding wooden walls, the purple-grey Paps of Jura rose. Appearances were deceptive. While she expected to arrive before the assembly day, Liddy knew she had at least a full day's hard walk in front of her. She had refused to travel in a boat since the accident which killed her young twins, Keita and Gilbreath.

Behind her, the footsteps which had been keeping pace with her for the last few miles stilled.

Liddy reached down and grabbed her wolfhound's collar. Her mother had objected to her taking Coll, even to the point of calling her by her proper name, Eilidith, and reminding her that she was a lady of the Cennell Fergusa, not an urchin without a noble kindred. Liddy had insisted and her mother had given way as she often did these days, commenting as Liddy left that for once she sounded like her old passionate Eilidith, the one who had vanished when her husband died.

Liddy rolled her eyes and continued walking. Her old self had vanished long before the day she heard of Brandon's demise. That self had ceased to be when her children drew their final rattling breaths and her heart had shattered into a thousand pieces.

Liddy reached down and stroked the dog's ears. Coll leant into her and gave a reassuring nuzzle of her hand.

In the aftermath of Islay's final fall to the Northmen, outlaws roamed the woods and desperate men were prepared to do desperate things. However, even a desperate man would think twice when confronted with a full-grown wolfhound. Coll's head came up to her chest. He had a scar running down his nose, a legacy from a tumble he took as a puppy, rather than a fight, but it gave him a fearsome appearance that made most people and dogs avoid him. But it made Liddy love him more.

She, too, had a disfigured face—a birthmark decorated the lower part of her jaw. When she'd been small and children teased her, her grandmother, her *seanmhair*, had declared her kissed by an angel at birth and that she'd bring good luck to the Cennell Fergusa. However, her late husband had considered the mark ugly and his mistress had declared her cursed at birth. After the twins died, she knew that woman had spoken the truth—she bore a curse. Her husband had even sworn in church, risking his immortal soul. Rather than risking the whispers, she shunned people and had become a virtual recluse, but now she had no choice—she had to act.

'We can do this, can't we, Coll? We can free my father and brother. Lord Ketil's promise to my father must mean more than empty words.'

Coll gave a soft woof and nudged her hand in agreement, as if he believed the words were truth rather than noise to fill the silence and bolster her flagging courage.

Liddy squared her shoulders. No one was going to stop her. She would get her father and brother released. There had been a misunderstanding. Unlike her late husband, her father had sworn an oath of allegiance to the Northman overlord at the first opportunity. To protect his people and the land he'd been entrusted with by his father, he swore. Peace brought its own prosperity and it was the land which mattered. Cennell Fergusa had to endure on this land. It was in their blood and sinew.

Her hand balled into a fist. Even the Northmen in their great fortress had to have some sort of honour. They, too, had laws and a king. The Northern jaarl simply had to be reminded of his obligations. He would see it was in his best interest to hold fast to the laws. He wanted peace and prosperity, not war with the islanders. And there was a tiny part of her which hoped that her *seanmhair* was right and she would bring good luck to the family.

'You walk with a determined step and a strong purpose,' a faintly accented voice said behind her, making her jump. 'Most people would shun this place at this hour.'

She half-turned and saw the same cloaked figure she'd been ignoring for the better part of an hour. The man had started following her a good mile or two back. He was tall and his face was hidden. There was no stoop in his back or shuffle in his step. Or rather not when he considered no one was watching. Under her gaze he seemed to shrink and hunch his shoulders as if he was attempting to seem less than he was.

She forced a steadying breath. No need to be frightened of a solitary man, not with Coll by her side and a knife stuck in her belt.

'What business is it of yours?' she asked and advanced another step on the path. She was glad that her remaining gold necklace was safely sewn into the hem of her gown. Nowhere that any robber would think to look. It was not much, but her mother had insisted. If she could not appeal to the Northman's honour and respect for the law, she could buy her father's and brother's freedom. Liddy had agreed more out of hope than expectation. There was no room for error. She knew what would happen if she failed, but she had to do something. 'How do you know where I go?'

'Unusual to encounter a lone woman on the road at this hour.' His gaze took in her cloak. 'Particularly one of high birth.'

'I've business at the Northman's fortress.' Liddy resisted the temptation to pull the hood across her face and hide the curse. Instead she curled her hand about her knife and threw back her shoulders. Maybe the stranger would take one look and decide a cursed woman was not worth bothering with.

Coll, sensing her mood, raised his hackles and gave a low growl.

The man stepped back a few steps and held up his hands. Coll flopped down at her feet, but kept a wary eye on the man.

'You are brave or foolhardy in the extreme going near that fort without a protector. Do you know how they treat attractive women?'

'My dog is my champion. He dislikes strangers, particularly Northmen who begin talking without a proper introduction,' she said between gritted teeth. Attractive? Hadn't he seen the mark on her face? 'Even the Northmen at the fort have to obey their own laws.'

'It has been some time since I have encountered anyone like you. Such bravery in the face of over-whelming odds. Unusual for a woman,' he said, slowly lowering his hands and risking a step closer. Coll gave another low growl.

'Flattery fails to work with me. I know what I am.'

His face took on a guarded expression. 'We both travel in the same direction. What is wrong with a little conversation to pass the journey? Have you considered how you will get into the stronghold to put your petition? It is well guarded these days. They don't just allow anyone in and lone unprotected women rarely emerge.'

'Have you been there recently? Is it true that they keep the entrance guarded, only allowing people in at certain times?' she blurted out.

The stranger tilted his head to one side and Liddy caught an intense blue stare before his hood obscured his features. 'The gate is locked at owl-light each night. They do not allow anyone in or out. During the day, everyone entering or leaving is searched. Thorbin, Lord Ketil's current repre-sentative, is cautious. There is resentment on the island.'

'You are one of the Northmen,' she said, hear-ing the faint traces of the heavy Northern accent, but laced with the slight lilt of her native tongue. Normally Northmen growled their words, making it difficult to understand them. 'But you speak my language better than most. Unusual.'

'You are a Gael.' He looked her slowly up and down, from the bottom of her travel-stained gown to the top of her couver-chief from which a few tendrils of hair kept escaping. Again she resisted the urge to hide the birthmark. 'Most Gaels take better care of their women rather than simply pro-viding them with a large dog before sending them to bargain with one of the most notorious men in the North. Have you considered what he will do to you when you lose?'

Liddy kept her hand on Coll. He couldn't have

guessed about the necklace, could he? Using her knife on him would be possible, but he would have to be closer. She would have one chance and the point where his throat met his shoulder was her best option. The quickest way, according to her late husband, who had liked to boast of his expertise in battle.

Her body went numb at the thought of killing a man, any man, but particularly this one who seemed so full of life.

'Most men would think twice about tangling with my dog,' she said instead. 'They will let me go once I've finished my business. They will be men of honour. They will keep the promise Lord Ketil made to my father.'

The words rang even more hollow to her ears than before. But if she lost this slender hope, she might as well turn back. She had to believe this miracle was possible and that she lived for some reason beyond a cruel joke by God. It had come to her that perhaps she had been spared so that she could do this thing—rescue her father and brother and somehow atone for her part in the twins' death. She had tried so hard to rescue them.

'I've seen dogs die before. A pity. He seems like a good and faithful animal.'

'I've seen men back away from him before.' Liddy wrenched her mind from the day shortly after the twins' deaths when she'd encountered the Northmen on the track which ran along the headland. Coll had guarded her well that day.

The man shrugged and Liddy became aware of the strength of his shoulders. 'You throw them a bit of meat and they are happy. Instant friends. Dogs have a simpler view of life.'

Liddy crossed her arms. This Northman might think he knew dogs, but he didn't know Coll. 'Not my dog. My dog distrusts strangers, Northmen in particular.'

His eyes flashed an intense blue. 'I'm hardly one to refuse a challenge.'

'You may try, but you are bound for disappointment. I know my dog. He is an excellent judge of character.'

He reached into his pouch and held out a piece of dried meat. A slight keening noise filled the air.

Coll, the traitor, took it from the man's fingers with only a heartbeat of hesitation. The man reached down and stroked Coll behind the ears. Coll completed his surrender by lolling against the man.

'Not all Northmen.' The voice slid over her skin as if he had stroked her hair instead of Coll's ears. 'But maybe he senses that I could be a friend and an ally. You would do well to trust your dog's instincts if he is such a good judge of character.'

'I stand corrected and it is duly noted. I will not make that mistake again,' she said through gritted teeth. Anyone would think that she was some sort of maiden from a convent who had never experienced men and their ways, rather than a widow. 'Coll, come here.' To the man, she said, 'I will bid you good morning and be on my way. I've urgent business with Lord Thorbin, who will uphold the law once the truth of the matter is explained.'

Coll instantly bristled as if embarrassed by his actions and slunk away from his new friend. Liddy caught his collar and began to walk away with determined steps.

The man seemed to take the hint and let her go without a protest, but she felt his eyes watching her with a speculative glint.

Liddy hurried her pace, rounded several bends and went off on a different track. The trees were closer and the air silent. She turned her head to one side and her feet faltered. Trees with bodies hanging from them like overripe fruit blocked her way. She wanted to run, but her legs refused to work. Instinctively, she turned away as her stomach revolted. Coll began to bark in earnest.

'Lord Thorbin sacrifices women to the gods,' the man said behind her in a low voice. Coll's howls immediately ceased. 'He takes positive pleasure in it. He never does anything important without making one human sacrifice. Are you still certain about continuing on with your quest?'

'How do you know it was him?'

His eyes became narrow slivers of blue ice. 'I've seen his work before.'

'And the women? Who were they?' Liddy whispered, pulling Coll closer. A distinct shiver ran down her spine. This man was intimately acquainted with Lord Thorbin's work.

'Slaves who were freed before they were sacrificed. Lone women without families to protect them or women whose families had abandoned them.' His mouth twisted. 'Sacrifices must be made with a free will, lest the gods get angry. How much choice they actually had...well...they were slaves. Sometimes there are worse things than dying free.'

Liddy put her hands on her knees and tried to breathe. The heathen Northmen might believe such things, but she knew it to be false. Those women were murdered for no good reason. How could she appeal to the honour of a man who murdered women like that? Her idea seemed more and more naïve, but she had to do something. Pretending her mother could cope was wrong. The barren fields were a testament to that. 'I thought those were tales from the priests to scare people.'

'Do you want me to cut one down and show

you? Do you truly want to risk disturbing the dead?'

Liddy regarded the grove again and one of the bodies seemed to reach towards her. A scream welled up inside her. She wanted to run but her feet had turned to blocks of stone. 'I…I…'

He grasped her elbow and turned her firmly from the gruesome sight. The simple touch did much to calm her. 'Where I grew up, people normally avoided these sorts of places. Stay on the well-trodden path. It takes longer, but mingling with the dead is rarely a good idea.'

'I can see why some might go that way, but my time is short.' Liddy wrenched her arm away. Didn't he know that she had no luck left to lose? 'The dead are incapable of harming anyone. I must reach the stronghold in good time for the assembly. My voice will be heard. It will not be said that I was turned away because I arrived late. Going through that grove saves precious time.'

Her heart thumped as she said the words. She had to hope they were true. To take the other way would add another half-day to her journey and she had to get to the stronghold in time for the assembly. She couldn't do anything for the dead, but she could do something for the living.

'What do you plan on doing with this dog while you speak with Lord Thorbin?' He held out his hand to Coll again who gave it a quick lick. 'Thorbin has as little time for dogs as he does for women. He has disliked dogs like yours ever since he was a boy and a dog bit him. Of course, Thorbin had beaten the dog with a stick, so it was understandable.'

Liddy abruptly stopped and turned back to the man. He knew far too much about Lord Thorbin's habits for her liking, but he also did not appear to fear him like so many did on this island. 'Is it any business of yours?'

He shrugged. 'I like your dog. He has character, but such a dog might be used as a weapon to attack Lord Thorbin. Thorbin might use you bringing your dog as an excuse to take you into slavery and to put the dog to death. What better way to get the gold he requires than to acquire slaves?'

She tucked her chin more firmly into her shoulder, the better to hide her cursed mark. In her ignorance, she'd nearly condemned Coll to death. 'But you know of a way that might work, one which wouldn't lead to Coll's death.'

'There might be, if you are brave enough. We could be allies, you and I.' He jerked his head towards the trees. 'Better than ending up somewhere where you most definitely don't want to be.'

A prickle crept down her back. She tried to

dismiss it. It was no more than her priest or her mother had warned her before she set out yesterday.

Liddy raised her chin and repeated the same speech she had given her concerned mother. 'I will succeed. I will make Lord Thorbin listen to reason. His overlord's sacred oath must have meaning. He will honour it or be damned in the eyes of his war band.'

The man stilled. 'Do you have a token of Lord Ketil's esteem? Or merely the words of your father, who is now imprisoned?'

'Yes, I do.' Liddy dug into the pouch which hung from her belt and withdrew the ring her father had forgotten when he left home. 'A ring Ketil Flatnose personally put on my father's finger.'

She took quiet satisfaction from the way the man leant forward and the intensity of his gaze increased. That would teach him to mock her.

'Why did your father leave it at home rather than taking it with him?'

'His fingers had grown too fat and he took it off months ago.' She placed it back in the pouch. 'In his haste to rescue my brother, he must have forgotten about it, but I remembered and searched for it. Our priest told me that it would not make a difference, but I know it will.'

'You chose not to listen to your priest. My

mother was a Gael and I know how headstrong you Gaelic women can be.' He gave Coll an absent stroke on the head. 'A pity, but it will take more than willpower to defeat Thorbin and get your family back.'

Pity from him? From a Northman? What sort of fool did he take her for? She knew what form a Northman's pity often took. She'd seen the burnt farms and the slain men. And then there were the *sgeula-steach tana adhair*, the women who had vanished without a trace. Fewer now that the Northmen had control of most of the islands, but every year one or two were still stolen.

'So your father was a Northman. Your poor mother,' she said instead. 'She is the one I pity.'

He tilted his head to one side. 'Why do you say that?'

'I presume she was born free, captured and remained a slave to the end of her days.'

'You know nothing about it.' His voice dripped ice. 'You are the one jumping to conclusions. Perhaps I should leave you to your well-deserved fate, instead of trying to help you.'

'But it is what happens. The women are taken and no one sees them again. These woods, hills and fields are chiselled in my soul. I will return to them a free woman. I will not die in a foreign land or become like one of those bodies in the wood.' Liddy tightened her grip on Coll and hoped the man would overlook the trembling in her hand. She knew what happened to women when they were taken by Northmen, and how some had escaped after a ransom was paid. The necklace was something to bargain with and could get her home, if the ring failed. 'I will not be a slave nor will any of my family.'

'All for a matter of honour?'

'If you like. We Gaels take our honour very seriously.' She belatedly put her hand over her birthmark, her badge of shame.

'My mother proclaimed she was the daughter of a king.' His mouth twisted. 'I later learnt that nearly every second woman makes such a claim.'

'What happened to her?' Liddy let out a breath. She was glad that she hadn't told him of her parentage and that her father used to be a king before the Northmen came and settled. Islay had many kings then, too many as they always quarrelled and far too many men had died.

'She was freed before she breathed her last.'

The impulse to ask if her body had hanged from a tree in a sacred grove threatened to overwhelm her, but one look at his face made the words die on her lips. For once she swallowed her words. 'Who freed her?'

'I did. I freed her from all torment. It was what

she desired most in the world.' He put his hand on his sword and his cloak fell away from his face. The shaft of dawn light which pierced the mist showed her companion to be one of the handsomest men she had ever seen. His golden hair fell to his shoulders, his lips were full, but his other features were hard. His eyes betrayed a steely determination. Here was no ordinary warrior. There was something about the way he moved and the set of his jaw. He was used to being obeyed. A leader of men.

'Who are you?' she asked and then regretted it. Her late husband always proclaimed that her tongue would get her into trouble, one of his milder rebukes. 'If I agree to join forces with you, will you actually help me instead of lulling me into a false promise?'

She hated that hope grew in her breast. She should know by now that these things only happened in the bards' tales. There was no one she could depend on, particularly not a cloaked Northman. Thrice cursed, her brother-in-law had called her after Brandon's funeral. Meeting this Northman, rather than having an uneventful journey, proved it.

'Give me your name,' she said when he continued to stare at her. 'Your true name, rather than a ridiculous nickname like the Northmen often go by. Give it or we shall never be allies.'

'Sigurd Sigmundson, a traveller like yourself who hungers after justice.' He tugged his cloak, hiding his features again. His cloak was more threadbare than hers. And yet somehow she couldn't believe it was his. There was the way that he moved. And she had a glimpse of the sword underneath the cloak. It was far too fine for a sell-sword to use.

'You mean to pass into the compound un-noticed. That is why you are wearing that old cloak,' she exclaimed. 'I mean you must be, other-wise you would row your dragon boat up Loch Indaal and land beside the stronghold.'

Sigurd Sigmundson reached towards her. Liddy took a step backwards and half-stumbled over a root. Coll gave a low rumbling in the back of his throat and Sigurd's hand instantly dropped to his side.

'Why would I want to conceal my identity?' he asked, tilting his head to one side. She caught the sweep of his lashes and again the piercing blue stare.

'Because the other way is the surest way to end up stuffed in a barrel and sent back to Ketil. Even where we live, we've heard rumours about how Thorbin treats his enemies.' She covered her mark with her hand. 'My late husband was a warrior. You move with a warrior's gait, not a beggar's. If you wish other people not to notice, then you should shuffle rather than stride. Free advice.'

He bowed his head. 'What are you going to do with this knowledge of yours? Do you wish me ill?'

'As long as you mean me no harm, it is none of my concern. Once my business with Thorbin is satisfactorily concluded, you may do as you will with him.' She paused. 'I, Eilidith of Cennell Fergusa, have reasons for wishing this. He is no friend to my family. But I go first.'

He was silent for a long while. She felt his gaze roam over her body. It had been a long time since a man had looked at her in that appraising way. She tightened the cloak about her figure, hoping it hid most of her curves. She had few illusions about her beauty. Her figure was passable, her mouth too large and her hair was far too red. Flame-coloured, Brandon had called it when he courted her. One of his few compliments.

'I have come to complete the task Lord Ketil set me,' he said with a wave of his hand. 'This task comes before your quest, Eilidith of Cennell Fergusa. Thorbin answers for his crimes and then you find your father and brother. Provided they haven't been executed as traitors.'

White-hot anger flashed through her. Who was he to condemn them? He had no idea of her story or how her father had sought to protect their clan from the worst of the invaders. 'My father gave his pledge to Lord Ketil Flatnose the first time he travelled to this island. My brother was but a mewling babe at the time. The tribute has always been paid. No one has ever accused my father of treason…until now.'

Liddy shook her head. She refused to think about the pitiful state of the fields, barely tended in the summer sun. According to her mother, her father had hidden the seed and the gold before he left. Without fresh seed, they stood no chance of having a good harvest and making the tribute.

She gritted her teeth. 'If necessary, I will go to Lord Ketil and remind him of his sworn oath to my father.'

She hoped he wouldn't hear the lie in her voice. The last thing she wanted to do was to travel on the sea. The thought of being on the open sea, out of sight of land, terrified her.

'Will you indeed?'

'What other option do I have?'

Sigurd regarded the small woman who stood in front of him. The faint light showed him that Eilidith's hair was auburn, not black as he'd first imagined it. Like the sun setting on a clear summer's day. The butterfly-shaped mark under her lower lip took her face from bland to intriguing.

She'd shown courage to come to this place with simply a large dog for protection. The only other women he could think of who would have done such a thing were his mother and Beyla, the woman he had given his heart to back in the days when he thought he had a heart. Beyla had chosen safety over their passion, and his half-brother, the man who was now jaarl over this island, Thorbin, over him.

'I believe you could travel to Ketil and demand justice, as is any ring bearer's right,' he said to distract his thoughts from unwanted memories. 'But Thorbin might have a great reluctance to see a prize like you go. Have you thought about what you might do then?'

She thumped her chest, like a warrior, rather than a lady. 'I gave a sacred vow that I will see my father free or perish in the attempt.'

Sigurd stood straighter. Had his mother been like that once? Strong and resolute instead of jumping at shadows as she'd done during the last few years of her life? 'The world would be a poorer place if you died. You obviously have a family who care about you.'

She lifted her head and assessed him as if he

were a prize bull at the market. 'Does Thorbin fear you or someone else more?'

'Thorbin's long-delayed day of reckoning has arrived. It gives me immense pleasure to know that I will be the one to ensure it happens. I, too, have a vow I want to see fulfilled.'

Islay was the lynchpin in Ketil's strategy for the Western Isles. He who controlled Islay, controlled the lucrative trade between Ireland and Alba. All the sea roads flowed past this island. Because of the whirlpool north of Jura, the quickest way to transport goods was overland. Thorbin's rule had begun a year ago last spring. At first Thorbin's star flourished and Sigurd had despaired of ever finding a way to avenge his mother, but Thorbin's tribute had been short at Yule. In the early spring Ketil had sent a man to investigate. When he returned, pickled in a barrel with an insulting message, Ketil finally lost patience with his protégé and ordered Thorbin to return to explain himself. It was Sigurd's task to deliver the message and ensure Thorbin returned to face the accusation.

Sigurd had spent the last week scouting out the stronghold, coming up with a plan, once he realised sailing up the strait and landing his boats was doomed to failure. His half-brother was no one's fool. It was obvious that he considered himself immune from retribution. But he'd also taken precautions. The bay was heavily guarded as well as all entrances and exits to the fort.

He felt sorry for this woman's plight, but in all likelihood her brother and father were already sold or dead. She and the ring she carried, however, were tools he could use.

'I have learnt that things rarely happen by chance. Our paths have crossed for a purpose,' he said carefully, aware she had not answered him. 'Let us fulfil that purpose. Let us together hold Thorbin to account.'

Her jaw became mutinous and her blue-green eyes flashed, becoming like the summer sea after a storm. 'Why should I trust you, Sigurd Sigmundson? Why are you not going to be exactly like every other Northman? Exactly like Lord Thorbin?'

He ignored the flash of anger at being likened to his half-brother and forced his voice to sound placating, as if he were trying to soothe a nervous horse. He had to give her some reason to make her trust him. 'We knew each other when we were children. I know his strengths, but also his weaknesses. It is why Lord Ketil gave me this task. I am the only man who can defeat him, but to do that I have to get close to him.'

Her neat white teeth nibbled her lower lip, turning it the colour of the dawn. 'And you can save my family when you defeat Lord Thorbin?'

'If they are on Islay, I will. If not, I will go to Ketil and personally lay your claim at his feet.'

'Why are you suddenly willing to help me?'

'To prove to you not all Northmen are the same. I remember my debts and I keep my vows.'

She tucked her chin further into her shoulder, hiding the butterfly mark. 'I need some time.'

Sigurd carefully shrugged and pretended indifference as he handed the dog his last piece of dried meat. The dog put his paws on Sigurd's shoulders and licked his face with his great wet tongue.

'Coll, bad dog!'

The dog instantly sat, licked his chops and looked hopefully for another piece.

'Your dog believes in me. He wants me to save you. Will you join forces with me?'

She bent her head and spoke to the dog before she held out her hand. 'I may regret this, but we join forces until the time comes for the alliance to end.'

He closed his hand about her slender fingers and resisted the urge to pull her close and taste her mouth. Eilidith of Cennell Fergusa was a tool to be used, not a woman to be enjoyed. He never mixed business with pleasure. He reluctantly released her and stepped away, being careful to keep his face blank. He had discovered the perfect weapon to crack open Thorbin's fort and destroy him. He would fulfil the vow he'd made as he watched the glowing embers of his parents' funeral pyre.

'You will be glad you listened to your dog.'

Chapter Two

Glad she had listened to her dog? Liddy kicked a small pebble, sending it clattering on the path. Coll gave her a look as if asking permission to chase it. Liddy shook her head and the dog stayed beside her.

'Where are you taking me? We need to be going in the other direction towards the stronghold, towards Thorbin,' Liddy said when Sigurd turned down another fainter track.

Sigurd stopped so quickly she nearly ran into him. 'I promise you—we will arrive in time for Thorbin to hear your petition. In fact, I will make certain of it. But we do it my way.'

'You allowed me to think you were a lone traveller, but there are other Northman in your company,' she guessed, her heart knocking against her chest. Her curse had struck again. She was going to be the ruin of Cennell Fergusa, rather than its saviour.

'You failed to ask about the finer details. You can hardly blame me for that.'

'Northmen always travel in packs. I've been a fool. Of course, it is an invasion force and you need to get someone inside.' A sort of nervous excitement filled her. She had more options than taking Sigurd's promise to release her father and brother on trust. She could spy out the land, determine where her father and brother were being held and free them in the confusion of the attack.

His lips quirked upwards. 'Thorbin certainly thinks there will be an invasion. He has fortified his stronghold. It can withstand siege.'

'It is why you need someone on the inside—to open the gates.' She swallowed hard. 'I can get inside and then hide until late at night. I will be able to open the gates.'

He picked up a stick and threw it for Coll. The wolfhound chased it and then came to Liddy with a sheepish air as if he knew she wouldn't approve. 'I will set a trap that he won't be able to resist. The problem has been the bait, but you have solved that difficulty.'

She fingered her mark. Had he missed it in the dim light? Thorbin would turn away in disgust. 'You don't understand. He won't…that is… I am not desirable. You picked the wrong sort of woman.'

He merely picked up the stick where Coll had dropped it. 'I have the right woman.'

'But…but…' Liddy struggled to explain. If she mentioned her curse, he might abandon her.

'Why not wait until you hear the full scheme?' He put a steadying hand under her elbow. She jerked her arm away from him. 'Better than making wild guesses, I always find.'

'What happened the last time you and Thorbin met?' Liddy asked to distract her from the unintentional comfort the light touch brought.

'He thought he had killed me. This time I have the measure of the man. He has grown soft and arrogant. I will win this time, Eilidith of Cennell Fergusa. I have learnt from my mistakes.'

The breeze whipped his hair from his face. He appeared utterly determined. Liddy glanced down at the ground. He might be the best hope her family had of surviving. She'd be foolish to walk away from him.

'Then I am grateful you survived. I hope Thorbin will be less grateful.'

A rumble of laughter rang through the morning air. Soft and low, doing something to her insides.

'Is it something I said?'

'You are refreshing, Eilidith.' He gave a crooked smile. 'Come meet my crew. Come learn what I will have you do.'

'I would be better off being the one to open the gate,' Liddy said to the ground. 'I can't see Thorbin being interested in me.'

'You've never met him. I have. You will be perfect. Trust me on this.'

'Keep your dog under control until my men have been introduced. I would hate for anything to happen.'

At Sigurd's words, Eilidith curled her hand about the wolfhound's collar. He nodded, pleased she had obeyed. He knew he'd almost lost her when he started to explain about his scheme, but she had recovered and stayed, rather than running, proving his instinct correct. The time had come to avenge his mother and make good his vow.

Sigurd whistled softly through his fingers. Within a few heartbeats, Hring Olafson, an older warrior who Sigurd knew more from reputation and whom Ketil had decreed would be second in command of the *felag*, appeared from the shadows with a double axe in his hand, closely followed by his other oarsmen.

'Where are the rest?' Eilidith asked. 'You can barely number more than twenty.'

Sigurd gestured to his men. 'Except for the ones who guard the boats, they are all here.'

'This is your invasion force?' Eilidith knelt beside her dog. 'Perhaps I should have stuck with my first plan.'

'They will be enough, you will see.'

'We had given you up for dead. You were supposed to return three nights ago,' Hring said, enfolding him in a rough embrace. In a lower tone in Sigurd's ear, he added, 'Get rid of the woman. She will slow us down. She doesn't look the sort who would entice Thorbin to do anything. He prefers blondes with large bosoms. She won't get close enough to wield a knife.'

'This is the newest addition to our enterprise,' Sigurd said, ignoring Hring. The older warrior remained sore that he had not been confirmed as the leader of this expedition. 'Lady Eilidith is the key to getting in.'

'The key or the lock?' Hring asked, making an obscene gesture. 'Thorbin has only one use for women.'

The rest of men joined in the crude laughter. Eilidith's face went scarlet. She might not be fluent in the North language, but there was no mistaking the meaning of the disrespectful gesture. Sigurd ground his teeth. Hring was far from his first choice on this expedition, but Ketil had insisted.

'If I had needed a whore, I would have bought one, Hring.'

'Even still, is it wise to trust a woman like that?' Hring touched his lower lip. 'The gods have marked her.'

Sigurd held up his hand and the laughter instantly ceased. 'Continue along that line and I will assume you wish to challenge for the leadership.'

Hring held out his hands as the rest of the men fell silent and backed away. 'It was a bit of fun. Harmless banter. That is all. If you want to stake all on this woman, then as leader it is your privilege. You've got us this far. Allow me to formulate a plan on what happens when we fail.'

'Seven days ago you proclaimed that we would perish when we set foot on land. Has your ability to foresee the future improved?' Sigurd said, steadily.

The other man was the first to look away.

'We have a duty to help Lady Eilidith,' Sigurd proclaimed, ignoring Hring. Once he had succeeded, Hring would be the first to praise him. For now, he kept his focus on the ultimate prize—Thorbin. Everything else was a distraction. 'She bears Ketil's ring as proof of the great friendship Ketil bore her father. A man who turns his back on the ring's promise is a man who has broken faith with Ketil.'

'May we see this ring?' Hring asked. 'I know what these Gaels are like.'

Sigurd wasn't sure how much of the exchange she had understood, but Eilidith held up the ring with its seal without prompting. He gave Eilidith a pointed stare and she gave a faint shrug before examining the ground.

'Her father swore allegiance to Ketil,' Sigurd said, making sure he looked each of his men in the eye, rather than pondering on the mystery which was Eilidith. 'Thorbin has ignored the friendship and falsely imprisoned him. Should Ketil ignore the insult?'

'No!' his men roared as one and beat their swords against their shields. The roar caused Coll to howl along with them. At the noise, everybody laughed and the tension eased.

Hring inclined his head. 'I stand corrected. You were right to take up her cause. Lord Ketil should never be mocked in this fashion.'

'Ketil's wishes must be adhered to.'

'Ketil wants Thorbin alive.' Hring scratched the back of his neck. 'Do you think you can still do that? After what you have seen?'

'If possible, I believe is how the order goes,' Sigurd responded. 'One never knows what might happen in battle.'

'Indeed.'

'Ketil trusted my judgement. You should as well.' Sigurd pointed his sword towards the sky for emphasis. As if on cue, the sun broke through the clouds and made it gleam. He could not have planned it better. 'Without question.'

Liddy found the pace the Northmen used to travel across country was quick but not overly exhausting. The North language was fairly easy to understand and she was grateful that her father had made her learn it. She simply had to concentrate far more than she was used to.

The jibe about her warming Thorbin's bed rankled. She had failed with Brandon. He had not even waited until the cockerel crowed after their wedding night to abandon her bed. And she knew she was no assassin who could seduce and then stick the knife in. But she had kept her face blank and trusted Sigurd would see the folly of such an action without her having to confess to her many failures.

'How much about our leader do you know?' the warrior who had challenged Sigurd asked in heavily accented Gaelic. One half of his face was covered in a network of scars. Scars on men were different from birthmarks. Scars meant battles fought and won, while a birthmark made people turn away.

'I know Ketil has sent him,' she replied, digging her chin into her shoulder. 'He has promised to right the wrong which was done to my family. It seems the quickest way to achieve my goal.'

His smile made the scars on his cheeks seem more lurid. 'But do you know why?'

'I suspect he is a good enforcer. He moves like a true warrior. I understand the tribute was short and the last man who tried to enforce Ketil's will ended up in a barrel.'

'Yes, there were few volunteers for the job after that was made public. Sigurd was the only one who had the guts to put his name forward.'

'Why are you here?'

'Because I go where I am sent, but Sigurd wanted this.' Hring nodded. 'I, Hring Olafson, will tell you the tale. They are half-brothers— Thorbin and your warrior. Close until their father's death from a cart accident, Thorbin caused Sigurd's mother to be put to death and nearly killed Sigurd.'

Liddy missed her step. Sigurd's earlier remark about his mother took on new significance. It was why he knew Thorbin was responsible for what had happened in that grove. He had waited for his revenge.

'How did his mother die?' she asked carefully in the North language.

'Sigurd's mother was supposed to burn to death

as is our custom when a great lord dies. One of his women volunteers to join him in the after-life. Always.'

'Why did she do it?'

'I heard it was to save Sigurd's life after he attacked Thorbin. Thorbin inherited everything.' Hring shook his head. 'Thorbin lit the pyre, but an arrow arced from out of nowhere and killed her before the flames licked her feet.'

'And Sigurd is supposed to have fired the arrow. Is that your point?' Liddy said, staring at Sigurd's broad shoulders. Knowing Thorbin's reputation, she suspected he had deserved to be attacked. 'How difficult. To be faced with a choice like that. Knowing that she had tried to save him.'

Hring grabbed her elbow. 'That doesn't bother you? He dishonoured the gods. Some might consider him cursed.'

Liddy touched her mark. Would this warrior think she had dishonoured the gods as well? 'Do you?'

'Lord Ketil knows what he is doing and I trust him. He chose Sigurd, but Thorbin makes sure the gods favour him and they have thus far. Luckiest bastard I have ever heard of.'

Not the words of endorsement for Sigurd Liddy had hoped to hear.

'Everyone is defeated one day,' she said more

to calm her nerves than to Hring. 'Sigurd will make Thorbin hold to Lord Ketil's promise. He is Lord Ketil's emissary.'

'I like you, Lady Eilidith. You have faith. You are not worried about such things as curses.'

Hring clapped her hard on the back and Liddy stumbled, grazing her hands on the rough ground. She shook her head at Coll, who gave a low rumble in the back of his throat.

'A problem?' Sigurd asked, coming to stand beside her. 'You tripped over that large stone, Eilidith. You should watch where you put your feet.'

Liddy wiped her hands on her cloak, shrugging off his steadying hand. She was doing it again—trying to see the best side of things. The sheer impossibility of what she was about to attempt swamped her and she wanted to sink down into a heap of tiredness and never get up. 'Next time, I will pay more attention to where I put my feet.'

'We can stop and rest,' Hring suggested with a sly smile. 'If this lady is the key which will open the locked door, we want her in the best condition.'

He gave her a look that suggested, even in her best condition, she'd have no hope of catching Thorbin's eye.

Liddy straightened her cloak and tried to ignore the sinking in her heart. If they rested for too long, she'd miss her chance to petition Thorbin during the assembly day. 'I'm fine.'

'Look where you are stepping in the future.' Sigurd turned back to his men. 'We will get there, my lady, never fear. Even if I have to carry you. Hring the Grizzled, go bother someone else with your nonsense. The Lady Eilidith is safe with me.'

Hring immediately moved off.

'Are you going to explain what that was about?' he asked softly. 'You should have informed me that you speak the North language.'

She shrugged. 'The Northmen have lived here for most of my lifetime. Someone had to know what they were saying.'

'And what was Hring saying?'

'Hring saw fit to inform me of various rumours about your past. Apparently you dishonoured the gods and they will get their revenge whereas your *half-brother* always ensures that his doings find favour with the gods.'

Sigurd's face became hardened planes. 'The gods have more to worry about than mortal men and their deeds. I believe you are responsible for your own success or failure. If you believe in a curse, you are more likely to see things that way. My mother died free.'

'I see.' Liddy pressed her lips together to keep the truth about her curse from spilling out. Sigurd did not need to know about her dead children.

He shrugged, but a muscle jumped in his jaw. 'I would have saved her if I could, but I was too late and could only ease her suffering. It was a long time ago, back in the North Country. Does it make a difference to what I will do? I think not.'

Liddy gestured with her hand. 'Some of those women...back in the grove...did they suffer greatly?'

His eyes held a haunted quality. 'It is far from an easy way to die. Not one I'd wish on anyone.'

'But do you dishonour your gods by speaking this way?'

He gave a half-smile. 'My god is my own business, but I haven't followed my father's religion since that time.'

Liddy wrapped her arms about her middle. He couldn't be Christian. He wore long hair and was leading a pagan war band. And she had put her life in his hands. 'Will you make sure that isn't my fate?'

'It won't come to that.'

'Even still...'

A muscle jumped in his jaw. 'Stop worrying. Trust me. Your fate will be different.'

They arrived at a small knoll overlooking the fort just as the light turned to dark. Liddy was impressed that Sigurd had indeed known a quicker way.

His assessment proved correct. The fort's gate was firmly shut with great ceremony as the last few rays flickered in the sky. The carts trundled out into the gloom. Liddy could hear various grumbles about the way the Northmen treated the Gaels, but not too loud and they were soon hushed.

Liddy started forward, but was hauled back against Sigurd's hard body.

'Where do you think you are going?' His deep voice rumbled in her ear.

She half-twisted. His closeness did strange things to her body. She frowned. Ever since she had watched the two tiny coffins being lowered into the ground, her body had had no feeling. Right now she had no time to go back to that indescribable pain. She swallowed hard and concentrated on the fortress.

'To wait by the gate. To be first in the queue when they open for the assembly day. There are sure to be dozens of petitioners and I want to make sure mine is heard.'

'We stay here a while yet.' He draped his arm across her shoulders, preventing her from moving. Another warm pulse coursed through her. She screwed up her eyes and willed her lungs to fill with air. The trouble was that a small part of her wanted these pulses to continue.

Her gaze followed the line of his other arm. A group of Northmen rode up and demanded entrance. The gate swung open and another smaller group came out.

'What are they doing?'

'Searching. We wait until other islanders arrive. Then we will go forth as part of a crowd.'

'Will they find us here?' she asked.

Sigurd lifted a brow and exchanged a glance with Hring, who fingered his axe. 'I'd prefer surprise, but we would be more than a match if they did discover us. A small patrol holds no fears for us.'

Liddy caught her bottom lip, something she always did when she was nervous. 'Where should I hide?'

Sigurd settled down with his back against a tree. He patted the ground beside him. 'Keep close and you will come to no harm.'

Liddy sat down with Coll between her and the Northman. The last thing she wanted, if she survived, was rumours that she had taken up with a Northman. She touched her birthmark. Not that any would be interested in her in any case. She had nothing to charm a man.

Sigurd woke with a numb arm. Some time in the night, her dog had moved to her other side and Lady Eilidith had moved closer. One hand was splayed against his chest. It felt right to hold her in his arms. He tried to remember when he'd last held a woman like this, just to sleep. Possibly Beyla all those years ago when he thought the world a very different place.

In the pale light, he watched her softly parted lips and the curve of her neck for another heartbeat. Something panged deep in his chest. He would do his best to protect her, but Eilidith was the bait. She was going to give him the excuse he needed to finally complete the first part of his vow and avenge his mother. First he did that and then he fulfilled the second part—regaining his father's lands and becoming a great jaarl, rather than a half-breed good-for-nothing as Thorbin's mother had proclaimed. If he lost sight of his goal, he lost everything.

He gently eased Eilidith away.

She blinked up at him, momentarily unfocused. Then recognition set in and she pulled away. Her dog gave a soft woof.

'Time to begin, my lady,' he said. 'Are you ready? Shall we teach Thorbin a lesson?'

She nodded. 'Coll and I are eager to play our parts, but Thorbin may listen to reason.'

He leant forward and adjusted the kerchief so that her flame-coloured hair was completely covered and less of a distraction.

'You, yes, but your dog will stay with my men.'

She gave a hiccupping laugh. 'Good luck with that. Coll will find a way to be with me. Your men won't be able to hold him.'

'They can and they will.'

A tiny frown appeared between her brows. 'Why?'

'Thorbin's guards won't let you anywhere near him with that dog. For my plan to succeed you must make your petition. You must be able to show Ketil's ring to Thorbin yourself.'

The tension flowed from Eilidith's face. 'I knew Hring had it wrong. You would not have me play the whore.'

He stared at her astonished. She'd been worried about that? He captured her hand between his. Her fingers were long and narrow. The inside of her wrist was naked and vulnerable. Her eyes met his with a clear gaze. He realised he was staring. He hurriedly dropped her hand.

'You are not the type,' he said and knew from

the flash of hurt in her eyes, his voice was a tad too harsh and he had put it badly. Her sensibilities shouldn't bother him, but they did.

'I never considered a whore for this,' he said, trying again. 'Thorbin knows how faithless women can be. You are perfect for what I need.'

Her hand grabbed on to Coll's fur. Silently he willed her to see the sense. Making her a present to Thorbin would be something Thorbin would expect and would have planned for. His half-brother was thorough in that regard. They needed to be as inconspicuous as possible. Thorbin had to have no inkling until Sigurd sprang the trap.

'If Coll senses I am in danger, he will find a way to get to me, but he can stay here.'

The air went out of Sigurd's lungs and his neck eased. Eilidith was truly a gift. There was no pouting or demands that he list her undoubted charms as most of the women he'd dealt with would have done—instead, she turned her mind to the next problem. An attractive woman who was sensible—he couldn't ask for more.

'Hring will take care of him for you. I will inform him how to keep Coll under control.' He stood up and held out his hand. 'Now we need to move.'

She remained where she was.

'Do you think we will emerge alive?'

He reached out and cupped her cheek. Her soft skin trembled beneath his fingers. 'Thorbin failed to kill me once. He won't succeed this time. Trust me to get this right.'

Her tongue flicked out and moistened her lips. 'What are we going to do? Tell me now or I will go straight to the gate and proclaim that Ketil's men are here.'

With great reluctance he let her go. Soon, he promised his body, he would taste her lips, but he needed her courage first.

'Warriors are allowed to challenge for the leadership,' he said, forcing his mind to work, 'if, and only if, they are in the assembly. A decree from King Harald Finehair in order to stop disputes. Thorbin seeks to prevent anyone from Ketil's *felag* from reaching the assembly. That is where you come in, you are going to get me into the assembly today.'

Sigurd hunched down and outlined his plan, concentrating on the important aspects of it, rather than thinking about how her lips might taste or how her hair slowly turned a glossy red in the rising sun. Such considerations had no place in the here and now. He had to focus on his task as he had a thousand times before. Focus kept him alive.

Eilidith was useful to him as a reason to chal-

lenge something Thorbin could not duck or fore-
stall on—that was all. He knew what was important
in his life and where his future lay. It had nothing
to do with a flame-haired woman and her overgrown wolfhound.

The gates finally swung open mid-morning
after much grumbling in the growing throng that
they normally opened at dawn as they had done
on previous days. The crowd began to shuffle with
much jostling and shoving to get a good position.

Against her natural instincts, Liddy obeyed
Sigurd's instructions and waited. According to
him, they wanted to be in the centre of the stream
of people going in. They were less likely to be
questioned, more likely to make it to the great hall
where Thorbin would hear the petitions. Her stomach had twisted itself into knots. The last thing
she wanted was to be questioned about who her
companion was. Her ability to lie was laughable.

She put her hand out to pat Coll and encountered empty air. She curled her fingers into her
palm and wished Coll was there, but he was back
being fed dried meat by Hring and she was here
with Sigurd, trusting that her curse would not
ruin everything.

The queue moved forward and then stopped

abruptly. Sigurd changed his gait as they inched forward. To her sidewise glances, he appeared much more flat footed and slow, rather than possessing the arrogant swagger of a Northman warrior.

A large warrior jostled a fishmonger's wife and she told him what to do in no uncertain terms in Gaelic. All banter ceased. The man stared at her while other people nudged each other. When she finished her tirade, she said very loudly in Norse that she wanted to go in to sell her fish, the freshest in the land. He nodded and waved her on.

'Most Northmen don't know the Gaelic language,' Liddy whispered. 'They taunt him. It is what passes for sport in this country these days.'

'They should be careful. Not everyone from the North is ignorant or tolerant.' Sigurd watched the warrior who was inspecting the woman's basket of fresh fish with a dubious expression. 'Gorm used to be well thought of. Slow to anger, but when he does, watch out. His double-axe skill is legendary.'

'Is that his name? Gorm?'

'Yes, that is his name—Gorm the Two-Axed. We served together briefly a few years ago against Ketil's great rival, Ivar the Boneless, and his band of dark Northmen, the men from the Black Pool, or *Dubh Linn* as you Gaels call it.' Sigurd pulled his hood more firmly over his face and leant on his stick more, giving the impression that he was old and feeble. 'He fights with two axes and no shield. I saw him clear an entire ship of Gaels on his own and emerge with only a slight cut on one arm.'

A shiver went down Liddy's spine. The people were playing with fire. All it would take was for someone to point out what was being said. 'Is he still…a great warrior? He seems to be running to fat.'

Sigurd was quiet for a long heartbeat. 'He broke his leg in a fight after a feast more than two years ago. See how he still walks with a limp. I'd prefer him not to be against us should it come to a full-on fight.'

Her heart thudded. If he knew Gorm, then Gorm would know him. Any hope of surprise would go. Her mouth tasted like ash. And she would be condemned as an accomplice. Any hope of rescuing her father and brother would be lost. She stared up at the clouds. There were too many people behind them to run. She kept trying to remember the sound of her *seanmhair*'s voice as she declared that Liddy would do great things, rather than thinking about Brandon's scorn.

'Gorm will recognise your voice.' She kept hers to barely above a whisper.

Sigurd nodded. 'It is why you must speak if he acknowledges us.'

She risked a glance at him. He had straightened up a little and was surveying the crowd. 'No one will ever take you for a servant. Stoop and keep your eyes on the ground.'

His breath fanned her ear. 'Your lover, then.'

Something warm curled about her stomach. Lover? She was finished with such things. She'd been no good at bed sport with Brandon and Sigurd had made it very clear that she was undesirable—not meant for the jaarl's bed. 'A servant will provoke less comment.'

He raised a brow. 'Say what you will, but make it convincing.'

'Why did you choose me?' she asked as they moved ever closer to Gorm's inspection.

'I knew I needed a distraction. Luckily the fates sent you along. Thorbin has even given up hunting wild boar, something I never thought I'd see him to do. He used to live for the chase.'

Gorm was five people away and demanding the cart be searched. The farmer instantly complied. The hay and straw was stabbed repeatedly with swords from all sides.

'I can see why you didn't try smuggling yourself in a load of hay.'

'I saw this happen to three carts on my first

day of spying,' he said. 'Until then I had favoured that idea.'

Gorm started towards them, waving his hand and signalling to another guard that he wanted to deal with them. Liddy forgot how to breathe.

'Whatever you do, act naturally,' Sigurd said in a low voice. 'You look like a doe who has just heard the hunter's tread.'

'Turn towards me, pretend we are in close conversation,' she retorted. 'It won't be so bad then. I can't see him.'

He took a step nearer. He was nearly touching her. His breath fanned her cheek again. 'I still think my idea of lovers was a good one.'

Liddy wriggled to make some more space. Lies dripped from his lips as easily as honey dripped from the comb during the September harvest, the same as they had dripped from Brandon's when he'd courted her. In her mind she listed the reasons Brandon's mistress had given her for why she was undesirable to men, starting with her birthmark. Her breathing eased. 'You should have told me about this possibility before I agreed to help you.'

'I discovered too many people knowing my business leads to disaster. Has the danger gone?'

Liddy raised up on her tiptoes and peered around Sigurd's bulk. 'Yes, he wanted the farmer's lad to help him unload the cart. He wasn't signalling about us after all. I panicked.'

'Keep on the side closest to Gorm. I'm depending on you, Eilidith, and your dazzling smile.'

'My smile never dazzled anyone.'

'We are going to have to do something about your persistent lying.'

Liddy shook her head, smiling a little at his foolish words. She knew what they were designed for. It had been a long time since anyone depended on her. Mostly they looked with horror at her, the woman who had caused her children's deaths, and tried to forget she existed.

Sigurd walked at her side, leaning on his staff as if he had trouble standing straight.

'Keep your head bent and your mouth shut,' she whispered as they neared the gate. 'Someone else has joined your friend Gorm. They seem to be looking for someone. They are unloading the sacks of grain for a second time.'

'Thorbin always had a paranoid streak. Who would hide in a sack of grain?'

The guards finished with the grain and motioned her and Sigurd forward. His hand squeezed hers. 'For luck.'

She drew back, knowing that her cheeks flamed. One simple touch and the ice she'd been encased in ever since Keita had given a terrifying gurgling sound and stopped breathing vanished. It was as if all the vile things Brandon had said to her and about her meant nothing. This man had touched her voluntarily. No, not voluntarily—to distract her from what was to come.

She withdrew her hand rapidly. 'No more of that.'

A dimple flashed in the corner of his mouth. 'If you say so, I was merely trying to play a part.'

'We agreed on another part,' she said between gritted teeth.

'What is going on here? Why do you come to this fort?' a booming Northern voice asked.

Liddy jumped and then slowly turned towards the warrior. 'I come seeking my father and brother.'

The warrior's brows drew together. Liddy tried not to think about the axe which hung from his belt. 'And your father is?'

'Gilbreath mac Fergusa. Chief of Cennell Fergusa.'

'You speak the North language. Good. It is good to see the women make an effort.' He gave a coarse laugh.

'Enough to get by.' Liddy wriggled to keep her gown from sticking to her back. Now she had started, the words flowed more easily.

'Your companion? Why is he here? Why does he allow a woman to speak for him?'

She kept her gaze on the warrior, refusing to look at Sigurd. 'My servant has lost his wits and his tongue. They say a witch cursed him last New Year. A woman like me would hardly walk across Islay on her own.'

'The North's peace runs here. Women are safe.'

Liddy remembered the sacred grove and knew he lied. She lowered her voice. 'Outlaws. My mother worries about outlaws. But I believe that despite his lost tongue, my servant could use his staff if any outlaws approached us in the woods.'

Sigurd made some mumbling sounds and seemed to shrink deeper into his cloak.

'It is fine, Colum,' she said. 'The warrior simply wanted to know about your ailment. I don't believe the witch's curse will pass to the next unworthy soul.'

Sigurd reached a trembling hand out as if to paw the large Northman.

Gorm drew back. 'You may take your suit to the council, but keep your servant under control. You are in luck. Today is the day Lord Thorbin hears such things.'

'Hopefully he will see the justness of my cause.'

Sigurd made another series of mumbling noise and started spinning around.

Gorm averted his eyes. 'Keep your servant

under control, my lady, or you both will be in trouble.'

He then began berating the farmer behind them, demanding that the load of fish be completely unloaded. Liddy hurried through the gate and started up the crowded road.

A hand on her elbow detained her. 'Cursed by a witch? Lost wits? I thought we had agreed something else.'

Liddy gave Sigurd her sweetest smile. 'You let me choose.' Her low voice matched his. 'You should trust me. He never asked to speak with you. He believed you bewitched. He couldn't wait to have you gone.'

Sigurd rolled his eyes heavenwards, obviously not appreciating the role she had assigned him. 'Preserve me from independent women with come-hither smiles.'

'My quick thinking allowed us to pass,' she retorted. 'We are in.'

He raised a brow. 'Now it is my job to ensure we get out of this place alive.'

'With my father and brother.'

'I know the bargain we struck, Eilidith. But I promise you—your life is important as well.'

Liddy studied the road rather than looking at the variety of warriors who stood just inside the gateway, far more than she had considered. What hope did Sigurd and his men have against them?

'I will hold you to that promise.'

Chapter Three

People crowded everywhere inside the fort. Several market stalls had sprung up, offering fish, fresh vegetables and trinkets. The Northmen were easy to spot with their long hair and fine cloaks. For the most part, the Gaels kept their eyes to the ground and moved with furtive steps.

'Where do we go now?' Liddy asked, drawing her hood more closely about her face so as to avoid people staring at her mark. 'Where is the best place to wait? When will your men arrive? I assume they are waiting for their chance, slipping in one by one.'

'To the great hall where the overlord hears the petitions. We are here to offer your petition and to see if Thorbin will keep the law.' Sigurd pointed to the large gabled building which dominated the area. 'My men will remain in the woods unless I fail to return by sunset.'

'Shouldn't I try to find my family?' she asked more in hope than expectation. 'Let them know I am here and working on their behalf. Fa and Malcolm need to be warned and be ready to escape, if my petition fails.'

Sigurd laid a heavy hand on her shoulder. 'Escape would be foolish. Where would they go? All your lands would be forfeit. They will be released when the jaarl of the isle chooses.'

'You mean Thorbin. He is the jaarl here and you don't believe my petition will work. You don't want me to give my family false hope.'

'Stop trying to peer into the future.' He placed a finger against her lips. 'Until the time is right, the fewer who know I'm here, the better.'

A Northman warrior bumped into her shoulder, nearly sending her flying. Liddy gave a little yelp. Sigurd instantly put up his hood and sunk deeper into the shadows.

'Watch where you are going,' the warrior growled and strode on without even truly looking at her.

Liddy waited until he had disappeared into the crowd before breathing again. 'That was close. What are my orders now?'

'Speak in a loud but firm voice once Thorbin acknowledges you. If he refuses, step aside and let me take over. Can you do that for me?' Sigurd put his hand under her elbow. 'You have done very well so far.'

'Anything else?'

'If I tell you to scream, I want you to scream with all your might. I want you to scream so that they can hear you all the way to Loch Indaal.'

'It will bring Coll. I don't think Hring could hold him if I were really in trouble.' Somehow the thought didn't bring her much comfort. The warriors who stood at the back of the hall would not hesitate to cut a dog down. She'd spied one with a quiver full of arrows kick a mangy-looking dog as they came into the fort.

'Precisely. In the confusion you escape and return to your home. It will give you time to warn those remaining in your family. You then make for the Isle of Man and Lord Ketil.'

A pain developed behind her eyes. If he failed, she faced a sea voyage. She'd never call Coll to the fate that awaited him here! Liddy silently resolved to remain silent. 'Do you think it is hopeless? I deserve to know the worst.'

'It is always best to have an alternative plan in mind.'

'I have an alternative—you and your sword arm, not failing.'

His lips curved upwards. 'It is good that you have such faith in my sword arm.'

'I have to have faith in something.' She tried to quell the butterflies which had taken up residence in her stomach. 'And if Thorbin does what is right?'

'I will be the first to congratulate you.' He put a hand on her shoulder. The warmth of his touch spread throughout her body, making the butterflies die down. 'Keep your hopes low. Thorbin will run to his nature. I have succeeded against worse odds.'

A heavy staff was banged on the ground three times and the entire hall emptied of noise. 'Come forward! Come forward, all you who have business with Thorbin, jaarl of the Western Isles. Come forward and he will see justice done.'

The curtains at one end of the hall parted and a warrior wearing a heavy gold torc and gold embroidered clothes stepped out. He had a long pointed nose and a disdainful expression as if the proceedings bored him. But there was something about him that made Liddy wonder where she might have seen him before—the way he tilted his head and the shape of his hands. Her stomach knotted. Sigurd's half-brother. She risked a glance at Sigurd, but his hood obscured his features.

Sigurd jerked his head towards where Thorbin stood. A cacophony of voices rose as everyone vied to put their petition before the jaarl first.

'There are too many in front of us,' Liddy whispered with a sinking heart. 'We won't be heard. All this for nothing.'

'Leave this to me.'

Using his staff, Sigurd shoved his way forward and Liddy followed in his wake until they were standing under Thorbin's long nose. 'Go, as loud as you can,' he whispered and stepped behind her.

'I will have order,' Thorbin thundered.

'I have business here,' Liddy proclaimed loudly into the sudden stillness. 'Ketil Flatnose promised my father protection from the slavers, but your men have taken him and my brother into captivity and they are to be sold in the North lands. I ask you to honour the promise Ketil Flatnose made to my father. I ask you to free them.'

Lord Thorbin regarded her as if she was an interesting insect that he wished to examine before squashing.

Fighting against the growing urge to hide her face, Liddy squared her shoulders and glared back at the tyrant.

'Is this true? Who told you this story?' Thorbin barked out. 'There are many who claim Ketil Flatnose gave them this or that right, but have little to show for it.'

'My father's servant returned to our hall with his bloodied cloak and the message. My mother has taken to her bed.' She dug into her pouch and brought out the gold ring. 'I bring the token Ketil gave my father when they swore eternal friendship and peace.'

Thorbin had leant forward and peered at the ring. He gave a non-committal grunt. 'Who is your father? You appear from this isle rather than from the North lands.'

Liddy wanted to wipe the bored smirk from his lips. 'My father is Gilbreath mac Fergusa, a man who freely gave his allegiance to Ketil Flatnose after his lands had been ravaged by Irish pirates. A man who convinced others to do the same. A man deserving of your continued protection.'

The North lord stroked his chin and his eyes narrowed. 'Gilbreath mac Fergusa is a traitor with a traitor for a son. The son would have killed me if he had had the chance. He broke friendship, not I.' He waved his hand. 'Application dismissed.'

Liddy put her hands on her hips. 'You lie! My father is an honest man! All he wants is peace and justice for his family.'

Thorbin leant forward. 'Hmm, are you challenging my word? A woman like you? A Gael? Mayhap you are a warrior who wishes to fight me and let the gods decide who is in the right.'

The room broke out into nervous laughter.

'A misunderstanding,' she whispered between

her parched lips. 'I am certain it can be solved, but my father must be released. He took no part in whatever happened when my brother came here.' Sweat poured down her back. What had her brother done? Malcolm could never hurt another human being in cold blood. He would have been a priest had he not been the only son. Had her mother known? Was that why she counselled Liddy against making the journey?

'There is nothing to be done about it. Give me the ring now! It is forfeit. Be grateful I don't make you fight.' Thorbin waved his hand and the North warrior who had opened the ceremony snatched it from her palm. 'Next.'

'But it is wrong!' The words emerged from her throat before she had a chance to check them. 'You have no right to take that ring! You have stolen it. That is against the North laws! I demand justice!'

Thorbin checked his movement.

'Are you calling me a liar? Both your brother and father are traitors. They broke the truce, not me. At the end of this assembly, they will be declared outlaws and all their lands forfeit.'

Liddy balled her fists. She wished that she was a warrior and could take on Thorbin. Sigurd had been right—there could be no justice in Islay while this man ruled the land. 'It is up to you to decide what you are. I merely state the facts. My father never knowingly broke a promise in his entire life up to now. Why should he start? He was one of the first to accept the Northman overlordship. He has never failed with the correct amount of tribute. Ever.'

Thorbin gave a pitying smile. 'The facts are that I am in charge, my dear. And it is I and I alone who judge if a man is a traitor. However, I am in a generous mood and can see you have no champion to fight in your stead. You may live. Quit this hall and never return. Be glad you have your life. I, Thorbin Sigmundson, am the ruler of this island and I decree this!'

'This lady has a champion!' a loud voice thundered out.

Thorbin started and seemed to pale, but then he recovered himself. 'There is none who cares to challenge. This has been settled. Be glad I am in a good mood, my dear. You may go, but your family's tribute has been doubled. I will expect it at harvest time. Then we can discuss your father's release.'

He tossed the ring and it landed with a clunk at her feet.

Sigurd stepped in front of Liddy and put his boot on the ring. 'I challenge you, Thorbin the Two-Faced! You failed to act on a solemn promise given by your jaarl. You broke the fellowship. You have forfeited your right to lead and I claim the right to challenge.'

'How dare you come before me with your face cloaked? How dare you call me that name? Who are you?'

Sigurd lowered his hood and threw back his cloak so that his sword was revealed. 'Sigurd Sigmundson. Deputy of Ketil Flatnose. I challenge you on behalf of this woman and her family. I challenge you for the leadership to settle the question once and for all.'

A collective intake of breath echoed about the hall, swiftly followed by an all-pervasive silence. Sigurd waited, knowing that this was the crucial time. Either Thorbin's men were up for a fight or they would force Thorbin to accept the challenge.

The colour drained from Thorbin's misbegotten face, making the white scar which ran from his temple to his chin stand out clearly. 'It is not possible. You are dead. Long ago. I saw you fall from that cliff in Ireland near the Black Pool.'

Sigurd bowed, enjoying his half-brother's discomfort. He had waited a long time for this day. It was gratifying to know that Thorbin had been behind the attempt on his life two years ago. 'But here I am, standing in front of you. Real and whole.'

'What connection do you have to this woman?'

'Will anyone deny me the right to challenge? To fight for the fellowship?'

There was a stamping of the floor and shouts of approval. The muscles in Sigurd's back eased. If there was anything a Northman loved, it was the opportunity to watch a good fight. None would interfere. From the look of it, Thorbin would be no match for him now. Not like years ago when Thorbin had left him more dead than alive.

Sigurd could see signs of heavy living in Thorbin's red-rimmed eyes and the way his hand trembled when he picked up the ring. This was his time.

'You leave me with no choice, Sigurd the Scavenger.' Thorbin gave a crooked smile. 'You will have your fight. With swords. I assume you will put the one which hangs from your belt to better use than the one of our father's which you broke.'

'That sword has been remade.'

Thorbin nodded. 'You should have died five years ago when you dared show your face at the funeral.'

Sigurd shrugged. He had gone to the funeral to show that he, too, wanted to honour his father and to rescue his mother. He had been naïve in thinking that it wouldn't be a trap. Beyla's timely emergence from the tent showed him his folly and he had to resort to ending his mother's suffering. 'You failed to kill me then and you will fail this time.'

'Shall we fight?' Thorbin wiped a hand across his face. 'The winner will take the woman.'

'That will be for the winner to decide. But no one touches my woman without my permission.' Sigurd damped down any protective feeling he had towards Liddy. She was a means to destroy Thorbin, nothing more.

Liddy went into the hut where Sigurd sat preparing for the fight, rather than stand outside and be jeered at by any more of Thorbin's men. She had stood it for as long as possible, but when the jibes became too crude she ducked inside.

She had never considered Sigurd volunteering to be her champion. He made it seem like she was little better than a whore. His woman, indeed.

What was worse, everything that had happened today increased the danger her family was in. If Sigurd lost, then they would all be branded traitors and lose everything. And if he won, could she count on him to keep his promise now that he had heard her brother had rebelled?

Liddy moved her mind away from that possibility. Brandon was right—her curse would destroy her family.

'I apologise for the men outside,' Sigurd said before she had a chance to complain. 'Manners are singularly lacking in this place.'

Liddy forced the impulse to laugh hysterically down her throat. She had come in all set to rant and he apologised as if it were his fault for causing her a minor inconvenience. As if their only trouble was the rudeness of the Northmen.

'How many times have you fought Thorbin? Was he the one to break your sword? You owe me that at least.'

He raised his head. His features seemed to be carved from stone. 'We fought many times growing up. We shared a father. While our father breathed his last, my half-brother arranged for my murder. I survived the attempt, but my mother agreed to be sacrificed. She did it to save my life. She thought the woman I professed to love and I deserved to be together. She believed in the power of love conquering all. She never knew how wrong she was.'

'What happened to the woman?'

'She chose another.' He gave a half-smile. 'Someone with more land and power. Another country. It taught me a valuable lesson—love will get you killed.'

Liddy stared at him in astonishment. This warrior was far more dangerous than she had thought.

'You wanted this not because of Ketil's pledge to my family, or any noble reason, but because of something that happened long ago. You wanted another chance.'

'The odds are in my favour. Trust me.'

She stared at him. 'You failed to trust me. Why should I trust you now?'

Liddy heard her heart thumping in the silence. He came forward and lifted her chin so that she was forced to look into his piercing gaze. His eyes would be easy to drown in. 'Leave this hut if you believe I will lose.'

'I remain here.' She wrenched her chin away and struggled to breathe normally. 'His men will kill you if you kill him. They have nothing to lose. They are betting on how short a time it will take to kill you.'

'Let me worry about such considerations.' He stepped away from her. 'You were magnificent back there. Better than I could have hoped for.'

A tiny bubble of happiness filled her breast. He had thought she'd done a good job. She struggled to remember when she had last had a compliment like that. And the part of her that wanted to believe she had been touched by angels at birth grew louder. 'It didn't do me much good. I lost my father's ring.'

'What do I see here?' He reached behind her

ear and produced the gold ring. 'Next time, pick it up. I may not be there to retrieve it.'

'I shall.' Her hand closed about the ring and she regarded his well-worn boots. 'It will take more than tricks to defeat Thorbin, but I do believe you can win out there.'

'It makes all the difference—having one person believe in you.'

'Do you want me to let your men know? About the fight? Everyone out there, waiting for you to return from your mission.' She made a little gesture and hoped it hid the sudden flaming of her cheeks. 'As I said, they are betting against you out there. Every single one of them.'

'Pity there is no one to place a bet for me. I could make a fortune.' He put up his hand. 'Don't even think about offering. They would not bet with a woman.'

She pleated her gown between her fingers. 'It is possible that Thorbin plans some sort of treachery.'

He shook his head. 'Thorbin knows that he will lose his men if he isn't seen to fight fair at the start. Once the battle begins, anything is possible between us, but no one else may intervene. I've learned a trick or two since he broke my sword.'

She pressed her hands together and tried to

hang on to her sanity. Sigurd seemed unnaturally calm about it. 'Have you done this before?'

'Challenge for leadership of a *felag*?' He tilted his head to one side. 'No, but I have fought many times, since Thorbin left me for dead. The surest way a man like me can rise. And I have risen, Eilidith, from the mud of society.'

'Call me Liddy,' she said before she lost the courage. 'We are friends after a fashion and I loathe Eilidith.'

'Liddy.' He made her name sound exotic and mysterious, rather than plain. 'It suits you better. Why are we friends suddenly?'

She gave an artless wave. 'Because you need one.'

He tilted his head to one side and she felt the full force of his gaze. She was aware of how small this hut suddenly had become. 'You may be right. My mother used to say a true friend was a pearl beyond price.'

'I have heard that saying before.' She watched her hands, feeling her cheeks go suddenly hot. She was bad at this sort of thing.

He stood up and walked over to her and put his hands on her shoulders. 'Allow me to do the worrying. You bring me good luck—that is why I need you there.'

She turned her face away, tucking her chin

into her shoulder to hide her mark. Now was far from the time or place to begin to explain about her problems, starting with the two tiny graves on the hillside and her part in making that boat capsize. Or her problems with her volatile ex-brother-in-law who blamed her for much that had gone wrong in Brandon's life—the woman with the cursed face who lied to hide her inadequacies. 'I am a woman of Cennell Fergusa. Worrying is something we do. What I do know is that my late husband, Brandon, would not have risked his life as you are about to.'

'Only the fates know when you will die.' He put his finger under her chin and raised it so her eyes met his piercing blue gaze. They were pools to drown in. Liddy hated that she wanted to believe in him. 'I am trusting that my life's thread runs longer than today. The three fates will have spun it longer.'

'We come from different cultures,' she whispered, watching his mouth. 'God, not the fates, decides when we die.'

'My mother used to say something similar. I can almost hear her voice, echoing down the years. Thank you.'

'My pleasure.' She watched his mouth as their breath interlaced. Her heart thumped so loudly she thought he must hear and guess her attraction to him.

He dipped his head and his lips touched hers. This time was not a fleeting butterfly touch, but solid and real. Her mouth parted and she drank from him.

For one wild heartbeat she forgot everything but the taste of him. Her breasts brushed against his hard chest. Then she stepped back, knowing that her face burnt far more than before. She fingered her birthmark, placing her hand to hide the ugliness of it, her badge of shame. He had kissed her voluntarily and she had no idea why.

'Did you take pity on me?'

'I have never kissed a woman out of pity yet.' He watched her with hooded eyes, making no move to recapture her.

'What was that for?'

'So that some of your excellent luck will rub off on me,' he said. 'You might not believe in such things, but I figure I need all the help I can get.'

'That is fine, then.' Her voice came out as a husky rasp. 'I figure you need as much as possible.'

She turned on her heel and marched out of the hut. Behind her she heard a soft voice saying thank you, so soft that she wondered if she'd actually heard it.

* * *

A good-sized crowd had gathered about a makeshift arena. The atmosphere had altered since she was in the hut. It was now far more restless as if there was change in the air. Liddy hung back, wondering where she should stand.

A cold nose nudged her hand and she saw that Coll had quietly joined her. Next to him stood Hring with a superior expression on his face. Liddy took a deep breath. She might not trust him, but at least he was on Sigurd's side.

'How did you get in?' Liddy gasped out.

'It is amazing how distracted guards can become when a big fight is about to happen.' Hring shook his head. 'The discipline.'

'You disobeyed his orders,' she said. 'You were supposed to stay outside the gates unless I screamed.'

'Sigurd's a good fighter.' He patted his chest. 'I predict my purse will be heavier tonight.'

'What will he say when he discovers what you have done?'

Hring bared his pointed teeth. 'I've never been one for following orders precisely. Sigurd knows that. And your dog pined for you. What should I have done—allowed him to take a chunk out of my arm?'

Liddy gave an uncertain laugh. Somehow it

was easier to have Coll with her. She curled her fingers around his collar. With Coll there, she had at least one protector. Heaving a great sigh, Coll flopped down at her feet.

'Sigurd is going to fight, but I worry Thorbin may not fight fair.'

'Thorbin is arrogant, but he isn't stupid. The men would turn against him if more joined in. Two men challenge and fight to the death in these situations. It is our law and our heritage. It works well.'

'Killing your brother cannot be considered a good thing where you come from.'

'Half-brother, and it has been known to happen, but Sigurd isn't planning on killing him.'

Liddy blinked in surprise. 'Why not?'

'Ketil Flatnose wants that pleasure.' Hring rubbed his jaw. 'If it was up to me, I would disobey that order during the fight, but Sigurd is different. He knows when to stop. I've seen him fight before. There are reasons why I backed him. But you needn't worry, my lady, any sign of trouble and I will get you out of here. You've held your side of the bargain, I reckon we can hold ours.'

Liddy tightened her grip on Coll's collar. The large Northman with strange pointed teeth no longer frightened her. 'Good to know.'

Sigurd was the first to emerge. He wore his tunic and carried his sword. Someone threw him a shield which he caught easily. In the sunlight, his hair gleamed gold and he moved with a great purpose, like one of the angels in church come to life. Her breath caught. It was hard to believe that he had actually kissed her.

'I was simply the nearest woman and he's a Northman with different beliefs,' she whispered to Coll. 'That was the reason.'

Coll opened one eye and gave a low growl of disapproval.

Sigurd banged the sword against the shield. All his muscles had tensed. It was good to be out in the open, good to be doing something, rather than skulking in the shadows. 'Thorbin. I am waiting. We are all waiting. Are you a warrior or a coward?'

Thorbin came out of the hall, dressed in a finely wrought tunic and tight-fitting trousers. In his right hand he carried a gleaming sword and in his left a highly polished shield.

'Is this how you dress for battle?' Sigurd roared, not bothering to control his anger at the contempt Thorbin showed him. 'You will rip your trousers and show your bare arse to the world before you take five steps.'

'Maybe that is all I will need.'

'You will need more than that, Thorbin, as you well know.'

'I would have a deputy fight for me. Do you wish to nominate someone as well?' Thorbin gave an ice-cold smile. 'A courtesy as we share a father. Blood will out, even if one has the blood of a whore.'

Sigurd glared at him. Trust Thorbin to bring up their heritage. Thorbin had been the legitimate son, the one with all the advantages. Thorbin's mother had made sure of that. 'Under the terms our mutual overlord has set, it is not permissible for either of us to have a deputy.'

'King Harald…'

'Ketil Flatnose has decreed no deputies in fights of this nature.' He dug into the pouch and withdrew a rune stick. 'We thought you might attempt this.'

Thorbin took the stick and read it with a curled lip. He tossed it away.

'I had no wish to kill my brother, but you will keep returning.'

'Don't worry,' Sigurd retorted. 'I have not considered you my brother for years.'

'I have no idea why the fates spared you, Sigurd,' Thorbin sneered. 'But it will be my pleasure to cut your life thread and then take the woman you desire. Like old times, Sigurd the Tender Hearted.'

Sigurd damped down the rage. He had used Liddy to get in here and owed her something for that. That was all. So why did it bother him that Thorbin could get under his skin in this way? He barely knew the woman. Women were not part of his existence. He used them when necessary, but mainly he focused on his vow and regaining his honour. His belief in love had died the day of his mother's death. And yet, his lips still tasted of Liddy's sweetness.

'Your pathetic attempt to unsettle me does you no credit, Thorbin. I only met the woman yesterday. A means to an end.'

'Then you know nothing of her past or her family. Why do you seek to protect her?'

'I have my reasons.'

'We could end this now. There are opportunities for men like you if you pledge your loyalty to me.'

Sigurd struggled to contain his temper. He would barely last a day before he encountered a knife in his back. 'I will pass. Shall we begin?'

'Your funeral.'

'Your meeting with destiny.'

Sigurd lifted his sword and drove forward. As he expected, Thorbin easily blocked it with his shield and tried to rain a blow of his own. Sigurd lifted his shield with plenty of time to spare.

'Getting old?' he asked, mocking his half-brother.

Thorbin shook his head and made a furious stab forward. This time the sword was harder to block.

Sigurd concentrated and began to fight in earnest, matching blow for blow and drawing on all the skills he'd learnt during his time as a sell-sword.

The crowd roared with encouragement every time Thorbin landed a blow and catcalled Sigurd. Liddy's stomach twisted. Even if Sigurd won, would he really be able to command these men?

However, very quickly the crowd became silent as it was obvious Sigurd was the better fighter and Thorbin was quickly tiring. Thorbin made one last attempt and forced Sigurd to his knees.

A scream echoed round and round the crowd. Liddy realised with a start that it was her voice.

She hid her eyes, unable to watch. Coll nudged her with his cold nose and she peeked through her fingers.

Somehow Sigurd had managed to twist and Thorbin's thrust forward missed. Sigurd half-pivoted and crashed his shield down on Thorbin's outstretched arm.

The sword dropped to the dirt as Sigurd brought his sword down onto Thorbin's neck. Liddy risked a breath. Sigurd was going to win. He was going to live. She quickly amended it to her father and brother were going to be freed. Whether a Northman lived or died meant nothing to her.

She fingered her lips. She could almost feel the imprint of his mouth. He'd kissed her voluntarily. It was almost enough to make her believe Brandon's mistress had lied when she said that no man would voluntarily touch her.

She pushed the thought away. Passionate encounters belonged to women who were made differently than she was. After today, she would never encounter him again. All she wanted was for him to keep his promise and free her family. Then maybe people would say her birthmark brought luck rather than shame.

Sigurd became aware of distant noises as the fog of battle cleared. He had done it. Thorbin was at his mercy. But he also knew that it had been Liddy's cry that had given him the extra surge of strength he needed.

He had fought better because Liddy believed in him. And that scared him more. Since his mother's death, he'd been alone, caring for no one but himself and the men he fought with. Finer feelings and tenderness had no place in his life. He barely knew her and already she was under his skin. She'd be returning back to her lands with her father. Liddy was not going to be part of his life. And the fact made him annoyed.

'You cut my ankle,' Thorbin whined, bringing him back to the reality. 'Unsporting.'

'Do you surrender?'

Thorbin made a noise.

Sigurd kept the point of his sword touching his half-brother's neck. For many years he had anticipated the pleasure he'd have when he killed this man, but now that it came to it, he found the desire vanished. Something deep within him revolted at the thought of killing his brother, even though he knew Thorbin would not have had the slightest hesitation.

'Louder, so all can hear. I am wise to your tricks.'

'I surrender.' His face showed real fear. 'I can't rise, Brother.'

'Louder!'

'You have won, Sigurd!' Thorbin screamed. 'You have defeated me!'

The silence was deafening. Sigurd knew the

majority of the crowd expected him to drive the sword home. He was well within his rights.

'Let Ketil decide what to do with you!' He tossed the sword aside as he motioned to Hring who stood next to Liddy. The warrior had obeyed him in his fashion.

The colour had rapidly returned to her face. He hated that something twisted in his gut, a reminder to keep people at a distance. Allowing them to become too close risked losing everything that he'd worked for. He'd seen it before.

After he dealt with Thorbin, they would say their goodbyes. It was how it had to be. He kept no one close. Beyla had taught him that lesson. Women were self-interested and their protestations of love meant nothing in the clear light of day.

The big man came forward, withdrawing the chains from the pouch he carried. Sigurd clamped the irons on to Thorbin's wrists and then shackled his ankles.

'You had best hope Ketil is in a forgiving mood.'

Thorbin paled. 'A misunderstanding. I can explain everything. You know what he will do to me. How I will suffer. I want a quick death, Brother.'

'You should have considered that before you

cheated Ketil Flatnose, before you sent his representative back in a barrel.'

Thorbin grasped his ankle. 'Blood flows from me! I'll never walk again. I might die on the voyage. End my life now. Show me some mercy.'

'You might die of your wounds, but I doubt it.' Sigurd shook his head. 'Did you show my mother mercy? Did you show anyone mercy? You will suffer, Thorbin, as your victims suffered and no one will care.'

'I have a child.' Thorbin's face showed real fear. 'The child is Beyla's, Sigurd. Just over seven years old. For pity's sake.'

Sigurd paused. Beyla had a child with Thorbin? 'Does Beyla live? Is she still your wife?'

'She does.' Thorbin shook his head. 'She screamed your name when she gave birth. I've brought up the child as mine. They are on their way here. Please, Sigurd, on what we once shared— give me an easy death. You can claim her as your own then.'

Sigurd's gut tightened. Beyla had screamed his name as she gave birth. It signified nothing now. That boy belonged to Thorbin. He would share Thorbin's disgrace and dishonour. 'What was between us once was finished long ago. The boy is yours. You sealed his fate.'

'Your mother!' Thorbin's voice cracked with

desperation. 'I was the one. I was the one who took her from behind. The old woman hadn't given her enough potion. She knew what was happening to her. Did you know that?'

Sigurd concentrated on retaining his last vestiges of control. 'I know that now.'

Thorbin jerked his head towards where Liddy stood. 'I swear I will come back and do the same to that one. I bet she'd like it.'

A red mist descended over Sigurd. Thorbin had been the one to rape his mother, making her scream like a demented creature, screams which haunted his dreams for years. And he threatened to do the same to Liddy. His promise to Ketil be damned. He reached for his sword.

'Go to the gods,' he said. 'Make your peace with them.'

Chapter Four

Liddy gasped in horror as Sigurd brought down his sword, ending Thorbin's life and his rule. When he had called for Thorbin to be chained, she thought Sigurd might be different, but then he killed Thorbin in cold blood. A cacophony of cheers intermingled with boos and catcalls broke out.

She struggled to breathe easily. Thorbin could no longer hurt her or her family. But who was the new Northern jaarl?

'It would appear our mutual friend has trouble following orders despite his oath to Ketil,' Hring remarked.

Liddy stared at Hring. 'You knew Sigurd planned on doing something like this.'

'I suspected as much. Ketil Flatnose took me into his confidence. He wanted to mete out his vengeance on Thorbin himself. He dislikes being thwarted. A death in battle is fair enough, but this went beyond his orders. Sigurd will have to face the consequences.'

Sigurd raised his bloodied sword to the sky.

'I, Sigurd Sigmundson, defeated Thorbin Sigmundson in lawful combat,' he roared. 'Will any challenge me for the right to lead? I will take on all comers! Speak now or swear allegiance!'

The crowd of warriors began to chant his name. Softly at first, but louder and louder until everywhere rang with it. He turned round and round, accepting the acclamation.

'He's done it, Coll. He's really done it.' Liddy dug her hand into Coll's fur. 'A new start for the island. He will be a different jaarl. He will uphold the law. I know this in my heart.'

Her eyes searched Sigurd's face for any sign of injury, but beyond the grazing on one cheek and bruising on his jaw, he appeared fine. Her throat closed. Was it bad that she had received more tenderness from him than she had ever received from her late husband? But would Sigurd have been so quick to offer tenderness if he knew what she'd been responsible for? asked a little voice in the back of her brain. Causing the death of two innocents by her own arrogance? Liddy tried to silence it.

Coll slipped from Liddy's grasp and bounded

towards where Sigurd stood in the centre of the other Northmen. To Liddy's horror, the dog jumped up and put his paws on Sigurd's shoulders, giving his face a wash.

'Bad dog!' Liddy cried and pulled him off. She stopped and was aware everyone was looking at her. 'I...I mean...he...wanted to make sure you were unhurt.'

Sigurd gave a heart-stopping smile. 'It is good to know your dog cares about me. Thorbin landed a few blows and I will be sore in the morning, but I've survived. This land is mine.'

He draped an arm over her shoulders and pulled her against him. Liddy stood for an instant, revelling in his nearness and the fact that he was alive. Then she realised where they were and that people were staring. Belatedly she covered her telltale mark.

'It's the Lord of Kintra's widow! I spotted her birthmark!' a voice shouted. 'Bet Aedan mac Connall did not know of this!'

Liddy went rigid. Should this get back to him, the last thing she needed was another lecture from her brother-in-law about how she needed to retire to a convent in Ireland. Rather than seeing her actions as the only way to rescue her family, Aedan would consider this as another insult to his sainted brother's memory. He'd chosen to see Brandon as the bright and shining warrior who vanquished his foes, the boat-maker whose boats did not capsize in rough water and the devoted family man who had plenty of time for his children, instead of seeing him as he was. Far too late to worry about Aedan's reaction now.

'Is something wrong?' Sigurd's voice rumbled in her ear.

'Coll wants more dried meat and has worked out that you are the man to give it to him. That's all.' Her voice sounded far too breathless for her liking.

Sigurd reached down and stroked Coll's ears and seemed oblivious to the shouts for him to give her a kiss. 'I will arrange for some.'

'Thank you.' Liddy pressed her hands together. Sigurd might say that he was not injured, but he moved his left arm as if it pained him. She knew how perilously close he'd come to losing. 'Thank you for everything. You must see to your injuries. Ignoring them can lead to complications. Having just won your jaarlship, you'd hardly want to lose it swiftly.'

His eyes narrowed. 'I've looked after myself for a long time, but thank you for the advice.'

Liddy's heart sank. The finality in his voice rang out. She had served her purpose and their alliance had ended.

'When will I see my father and brother?' she asked, once again trying to hide her birthmark. 'When will you keep your end of the bargain?'

'The prisoners will be released unconditionally. If they are on Islay, they will go free.' All the warmth had leached out of his voice. 'They will be down by the harbour. You can wait for your father and brother there if you wish.'

'About earlier…' she began, twisting her hand about her belt. She should go, but once she did the strange connection she felt with this man would vanish for ever. 'I am not usually like that— kissing men I hardly know…even for luck.' Her voice faltered as his brow darkened. 'I'm explaining this badly. I want to thank you from the bottom of my heart for releasing them in case we never encounter each other again.'

'Go wait for your father and brother. If the fates allow, they will be alive.'

'Is that what you were sent to do?' Gorm asked Sigurd after he swore his oath. 'Kill Thorbin? I understood Ketil wanted him alive.'

Sigurd pursed his lips. It was intriguing that Ketil's wishes should be the first thing Gorm mentioned. 'If at all possible is how the orders went.'

Sigurd concentrated on the ground. He refused

to think about the ice-cold rage which had filled him when Thorbin spoke of raping Liddy the same way he had raped Sigurd's mother. He had guessed years ago about Thorbin's involvement in the night. His mother's screams had haunted him for years. He had known then his father's gods were false and his mother's god had forsaken her. He had controlled his anger, but it had spilled over when Thorbin mentioned Liddy. He might not have been able to save his mother, but he could save Liddy.

'Ketil…'

'Ketil is pragmatic. I've no doubt you will inform him of your recollection of events in due course.'

'Yes, my liege. I have always been Ketil's man.' Gorm thumped his chest. 'He had sent word to be prepared. It is why I allowed you into the fort. Spotted you straight off. Be sure to tell Ketil that.'

'Indeed.' Sigurd kept his face carefully blank. Gorm was playing a dangerous game, but it made sense that Ketil had a spy. Both here and in his own *felag*. Hring also would be reporting the events to Ketil. The key to remaining jaarl was finding the missing tribute. After that he could put other parts of his plan into action, like obtaining a wife whose family would help him advance still further. The slave girl's son would rise. 'And the gold Thorbin kept from Ketil? Don't even think about lying, Gorm. Your ears go red. They did just now when you said you helped me to get into the fort. I know who was responsible for that.'

Gorm retreated backwards. 'I was not a member of his inner circle. He said repeatedly that we would be rewarded if we followed him, but we haven't seen a single gold piece. I heard a whisper that he has used it to entice Ivar the Boneless as a counterweight to Ketil. I have no love for that particular son of a sea serpent after he murdered my brother and cousin.'

The other Northmen confirmed what Gorm had said about the gold. Sigurd frowned. They had little reason to lie now that Thorbin was dead.

'Where is Thorbin's wife? Where are his women?' Sigurd asked Gorm after he had questioned all of the men.

Gorm shook his head. 'His wife stayed in the North lands with their son, attending their estates. She let him have his fun. But he has had no women since the last disappeared. The others… their bodies adorn the sacred grove.'

'Beyla stayed in the North country?'

'Do you intend to marry her? Everyone has heard the rumours about you and her. Why Thorbin wanted you dead.'

Sigurd clenched his jaw. Years ago, marriage to

Beyla would have been sweet reward. His mother had thought they belonged together—two halves of the same whole.

Now? He wanted to see her. He wanted to look Beyla in the face and show her what she had spurned. And Thorbin would not have left his son destitute. She would know where the gold was. Beyla was clever that way. He simply had to set a trap for her.

He drew his sword and put the point of it under Gorm's chin. 'My business, not yours.'

The wind from the harbour whipped tendrils of Liddy's hair into her mouth. She pushed them away with impatient fingers and tried not to think about the sea and what it could do to the unwary. She had gone over that day in her mind so many times. It still returned in her nightmares.

Coll had given up barking a greeting to every seagull who happened to land on the beach and now lay at her feet. She shielded her eyes against the sun and tried to concentrate on the long queue of prisoners who were shuffling off the ship. Things could go back to what they were before Malcolm and her father were captured, before this nightmare started, once she was reunited with them again.

A small traitorous piece of her disagreed. She

had felt alive in Sigurd's arms. She wanted to be something more than the cursed woman. When they were back on the estate, she would move out to a small cottage and spend her time cultivating a garden. She would plant rosemary for remembrance on either side of the door. Life would be quiet, but the solitude would be welcome.

'Everything worked out, Coll,' she whispered. 'And when we get back home, people will have to say that I was kissed by an angel. I did save Cennell Fergusa from certain destruction. There will be no more talk of Irish convents where the devil would be beaten out of me and where you couldn't go.'

Coll's soft sound of agreement turned to a sudden bark of recognition as two scarecrows stepped from the boat that was used to ferry prisoners.

It took her a heartbeat to recognise her father. He appeared to have aged several years in the time he had been away. His hair had turned completely white and his shoulders were hunched. He stood, bewildered as the shackles were removed. Then it was Malcolm's turn to be freed. Her brother's face was a mass of healing bruises and cuts. When he'd left their hall, she'd joked that he'd soon have to have a new larger tunic, but now it hung from his frame like an empty sack.

She gave a cry and raced towards them. Coll

reached them first, putting his paws on her brother's shoulders. Only then did some spark of humanity return to her brother's eyes. He looked long suffering as the dog washed his face.

'Liddy! What are you doing here?' her father cried. 'Can't you keep that great beast of a dog under control? What will everyone think? Where is your sense of propriety? Did you not remember my last words—you were to stay on the estate and look after your mother?'

Liddy looked heavenwards. Trust her father to be more concerned about appearances than about being free.

'*Seanmhair* always said that I would bring great fortune to this family and I have. I saved you.'

'My mother always had a soft spot for you,' her father said.

'No, it is true.' Liddy rapidly explained all that had passed, but she kept the kiss she had given Sigurd before the fight a secret. Her brother's and father's faces showed enough incredulity at her story without adding that little snippet. She kept thinking that she'd been mistaken about it.

Something panged deep within her. Why did she feel so upset about what might have been? Their friendship such as it was had always been doomed to be short lived.

'You convinced a Northman to free us? Don't make me laugh, Liddy,' her brother scoffed when she finished her edited recital. 'Why would he do that? What could he possibly want from us? What did you promise him? What did you give him? Fa, this explains…'

'Hush, Malcolm. You know little about it,' Liddy retorted, aware that her cheeks had flamed. 'We made a bargain because of Fa's ring. He needed an excuse to challenge Thorbin.'

She handed the ring back to her father as well as the necklace she'd retrieved from her gown's hem. Her father watched her with a thoughtful expression.

'An honest Northman. Today has been a day of miracles. The prayers from the Kells obviously did their work,' her father said.

Prayers indeed! Where had praying got them? 'It was only when I started to take action that things happened.' Liddy clenched her fists. Today proved that she had been mistaken to listen to Brandon's self-serving prattle. Not everything she did was destined to fail. But she refused to fight with her father here with all the Northmen looking on. Later, she'd try to make him understand.

'He fought for you,' her brother muttered. 'I heard what the guards said. About Sigurd's woman with a marked face. Now I find out it was you! I'd have rather rotted than know my release was due to you opening your legs for that man.'

Liddy marched up to her brother, sticking her face a few inches from his. 'Say that again, Malcolm. Say it and you will know the meaning of my fury. He fought for you and Fa, not for me.'

'Stop it, you two!' her father thundered, pulling them apart. 'Your sister did what was necessary to rescue us, Malcolm. Leave it at that.'

'It was because of Fa's ring that I had the sense enough to bring.' Liddy flexed her fingers, wanting to throttle Malcolm. First he had caused this by aggravating Thorbin in some way when he was supposed to be selling winter cabbages and then he accused her of being Sigurd's mistress. As if she would. As if she could! Now that he was the undisputed jaarl of Islay, women would flutter about him.

Malcolm rolled his eyes. 'You can be so naïve, Sister. You would think you would have had more dignity. That you wouldn't have wanted to disgrace your late husband's name by begging a Northman for help.'

'A dead man cannot have his reputation altered by actions of the living.' Liddy concentrated on her wolfhound's ears.

Even before their children died, Brandon had had the habit of talking over her as if she didn't exist or wasn't important. He'd been an attentive enough husband, but his passion was elsewhere. The sea had been his first love and his best mistress, but there had been other women.

His then-mistress made that very clear the morning after their wedding when she confronted Liddy and listed all her failings. Brandon had gone straight to this woman's bed that night. And when he left on his last sea voyage, he had muttered to Liddy about forcing her to go into a convent so that he could marry a woman who would actually warm his bed and ensure any children were kept safe.

'Brandon had no love for the Northmen,' Malcolm said, kicking a stone. 'He never bent his knee. He would be spinning in his grave to learn you had assisted any Northman.'

'Malcolm, do you wish to return to chains?' Liddy said through gritted teeth. After all the hardship she'd encountered, her brother was being vile. He should be grateful that she had saved him, rather than reacting to what were nonsensical rumours. 'I've no influence over our new overlord. I'm not his mistress and am not likely to become one either. Coll and I are returning home. You may accompany us or take your chances here.'

Liddy kept her back straight and prayed that

her cheeks did not burn the way she suspected they did.

A movement made her turn and she saw Sigurd standing at the water's edge. He had washed and exchanged his threadbare cloak for a fur-lined one in the time she'd been waiting for her family to appear. Rather than a raggedy beggar he appeared like the Northman jaarl that he was.

Liddy's heart leapt, but she damped it down.

Sigurd had no reason to make an alliance with her family. He needed the sort of woman who could advance his career or bring great wealth. Brandon had squandered her dowry.

'Fa, now is not the time to mention any potential trouble with paying the tribute,' she whispered, turning quickly to her father. 'I would hardly like you to get off on the wrong foot with Sigurd.'

'Nothing to worry your head about, my Liddy,' her father said, giving her a speculative look. 'Let your father handle it. You've done more than enough and it's good to see your old spirit returning.'

Her insides twisted. Her father appeared far too frail to even manage the journey home. His hands trembled. He would have to spend months in bed, rather than months out in the fields. 'That is what you said when you went off to rescue Malcolm.'

'And he has been rescued.' Her father patted her shoulder. 'Just like your mother, worrying over nothing. You have to believe that everything happens for the best. And it will. Cennell Fergusa will prosper again. When has your fa ever lied about something as important like this?'

Liddy arched a brow. 'Since when is being imprisoned and about to be sold for a slave for the best? Sometimes, Fa, I have to wonder about you.'

'I found out that my daughter cared enough to rescue me and that surely counts for something. Ack, I've missed the way your eyes flash. You've been one of the living dead, Eilidith. You have come back.'

'I never went away.'

'A matter of opinion, of course.' Her father swung his arms and breathed deeply. 'I'd considered that I would die a slave in the North and now I breathe the free air in Islay. I don't believe I properly appreciated it before.'

'Fa!'

'It is not open for us to understand the mysteries of God and his angels. We can only marvel.' Her father cocked his head. 'And who is this coming to greet us?'

'Is this your father, Eilidith?' Sigurd said, bowing low. 'A pleasure to meet a man who wears Ketil Flatnose's ring.'

'I rescued Ketil Flatnose from Irish pirates. He owed me a life debt.' Her father tilted his head to one side. 'And the arrangement has worked for the both of us.'

'Your daughter risked a great deal to rescue you, Gilbreath mac Fergusa. I hope you realise the debt you owe her.'

'My daughter possesses more courage than any man I know,' her father said, bowing low. He had the same look about him as he did when he was bartering cows or sheep in the market. 'Truly a woman beyond price, your lordship.'

'Indeed.'

'I have heard of you and your fighting ability. You were with Ketil when he fought the Northmen from the Dubh Linn last year.' Her father made another low bow. 'I trust you will do a better job of honouring your overlord's agreement than the last one did. An oath should be binding on both sides.'

'And you will have the tribute on time, I trust. To honour your side of the bargain.' Sigurd's smile was cold. 'I would hate to think any of Thorbin's claims were *true*.'

Her father scuffed his toe in the dirt. 'I plan on it. The weather will have something to do with it.'

Her brother made a cutting remark in Gaelic. Before Liddy could warn Malcolm, Sigurd bowed low and answered back that he was not greedy, but merely seeking his due for the protection he planned on providing. Malcolm's face went bright red.

'A Northman who speaks Gaelic. This is indeed a change,' her father said, rubbing his hands together. 'I would never have guessed such a thing was possible. Would you have, Liddy?'

'One of the reasons my half-brother gave for being late with Ketil's tribute was that his tenants were late with their payments. I have inspected his strong room. Remarkably empty. As are the granaries.'

'To be sure it is early in the season,' her father replied far too smoothly. An uneasy prickle went down Liddy's back.

Sigurd tapped his fingers together. 'A mystery, wouldn't you say? I know how prosperous Islay once was and how much tribute it sent off to Ketil last year and the year before.'

'There can be many reasons for an empty strong room, including Thorbin storing his gold elsewhere,' she said before Malcolm exploded. 'Thorbin expected someone to visit him. You said that several of Ketil's emissaries failed to return alive. Thorbin will have wanted to protect his ill-gotten gains.'

Sigurd nodded. 'You have a point, Lady.'

'Sensible woman, my Eilidith,' her father said, swaying slightly and closing his eyes as if it was all too great an effort. 'Forgive me, my lord. It has been a while since I last saw the sun.'

'My father has been through much.' She came forward and grasped her father's arm. He leant against her as if he was an old man. She realised with a start that it was no sham. He did need Malcolm rather more than he wanted to admit. In her mind's eye she could see the barren fields that she had walked past on her journey here. They should have been planted weeks ago, but her father had gone to rescue Malcolm instead. And her mother refused to do anything except sit in a chair and pray, claiming she did not know where the seed or gold was stored.

Sigurd stroked his chin. 'Are you certain you can make the full tribute?'

Liddy could hear the unspoken words and struggled to control her temper. Despite her help, Sigurd was going to act just like any other Northern lord. 'The only reason my father might struggle is because he was unjustly imprisoned.'

'Hush now, Daughter.' Her father patted her back. 'Let the man speak. He has only just become my overlord. He needs proof of his own eyes, rather than mealy-mouthed words. I can appreciate that.' He inclined his head, but there was a faint spark in his eye which Liddy thoroughly distrusted. 'Forgive my daughter, your lordship. She speaks from the heart, rather than from the head. Know our door is always open to you and your men, but it is a long way and I have been away too long. The tribute will be paid.'

Liddy's heart pounded in her ears as she waited. Her father was trying to save her. Sigurd was not her lifelong friend. They had parted ways.

Sigurd clamped his hand about her upper arm. Coll bristled and gave a low growl, but when Liddy shook her head at him Coll sat.

'We have nothing more to say to each other,' she said between gritted teeth.

'Your daughter may act as surety so that I can be certain of your good behaviour. Once the full tribute arrives, she will be free to go, but for now, caution.'

'Why are you doing this?' Liddy said in a furious whisper. 'You have no need of a hostage. Least of all me.'

Sigurd regarded her with an upraised brow. 'This is between your father and his overlord.'

Her father rather than protesting hung his head. 'You heard about what my boy did.'

'What did Malcolm do?'

'He attacked my predecessor with a knife.'

'He lies!' Malcolm shouted.

'There were witnesses to the attack. Several have spoken to me about it.' A cynical smile crossed Sigurd's face. 'I am to watch my back when I am dealing with you.

Liddy's mind raced. Malcolm had been stupid and impetuous, but her brother was no natural warrior, not like her late husband or his brother. Malcolm preferred talking about battle, but he obviously had done something or otherwise why would Thorbin arrest him? 'But if he had had proof, Malcolm would be dead. Malcolm went to sell vegetables—winter cabbages.'

'You are interrupting, Eilidith. A very bad habit you acquired from your mother, no doubt,' her father said. His eyes half-closed as a bout of coughing racked his frame. His time as a prisoner had obviously taken quite a lot out of him, but she couldn't shake the sneaking suspicion that he was in the midst of some trading scheme. 'My daughter as surety against this year's harvest. I am happy to agree to this condition. You see how confident I am about the harvest as I love my daughter dearly.'

'Fa!' Liddy hooked her arm about her father's and lowered her voice. 'You have no idea what will happen to me if you don't make the tribute! You know what the barley fields are like. They have not become any better in your absence.'

She clasped her hand over her mouth, unable to believe she had said the words out loud.

Sigurd tilted his head to one side. His eyes had become deadly. 'Do you fear your father will be unable to get the required amount of tribute, Lady Eilidith?'

Liddy swallowed hard. She was trapped. If she confessed her fears, he would take away the estate right now. Sigurd Sigmundson was first and foremost a Northman who had no heart or compassion. He required gold. The tribute for him was a business transaction, for her it was about a land that had entwined its way about her sinews.

That estate was all her family had left. It was why she had risked her life coming here today. Now everything was going wrong because of her outburst. 'My father will get the tribute to you, whether or not you have a hostage. That is all I meant. His word is his bond. Take the ring as surety.'

Her father shook his head. 'That ring will always be on my person from now on, but I understand what Lord Sigurd is asking. A hostage is to be expected.'

A ghost of a smile played across Sigurd's features. 'You see, your father agrees with me.'

'Will you be requiring other hostages?' she asked. 'Or am I to be singled out?'

'It depends on the circumstance. Your brother swears he acted alone. Of course, your brother might like to be the one who stays.' Sigurd gave her brother a hard look. Malcolm pretended to examine the dirt.

'I need Malcolm, Liddy,' her father said in a low voice. 'We don't stand a chance of paying the tribute without him. Your mother can cope without you.'

Her brother pressed her hand. 'I'm so sorry, Liddy. I never thought. I will find a way to get you free.'

'It is fine,' Liddy said around the sudden tightness in her throat. 'You are going to have to prove your worth, Malcolm. Get all the harvest in and I go free.'

'I know.' In that instant Malcolm looked like her little brother again, instead of the would-be warrior. She clearly remembered the tender-hearted little boy who had cried when she married as he was never going to see his beloved Liddy again.

She moved away from her brother and straightened her back. 'You need not worry, Fa. I volunteer to be the surety. I believe in your ability to get all the tribute required.'

'That's my Liddy of old.' Her father's elbow nudged Sigurd in an overly familiar way. 'The courage of a good woman, eh?'

Sigurd's features became even more remote. 'We go now, Eilidith.'

'Coll comes with me. Where I go, he goes. My shield and my comfort.'

Coll gave a sharp bark of agreement before darting over to Sigurd and flopping down at his feet in rapt adoration.

Sigurd's lips twitched briefly upwards before setting into a stern line. 'Your dog approves of the arrangement.'

Her father's eyes darted between her and Sigurd. He cleared his throat. Liddy instantly distrusted that throat clearing. She had seen it before when he sold horses and thought he had a gullible customer. She wanted to reach out and tell him to be quiet. Sigurd was not a man to be cheated.

'Of course, I might be willing to sell my daughter,' her father said, rubbing his chin. 'You may have her in lieu of this year's harvest.'

She blinked twice. Her own father was prepared to sell her? As a slave? Hostage was bad enough, but she had never reckoned on being gifted as a slave. 'Fa! You have no right!'

Her father gave an exasperated sigh. 'There will be grave consequences if the full tribute is not paid.'

'But you can pay it.'

'You refused the convent, Liddy, and who will

have you after you have spent time in the Northman's household? If this Northman will not take you, there is always the open market after I redeem you. You are acting like one of the living dead.'

Liddy balled her fists. Her father was behaving irrationally. The time in prison had addled his brain. She had refused the convent that Brandon wanted for her, the one which would beat the devil out of her. 'If you are trying to be funny, you are not succeeding.'

'I am deadly serious, Daughter. Paying tribute is my most important act. It is not just your future, but the entire future of Cennell Fergusa. For a king, the *cennell* must be more important than his immediate family. He has a responsibility to all his people.'

'And what will my mother say?'

'Your mother will refuse to speak to me for a week, but she will come to understand. She knows the need for sacrifice.'

'I volunteered to be a hostage, not a slave,' Liddy cried. 'A hostage has certain rights. A slave has none.'

'You offer your daughter as tribute?' Sigurd asked in a tone chipped from last winter's ice.

'Aye,' her father said heavily. 'I may have to sell her on the open market to raise the amount required if the harvest fails. She will fetch a pretty price. Worth her weight in silver and gold is my Eilidith. Her housekeeping skills are second to none. How can I look my people in the eye if I lose these lands through the action of my children? Duty must come first.'

Something flickered in Sigurd's eyes and his face became more carved in stone than ever. 'I will buy her from you…if the price is right.'

Her father rubbed his hands together. 'My price is this year's tribute. Not a gold coin less.'

Sigurd's eyes became blue ice. 'Half. There are other women.'

Her father shook his head while Liddy watched in disbelief. Her father was prepared to sell her, as if she was a yearling calf. If anyone else had told her about it, she'd have denied her father capable of such a monstrous thing, but here he was, haggling worse than a fishwife.

'Without my daughter, you would be outside this fort, possibly dead. Eighty per cent is the lowest I would be prepared to go.'

Time ceased to have any meaning. Liddy kept a grip on Coll. The dog gave her hand a lick.

'Three-quarters and I take the dog as well. My final offer.'

'Coll belongs to me!' The words burst from Liddy's throat. 'He is not for sale!'

Sigurd's face became grim and unyielding. 'If Eilidith is merely a hostage and you fail, Gilbreath mac Fergusa, I will take everything. Ring from Ketil or not.'

Her father gave her an unhappy look. 'I have to take the offer, Liddy. I will accept the price. You, my lord, now own my only daughter and her dog. The rest of the tribute will be paid at the harvest.'

Sigurd snapped his fingers and a piece of rope was brought. He tied it in a loop and put it over Liddy's head.

Liddy knew then that there would be no going back home. Her home had gone for ever. With a few words, her father had abandoned her. No, more than abandoned her, he had sold her.

She was Sigurd's slave. She belonged to a Northman.

Chapter Five

Sigurd struggled to contain his anger. At Eilidh's father. At himself. Instead of bidding goodbye to the woman who had helped defeat Thorbin, he had made her first a hostage and then a slave. He wasn't sure who he despised more—her father for selling or himself for buying.

He'd always sworn that he wouldn't be like his father in that way and yet all choice had been taken from him. Sigurd renewed the vow he'd made standing beside his parents' funeral pyre—until he became greater than his father ever was, he would keep his heart safe. Unlike his mother, he knew how much love could hurt.

'I will give you time to make your goodbyes, Liddy.'

Her eyes flashed a deep sea-green. 'Should I be on my knees thanking you for that as well?'

Not trusting his temper, Sigurd tossed the rope

to Hring, who hastily caught it. 'When she has finished saying goodbye, bring her and the dog to my hall.'

'Shall I cut her hair, Lord?' Hring asked, drawing his brows together in a disapproving frown. 'Make the lady more like the slave she now is?'

'Eilidith keeps her hair. I may wish to run my hands through it.' Sigurd turned on his heel and marched away, ignoring Liddy's horrified gasp. She would learn who was master here.

Liddy struggled to breathe. Sigurd had bought her and he wanted her the way a man wanted a woman. She shook her head to clear the buzzing sound. Obviously, he had taken a knock on the head during his fight. Men did not want her in that way. She went over her lack of charms again, about why she was doomed to never please a man in bed. Brandon had confirmed it after the twins were born and then again after they died. Then she hadn't minded as much, as she never wanted him to touch her again.

Coll gave a low growl in the back of his throat as Hring started to lead them away. Hring dropped the rope. 'Keep your dog under control.'

'I am allowed to say goodbye. Sigurd gave the order.'

The old warrior gave her a look almost akin to

pity. 'You have a little time. Make your goodbyes. Then come find me. I can't abide such things.'

He strode away, shaking his head.

'Well now, Eilidith, I think that went very well indeed,' her father said with a smug smile. 'You will make a lot of people happy. Maybe my mother was right after all. Maybe an angel did touch you at birth.

'This is how you treat me?' Angel-touched indeed. 'After everything I have done for you? This is my reward? Being sold like I am a bag of grain or a flock of sheep?'

'A prized cow?' her brother said.

Liddy balled her fists. 'You wait, Malcolm. I will get free and you will be laughing on the other side of your misbegotten face.'

'I need to be pragmatic and put the needs of the *cennell* first,' her father said in an undertone. 'I know the state of the fields as well as you. One day you will understand.'

'I will never thank you!'

'Sometimes God provides an opportunity. An answer to my prayers. I must give thanks to the monks for finding a way out of my dilemma. A story I heard in my youth provided me with the way. These Northmen can be sentimental at times.' He paused. 'You have become my old feisty Liddy, the one who fought so hard to save her children.'

Liddy tucked her chin into her shoulder. 'I lost that fight.'

'Your husband tried to extinguish that spark. I feared he had and a daughter who is more dead than alive has little use. But the saviour of the *cennell*? Now *that* is a daughter worth having and you will save us, Liddy. I can see that now. Your mark is a blessing and not a curse.'

'I was willing to be a hostage, but not a slave,' she whispered. 'Your experience has addled your wits. If being sold for a slave by your father isn't a curse, what is?'

Her father hung his head. 'The tribute Thorbin set is too great. Everything would have gone. This gives us a chance. You can do us proud. Soften his heart towards us.'

'But surely we have gold. The treasure you buried when the Northmen first came…you can use that.'

Her father pressed his hand to hers and leant in. 'I sent the gold to Kells, so that the monks would pray for us. Our immortal souls were in danger. I will send the necklace as well. You need all the help you can get, but I trust you will prevail.'

Liddy stared at her father in astonishment. Was he truly that unworldly? When she'd been small, he had run his tiny kingdom reasonably well, but now she had to wonder—what sort of man sold his children after giving gold to the church?

'You should have consulted me. We have nothing to spare. That necklace could pay for most of the remaining tribute.'

'I am doing what is best for everyone, Liddy. Neither of us has a choice. Some day you will understand. Your mother understands.'

'Will she understand that you sold your only daughter?'

'Your mother understands my responsibility extends beyond my immediate family.' Her father patted her arm. 'You have been given an opportunity. Use it. He appears to like your dog which is more than Brandon did.'

She gave an unhappy nod, but it bothered her that she would have tried to pay whatever price to keep him from slavery and he had so readily sold her.

'Calm yourself before you explode, Liddy,' her father said, putting an arm about her shoulders. 'We have little time. There are things to discuss.'

Liddy shrugged off the arm. 'You sold me! You would have put me on the open market. There is nothing to discuss!'

'Liddy, stop being so overly dramatic,' Malcolm said. 'You will find a solution. You always do.'

Liddy took three steps backwards. Her brother and father seemed delighted by the turn of events. They had no consideration for her or her future. She had risked everything for them and this was how they repaid her.

'You ought to be ashamed.'

Malcolm mumbled an almost inaudible apology. Her father continued to smile benevolently at her as if he had given her some great gift. Over his shoulder, she could see Hring advancing towards her. Her time was up.

'Give my love to our mother, Malcolm,' she said in a low voice.

'Keep the faith, Liddy.' Her brother leant in. 'If I can think of a way to free you, I will send word.'

'You have already done enough. Go before they shut the gate.'

Her father and brother stumbled towards the gate, but Liddy remained where she was. Hring could come to her.

Coll looked up at her and she absently stroked his ears.

'I might have freed them, but I have enslaved myself.' She clenched her fists. 'I might be a slave, but I was born a free woman and I shall die free.'

Sigurd paused in his perusal of Thorbin's effects in the dilapidated bedchamber. It surprised him that his fastidious half-brother had sunk this low.

The missing gold was nowhere to be seen. He could not believe his half-brother had beggared himself. No, the gold would be hidden somewhere. Once Beyla and the child arrived, he would get the answer. Beyla would be unable to resist the lure of gold.

He ran his hand through his hair. The last person in the world he wanted to encounter was Beyla Olafdottar. Once he'd loved her and had promised to give her his full devotion. But she had abandoned him for his half-brother. She had chosen comfort and safety over their passion and in doing so taught him a valuable lesson—love did not conquer all despite what his mother believed.

Ketil's annoyance at not being able to exact retribution personally would vanish once Sigurd found Thorbin's hidden gold and then he'd be confirmed as the jaarl. It would be one more step towards becoming part of Ketil's inner circle. He would be Sigurd the Scavenger no longer.

It had to be somewhere. This island should be productive, more than productive, a miniature gold mine. All the freight from Ireland to Kintyre went through this island as it bypassed the tricky currents around Jura. The whirlpool there had caused many a shipwreck.

He made a face. His half-brother had probably spent the bulk of it on drink and gaming. The rest? Gorm's story about a payment to Ivar the Boneless failed to ring true. Why willingly trade one master for a greedier one? Thorbin was many things, but he knew the value of a good master.

He ran his hand along the iron-bound trunk's lid. A pang went through him as he recognised the runes. It had belonged to his paternal grandmother. His mother used to point out the carvings on the lid.

'In here?' he asked softly.

On impulse he lifted the lid, but the trunk was empty except for several fine cloaks and a gold-embroidered tunic. His mother had been forced to work a tunic very like that one before she died.

He turned his mind aside and locked the memory away, as he slammed the lid down. Remembering his mother as a slave was not what he wanted to do. Particularly not now. Not now that he'd done the one thing he'd sworn he'd never do. He'd made a woman a slave and not just any woman, a woman he owed a great debt to. His mother would be ashamed of him.

'Do anything with your life, but make me and your father proud.'

His father only understood power and his mother believed wholeheartedly in love.

That was not the reason he'd purchased Liddy. His heart remained intact. He'd been left with little option. He could hardly have Gilbreath mac Fergusa flaunting the law. Or selling her to someone else. Renewed anger flowed through him.

A little voice in his mind asked if his father had felt the same way when he purchased his mother. He slammed his fists together. He was not his father and he'd never forced a woman. Liddy would have a choice…and it was up to him to ensure that she made the correct choice.

'Here is where I find you.' Liddy appeared in the doorway with Coll at her side. The twisted piece of rope marked her throat. Her jaw was set and her colour high. Her red hair had escaped from its cover and framed her face, but all warmth and vitality had fled from it. He struggled to remember the woman he'd held in his arms in the hut before the combat, the one who had kissed him with such passion.

'You didn't wait until you are spoken to.'

Two bright spots appeared on her cheeks. 'Was I supposed to?'

'Most slaves wait.'

Her gown highlighted the gentle curves of her body. Liddy was every inch the proud daughter of a king. In his mind, he could hear his mother's voice asking him if he knew what he was doing, what he was letting himself in for.

'You gave orders that I was to come here.' She defiantly tilted her head upwards. 'I have said my goodbyes. My brother and father have left for home. Good riddance to faithless baggage.'

Silently he lifted the rope from her neck. The red mark remained, mocking him and reminding him of what he'd done. How he'd given in to his anger at the situation. Or was it that Liddy had made a fight of it?

'Did Hring have to drag you here?' he ground out, ready to pulverise the other Northman.

She made a little deprecating gesture with her hand. 'Why? Is that how you treat slaves? Dragging them behind you? I will remember for the next time, but I walked beside Hring after the first bit. It made it easier for us both.'

Inwardly he cursed. He'd gone about it wrong. He ran his hand through his hair. 'Your skin should remain unharmed.'

'That is good to know.' Her mouth held a cynical twist. 'You are willing to make a woman who helped you a slave, but you don't want her skin harmed. You must explain your reasoning some time.'

'Do I owe you an explanation?'

She looked him up and down. 'It depends on what sort of man you are.'

Sigurd winced. The barb hurt far more than he expected it to. He had done the right thing. He had done it to protect her, to prevent her father from selling her off to someone else. But with her in this mood, what was the point of explaining it? 'You serve at my pleasure and it is my pleasure to keep your hair long and your skin unblemished. I may change my mind.'

'My father and brother have departed.' She held out her arms. Her wrists looked very slender and vulnerable. But there was a defiant tilt to her chin, making the mark on her face tremble like a butterfly about to take flight. 'You promised freedom when I met you.'

'I promised your brother and father freedom. We said nothing about you.' He picked up some light golden bracelets and anklets and swiftly fastened them about her ankles and wrists before he changed his mind. The gold marked her out as his official concubine, rather than an ordinary slave. All of the men would leave her alone. But right now all they showed was the paleness of her skin.

'Some day you will find a woman you care for and you will seek to keep her from harm'— his mother's explanation about why she wore the golden shackles.

'To mark you out as mine,' he explained at her look of horror. 'I would not have you mistreated by anyone.'

'A shackle is a shackle.' Liddy curled her hands into fists. She hated the unaccustomed weight on her ankles and wrists. 'I thought we were friends.'

'You were the one to end our friendship,' his soft words reminded her.

'We were never supposed to see each other again!'

'It's a small island.' His eyes glittered. 'And the truth is that your father was prepared to sell you. I merely took him up on the offer. If you want to be angry, be angry with him.'

She bowed her head and allowed her arms to drop. Her shoulders hunched and the defiance leaked from her like water running out of a dam. He was right. Her father had engineered this and she could never forgive him for that. 'I know who to blame and don't need reminding.'

'Well, then...'

'I've no idea why you would want a woman with a curse on her face.' Her voice wobbled on the words.

'A curse?'

'My birthmark.'

He laughed. The sound bounced off of the walls, causing Coll to bark.

'What is so funny?'

'Curses like that fail to frighten me.' All merriment fled from his face. 'If I am cursed, then the cursing happened long before I met you.'

'It is a bad curse. I can prove it.' She pressed her hands together, but the words about how the ship capsized and Keita and Gilbreath met their end stuck in her throat.

'My husband died and my father sold me as a slave,' she finally gasped out.

His fingers brushed her birthmark. 'As far as curses go, it is but a little one. Forget about it. Whatever you have done in the past, your life starts again now.'

Liddy stood completely still, unable to move. She wanted to turn her face into his palm. He had touched her voluntarily, knowing that she bore a curse. But if she told him about Keita and Gilbreath and how the guilt ate into her soul, he would back away from her in horror. She couldn't face that today. She had a responsibility to her *cennell* and needed his good will.

'I will keep your words in mind, but I always will be of the Cennell Fergusa.'

'Did your *cennell* declare you cursed?'

'It is something I can't change.'

'Have you tried?'

Her tongue moistened her lips. She didn't know

why, but her heart sang slightly. 'You know nothing about me, not truly.'

'Nevertheless…you are Eilidith, property of Sigurd.' His stare grew ever more intense, calling to something deep inside her, to that small part of her that wanted to believe he was different from the other Northmen. 'I am your master and what I say happens. No more talk of curses. You brought me good fortune and will continue to do so.'

'I will keep your wishes in mind,' she whispered. Inside she felt as if a gigantic door was slamming shut. Nothing was going to be the same again. She did not belong to Cennell Fergusa. She belonged to him. 'My grandmother thought it fortunate as well.'

'You see. It is up to you to choose.' Sigurd brushed the red welt. She winced and it made his guts ache. He noticed her pulse beat slightly quicker. She was not as indifferent to him as she might like to pretend.

He noticed that she kept her eyes away from the bed. Sigurd grimaced. His body ached far too much to do anything about bedding her, even if that bed was in a fit state. He would wait for the arrival of his linen, furs and tapestries before seducing her, but he would do it. He wanted to taste her mouth again.

'What do you want from me?' She took a step backwards and glanced towards the bed again.

'The usual,' he said.

'The usual?' She paled and her eyes flitted to and fro. 'That…that is not possible. Even my husband…found other women…when I… Is this how you repay my help?'

He instantly regretted his impulse to tease her. She was acting like a trapped animal. She had been married before. She knew what passed between a man and woman. An unexpected stab of jealousy hit him. Her husband must have been a blind fool if he took other women. Or perhaps Eilidith had found the experience distasteful and had encouraged it.

'I've never forced a woman, Liddy, and I have no intention of starting with you. When you come to my bed, it will be because you want to be there.'

All colour except for a spray of freckles across the bridge of her nose drained from her face. 'Why would I want that?'

'Because you will.' He inclined his head, wondering what sort of blind brute her husband had been. Her insistence at being cursed showed her fear. Liddy had flame-coloured hair and passion to match when she forgot her fear. He planned on making her forget—a pleasant challenge for him. 'I tasted your mouth, but I am a patient man and can wait for the final surrender. Far sweeter that way.'

She chewed her bottom lip, turning it the colour of berries in the summertime. 'The kiss before you went out to the fight…it was a mistake. An impulsive mistake.'

Sigurd pretended indifference, but his body thrummed as if someone had plucked a harp. 'Pity. I quite enjoyed it.'

She backed up three steps. 'My heart is buried on the hillside where…where my husband lies.'

Sigurd let his hand fall to his side. An unaccustomed flare of anger and jealousy surged through him. 'Who said anything about your heart? I am talking about your body meeting mine.'

Liddy spoke to the ground. 'I am trying to be honest… My husband…'

He captured her chin so that she was forced to look into his eyes. 'Lie to yourself by all means, but don't lie to me. I have no interest in your heart. You are free to love who you want. I'm not interested in love or emotional attachments. I was cured of that years ago. Beyla—'

Liddy wrenched her chin away. She had made a grave error. Sigurd lacked pity or any of the finer emotions. She was pleased she'd used Brandon as an excuse rather than explaining about Keita and

Gilbreath and their deaths. Her children were not going to be served up so that he could mock them. She might have lost everything, but her heart was theirs. 'Thank you for telling me the truth. I won't make that mistake again.'

Coll gave a low growl.

'You seem angry about something,' he said with deceptive casualness as he put a restraining hand on Coll's neck. 'You are making Coll nervous.'

Liddy clicked her fingers and Coll moved to stand beside her. 'Coll is my dog. I know his mood better than anyone. Thank you.'

He raked his hand through his hair. 'You are beyond a doubt the most perverse of creatures. You always have to be right, but you are wrong to fear me.'

'I don't fear you.'

'I see...thankfully I have other things to do besides sparring with a rebellious slave.'

She stared at him open-mouthed as he strode through the door.

'I will never have feelings for that man,' she whispered to Coll. Coll gave her a look which seemed to say that if she was indifferent, why did she feel so alive in his presence?

No good ever came from antagonising a Northman. That fact had been drummed into her head ever since she could remember.

Swallow her pride. How difficult could it be? Liddy shuddered. Apologising would be easier away from here.

Liddy discovered Sigurd standing beside the lake, looking out at the purple Paps of Jura. Coll went up to him and pawed at his trouser leg. Sigurd reached down and threw a stick into the water. Coll, the traitor, went bounding after it.

'It is better to lance a boil than allow it to fester as my mother would say. I had no right to take my anger out on you,' she said at his questioning glance. 'I haven't been a slave for long.'

He picked up the stick that Coll dropped at his feet. 'You have a nose for trouble. You need someone to ensure you are kept safe. Someone needs to protect you.'

She stared at him, astonished. Justifying his behaviour by saying that he was protecting her! Swift anger filled her, but she forced it back down her throat.

'You made me a slave to protect me?' she asked in a deceptively quiet voice. Coll bristled beside her.

'Someone had to. Your family singularly has failed thus far. He would have sold you, Liddy.' He threw the stick again. It arched in the sky before landing in the water. 'I know how the Gaels behave. My grandfather sold my mother.'

'My father is different,' she ground out and then closed her eyes. 'At least I hope he is.'

Sigurd threw the stick again for Coll. It arced high before landing in the lake with a plop. 'You'd volunteered to be a hostage. What is the difference?'

'A hostage has the hope of freedom. A slave...' Her throat tightened. 'A slave has nothing. You expect me simply to accept this change of status without a murmur. To welcome it. What sort of world do you live in?'

The huge dog returned with the stick in his mouth. He shook the water all over her, before covering his eyes with his paws. She sighed inwardly. Why of all the men did Coll have to take a liking to this one?

Liddy crossed her arms over her aching stomach. It hurt that once again she had made a mistake about someone. When would she ever learn? When Brandon had courted her, she'd been certain that he'd seen past her birthmark to the real person. Then on their wedding night, after he'd hurt her with his rough lovemaking, he revealed that he'd only been interested in her dowry and the land she brought.

'Why? You owe me that much. A hostage

would have accomplished the same thing.' She held up her hand, stopping his words. 'And don't go on about rescuing me from my father. You don't know him. He takes his duty to his people seriously.'

She hated how her voice wobbled on the word. Sigurd threw the stick again.

'As a slave, you belong to me. A hostage is at the whim of the jaarl,' he said finally.

'You are the jaarl here.'

He turned towards her. His face had settled into harsh planes. 'Who knows what the future holds? Ketil needs to confirm it. Many will desire it now that Thorbin is gone.'

Liddy's mouth went dry. They might yet face another Thorbin or worse? 'What will make you secure?'

A bitter laugh escaped Sigurd. 'Thorbin has hidden his tribute. He had promised Ketil gold and sent nothing. My late brother has been cleverer than I thought. It is not in his usual hiding places.'

Liddy looked out at Jura. The shifting sunlight had turned the paps a deep purple. 'You won the fight.'

'Ketil wanted Thorbin alive...for some reason. He could have returned.'

The stark words sank into Liddy's conscience.

Sigurd had exceeded his orders and Ketil was not the forgiving type. 'And you killed him after the fight, rather than during it. Wil Ketil punish you?'

Sigurd's brows drew together. 'I had my reasons. Ketil will forgive me once he has the required gold. My plans will happen. He will confirm me as the jaarl.'

'As long as you find the gold. Otherwise...' Liddy wrapped her arms about her waist as she struggled to see the kindness in his eyes again. She wanted to see the man who had given her dog the dried meat not long ago. Instead, this stranger with hard eyes stood there, telling her that the horror she thought she'd saved the island from might not be ended. 'You allowed my father to think that you were the jaarl. He'd never have sold me.'

'You don't know that and have no fear, the required tribute from your father's estate will be paid to Ketil. I don't cheat.'

'But...'

'I will find the gold. It is here. I have not come this far to lose everything.' He put his hand on her arm. She hated that the touch made a curl of warmth grow in her belly. She wanted to lean into him. She wanted to experience his mouth against hers again.

'If you do, you might have to sell me.' Liddy swallowed hard. Things like that didn't happen to her. Silently she listed again the reasons Brandon's mistress had stated when she explained why Brandon would never return to Liddy's bed after the first week of marriage, beginning with her birthmark and ending with her bony figure.

'You worry too much about a future which may never happen.'

His mouth came down on hers and claimed it. The kiss was different from the one they'd shared earlier. This kiss was about ownership. And yet there was something else to it. It ignited a fire deep within her. Her back arched towards him and she encountered the hard planes of his chest.

Her mind reeled. And then she froze. Where was her anger? And her promise not to warm his bed? She was behaving worse than Agnes on her husband's estate, who only had to have a man look at her with a hint of passion and she opened her legs. Pathetic.

She struggled against the bonds of his arms.

He let her go. Instantly. The corner of his mouth twitched slightly. 'A willing woman, Liddy. I am willing to wait for a little while. You were the one who asked for the kiss.'

Her fingers explored her tingling lips. 'How?'

'Your eyes asked for it.'

She crossed her arms over her suddenly tender breasts. 'Next time wait until my mouth does.'

He gave a soft laugh as his gaze homed in on them. 'Your voice or your lips?'

Her lips ached worse than ever and a warm curl started in her stomach. Brandon had never made her feel like this, not even when he was courting her. Her husband had deserted their bed before the first night was through. How could she hope to hold someone like Sigurd? And what would happen when he discovered about Keita and Gilbreath and how they died? It was best never to start or to have dreams.

'My voice, of course,' she answered and with as much dignity as she could muster inclined her head.

'Good.' His maddening smile returned. 'You wish to make this interesting. I will wait until you break...until you beg.'

Her body protested that she had been willing, more than willing. 'You will have to wait a long time, then.'

He gave a half-smile. 'You might not believe it, but I actually want you for other things than warming my bed. The wait will do me good. But it will happen.'

'What things?' Liddy asked as relief flooded through. Of course, he had been teasing her.

'I need someone I can trust to run my household, Liddy.' He gestured towards the various buildings. 'Thorbin may have been content to live like a pig, but I refuse to. Someone to tell me if anything unusual is found.'

Liddy struggled to breathe. There was a way to become free after all—one which would not involve bed sport.

'If I am the one to find the gold, will you set me free?'

He tapped his fingers together and assessed her under lowered brows. Liddy shifted uncomfortably, aware that she might have gone too far. 'Are you worried about your curse preventing you from finding it?'

'My curse doesn't work that way.' There was little point in telling him that it worked against people she loved. She could never have feelings for a man like him. 'You need someone to help you.'

She waited, certain that he must hear the thumping of her heart.

'If you find it and bring it to me, I will free you.' He lowered his brows. 'I expect you to spend time keeping my house, not hunting for gold. And I expect loyalty. You belong to me until this happens.'

'Loyalty should be earned, not bought.'

'Indeed.'

She took a deep breath. 'But I agree and I will be discreet. I would hardly want anyone else to discover the gold.'

His eyes danced. 'Do we seal this bargain with a kiss?'

She shook her head before the temptation to taste his lips again filled her. She held out her hand. 'A handshake will be the best.'

He tilted his head to one side. 'I never took you for a coward.'

Liddy moistened her lips to stop them tingling. 'I told you that wasn't going to happen. I'm not interested.'

He raised a brow. 'You are a very poor liar.'

'It is the truth.'

'Prove it. Seal our agreement with a kiss.'

Her mouth. If he kissed her again, he would know how much she longed to be in his bed and that would be a mistake. She needed to discover the gold before he discovered what a disappointment in bed she was. 'You won't get me that easily.'

He leant forward and brushed her over-sensitive mouth with his fingers. 'Anticipation makes everything sweeter.'

Chapter Six

Sigurd picked through the used straw and hay that littered the stable floor the next morning. The stables were at least well-kept, unlike the hovel where he was now expected to reside. He had kept away from the chamber last night, unable to trust himself with Liddy. He'd worked by torchlight trying to discover where Thorbin had hidden the gold until he had become too tired and slept.

He wanted to keep his mind away from Liddy and the problem she posed. He had told the truth—he didn't force women, but one taste of her lips had been nearly enough to send him over the edge.

He slammed his fist against the wall. Where had his famed control gone? He needed to be thinking of other things, not the curve of Liddy's neck or the way she chewed her bottom lip. He wanted her, but he didn't need her. He didn't need anyone. He had learned that lesson long ago.

'Where have you put the gold, Brother? How far did your treachery extend?'

'Do you know what you are doing? Or are you like your half-brother—intent on shutting everyone out?' Hring burst into the stables.

'Has everything been secured? What about the men who followed Thorbin? Did they allow for their belongings to be searched? I expect trouble.' Sigurd glared back at the man. What was it to him that he'd undertaken the search of the stables on his own? He'd left orders.

Hring slapped his hand against his head. 'Do you take me for an idiot? There was no trouble after I invoked your name. I swear no one knows anything, but Thorbin distrusted everyone. He was ever likely to order the murder of anyone who disagreed with him. To the point of paranoia. Two were hanged last week and their bones left out for the crows. Are you going the same way?'

Sigurd took a steadying breath. Hring was right about one thing—he couldn't become like Thorbin. He wouldn't behave like that.

'Where is his mistress? Did you discover her hiding place?' he asked, righting the manger.

'The last one disappeared over three months ago. He has not taken another woman.' Hring let out a sigh and the lines of tiredness were clear on his face. 'I questioned everyone closely and they tell the same tale. I mean, it is not like Thorbin to deny himself anything.'

Sigurd tapped his fingers together. The timing of the woman's disappearance would have coincided with the barrel arriving at Ketil's headquarters. Thorbin was no fool. He must have known that his time was limited.

'Find the woman, find the missing tribute.'

Hring shook his head in confusion. 'But where has she gone? Nobody knows.'

'Disappeared, not sacrificed? Are you certain?'

'Maybe he had other concerns. Maybe she knew that she would go the way of the others, saw her chance and took it.' Hring shook his head. 'It weren't right, hanging those women.'

'Dead bodies rarely whisper secrets.' Sigurd stared at the stable. Thorbin had to have calculated that he would be taken from the island, so where had he hidden the gold? It had to be in an easy place to access and where Beyla would be certain to look if the worst should happen. 'There is one place to search…'

Hring backed away. 'You might not fear that place, but others do.'

'Very well, I shall dig.'

'The priests might have something to say about that.'

Sigurd put his face close to Hring's. 'Ask me if I care.'

'I forgot you care nothing for our gods.' Hring rubbed the back of his neck. 'Just remember others might take offence. We need those men on our side and you quite frankly do not look fit to fight another battle.'

'First I question the priests and then I dig.'

'You won't find anything.'

Sigurd tilted his head to one side. 'Where do you think he hid the gold?'

Hring shrugged. 'Perhaps Thorbin spoke true. Perhaps it is the natives not paying up. Certainly I found nothing. You were wrong to kill him before you had made him divulge the whereabouts. And you never questioned him about this alliance with Ivar the Boneless that they are all talking about.'

'Thorbin sent our compatriot back in a barrel. What more evidence do you need? He could not hope to hold this island against Ketil on his own.'

'But Ivar the Boneless!'

'Perhaps he thought he could play both off against the other and build his own empire. My brother was like that—divide and conquer. I want the patrols doubled. We will be prepared if Ivar decides to make a move to avenge Thorbin's death.'

The man continued to stand there with a fierce expression on his face.

'What is it?'

'You never keep women long. You had Eilidith for one night.' Hring blew out a long breath. 'Once you are finished with her, sell her to me. No one else. I helped you achieve this. This is all I ask. The right of first refusal.'

Sigurd regarded the grizzled warrior. A stab of unaccustomed jealousy passed through him. Why should Hring have anything to do with Liddy? He knew little of Hring's private life. He had a wife and a daughter back in the North from what he could recall. 'Is that so? What will your family say about it?'

'My daughter, Ragnhild, runs the estate. She never questions my authority or at least not about slaves.' Hring slammed his fists together. 'Not if she knows what is good for her.'

Sigurd nodded. But the jealousy was like an itch he couldn't ignore. Why did people assume he was done with Liddy? He prepared himself to take a swing at the man. 'Why would you want her? What can she offer you?'

Hring stood there, stoically. 'We owe her a debt. She saved this whole enterprise. She deserves better than a life of servitude. Gorm says you have called for Thorbin's wife. Everyone knows you and her were lovers once. Would you have the woman who saved us serve a bitch like Beyla?'

'Your tongue runs away with you, Hring.'

Hring looked unrepentant. 'Somebody has to tell the truth or otherwise you'll end up like Thorbin.'

'You would free her, you mean,' Sigurd said, suddenly understanding. 'You think I should never have taken her as a slave in the first place. That she should return to a father who sold her as a slave and a brother so weak that he allowed a woman to be a hostage in his place.'

'Without her help, the bloodshed would have been much greater. You owe her a debt. A true warrior always pays his debts.'

'Do you run the *felag* now, Hring?' Sigurd asked, allowing his voice to drip with ice. 'I have my reasons. I know what Eilidith did and she will be rewarded in good time. You may tell everyone that. I paid a heavy price for her. Her family will keep its farm. I've made good my promise, but I will not have anyone think me weak or soft.'

Hring took three steps back. 'You are overly touchy today.'

'Do not question my authority again. I expect an honest report to Ketil as well.'

Hring nodded, but his eyes took on a speculative gleam. 'Do you intend to bed her? It is obvious that you haven't yet or you wouldn't be this touchy. It looks like you spent all night in here, searching rather than celebrating.'

'None of your business. That is private between the lady and me.'

Hring's face broke into a wide smile. 'It is good to see you are human, Lord Sigurd. Sometimes I've wondered. We've all wondered.'

Liddy looked over the Northman's banqueting hall with a practised eye as the morning sun shone through the door. If she concentrated on the hall, maybe the butterflies in her stomach would cease and she'd forget how awful it had been the first morning after her marriage when Brandon's mistress had led the jeering of her. She tucked her chin into her shoulder and moved into the centre of the room. The rushes on the floor had not been changed in a very long time. Then there were the badly moth-eaten tapestries. But there were no obvious hiding spots for the gold. Perhaps it was why Sigurd had readily agreed to her boast—he knew she had no hope of finding it.

'What are you doing here?' one of the servants asked her.

'I'm your overlord's new...new housekeeper,' she said. Her voice refused to utter the word *slave*. 'He has charged me with overseeing the clean-up of this place.'

The women shook their heads. One looked her up and down before jangling her rather large breasts. 'You? Aye, I know what the last housekeeper did and it weren't much of cleaning.'

'You don't appear to have much to offer,' another said, looking Liddy up and down. Liddy instinctively placed her hand over the birthmark and focused on the filthy rushes. If she needed any confirmation of her appeal to men, this was it—the judgement of strangers.

'His eye will wander elsewhere,' said another, preening.

'She can have him,' called a third. 'We all know what happens when a jaarl takes a woman to bed. Poor thing.'

The entire room went silent as the women nudged each other.

'What happens?' Liddy asked, jerking her head upwards and forgetting to hide her chin.

'She ends up dead!' the first one cried. 'A cursed position. It doesn't matter about all the gold-shot shawls or gowns if your body hangs from a tree, rotting.'

'Who was Thorbin's mistress?' Liddy asked, trying not to shudder. 'Which one of you graced his bed?'

The woman blanched. 'Shona disappeared about three months ago. Just after the last Northman came, demanding payment. She was the one who had to feed him the poisoned cup and she spilt it all down his front.'

'Shona disappeared?'

'They said that she had run away. The jaarl launched a big search for her, but she was never found.' The woman with the large breasts shook her head.

'I still say she is alive, hidden somewhere, waiting for him to return,' the first maid said.

'He never brought back a body. And she'd have done anything for him after he gave her that shawl shot with gold. She kept saying how he'd marry her.'

The women all began talking at once about the woman and their theories about her disappearance. Coll gave a sharp bark and the clamour died down. They all gave the dog a wary eye.

'You can either help me or not, but gossiping will never clean a house.' Liddy silently resolved to discover what had happened to this Shona. The woman might well know where the gold was and once Liddy had found that gold, she'd be free and could live out the rest of her life with honour. Maybe Sigurd was right—maybe her curse no longer had any power now that she didn't belong to Cennell Fergusa.

The women exchanged glances and there was

a hushed discussion behind their hands. Liddy waited with crossed arms.

'How come you are working here now?' one asked. 'I thought he fought for you and your family. Are you a hostage?'

'My father sold me to pay this year's tribute.' She pulled up her sleeves to reveal the golden bracelets. 'I wear Sigurd Sigmundson's golden chains.'

Instantly the atmosphere changed. One of the women shook her head. 'I have never seen golden shackles before.'

'It doesn't matter what they are made of, they are still shackles,' Liddy retorted.

'It ain't right, that. You helped free all the prisoners from Thorbin the Hangman,' one muttered and the rest agreed.

'Will you help? The hall needs to be cleaned before tonight's feast. It stinks of sweat and stale beer. I doubt the men will be as forgiving as they were last night.'

'They won't notice much when there is a warm body wrapped about them.'

'That is not an option for me.' Liddy fingered her mark. 'I know my limitations.

The woman gave a pitying smile. 'It wouldn't be so noticeable if you didn't hide your chin like that. And it ain't so bad—it looks like a bird.'

Liddy forced a smile. 'I know the extent of my charms, but thank you for being kind.'

The woman gave a half-shrug.

'Are you going to set your great beastie on us?'

Liddy gave the large-bosomed servant a hard glance. 'I will make certain Lord Sigurd knows who helped and who did not.'

She gathered the worst of the rushes up, while the women watched. After depositing them outside, she went back for a second load. Returning from her third trip, she stopped. Coll gave a soft woof. Several of the women had begun to help to sweep the rushes into piles.

'It smells better already,' one said with a smile. 'And Shona used to flip her red shawl and point, rather than actually do anything.'

'All right, all right,' the large-bosomed servant grumbled. 'I've no wish for a trip to the sacred grove. Women never return from there.'

'Sigurd was appalled when he saw the bodies,' Liddy said quietly.

'That is the first truly good news we have heard in months,' one of the maidservants said. 'I'm Mhairi, by the way. And I will see you right. No false airs and graces with you.'

Liddy rapidly listed all the jobs that needed to be done. To her relief, several women knew where the fresh rushes were kept and how to detach the tapestries from the walls.

In an odd sort of way it felt good to be running her own household again, instead of existing at her parents'.

If she kept busy, she'd have no time to think. If she kept busy, she would have no time to consider the implications of her wager. If she kept busy, she would fall asleep, exhausted, at the end of the day.

She'd learnt that trick after the twins died. She'd despised housework before their death. She did it because she had to. The outside had always called to her, but she'd learnt the value in hard work and being far too tired to think. Thinking about Keita and Gilbreath was too much for her heart to take.

After their death, she had wanted to cry great sobs or scream until the woods and the Paps of Jura across the water rang with her cries, but she didn't want to give Brandon the satisfaction of calling her mad. One day she discovered if she kept her hands busy and her mind occupied with little tasks, she had given the appearance of functioning normally and little by little the need to scream had diminished.

The things which had to go first were the bedding and the rushes covering the floor.

Several of the maids, once they realised that she was not about to beat them, assisted her and within a few hours the banqueting hall smelt far cleaner.

Beyond supervising from the doorway, Liddy had kept out of Sigurd's chamber, much to the amusement of the other servants. She had spied a convenient corner near to the kitchen where she and Coll could sleep.

The tapestry was being returned to the wall when Sigurd came into the hall. Instantly Coll rushed over to him, rolling over and offering his tummy to be stroked. Sigurd's hair sparkled with raindrops, making it look as if he'd been covered in diamonds. Liddy's breath hitched.

She frowned. 'Is it too much to ask that my dog remain loyal?'

Sigurd laughed and gave him a piece of dried meat. Coll took it and slunk off to a quiet corner. 'I'm pleased someone is happy to see me.'

'I hope this meets with your approval,' she said and gestured about the room. She could do distant. 'Or do Northmen prefer to live in a pigsty?'

A small smile played on his mouth, highlighting a dimple she hadn't noticed earlier. 'Gratifying to know that I chose the right person for the job. The women seem to obey you.'

'For now,' she said with a careful shrug. 'They are wary of Coll's teeth.'

'Coll is a sweetheart.'

'He dislikes most men.'

'Did he have an opinion on your late husband?'

Liddy shook her head. 'They mostly ignored each other after I refused to get rid of Coll, because he had barked at one of Brandon's...'

'Mistresses,' Sigurd finished for her. 'A dog of discerning taste.'

Liddy tapped her foot on the ground. 'Did you come here to speak about my dog?'

He laughed. 'I reckoned I'd find you here. You have accomplished more than I thought you would. We will be able to feast tonight without holding our noses.'

Liddy paused in her demonstration of the changes she had made. The tiny compliment made the hairs on the back of her neck tingle. She dreaded to think how long it had been since she had received a word of praise and the way he looked at her, she could almost think herself pleasing to the eye.

Deliberately she touched her birthmark. The man had bought her as a slave. Melting and making excuses would not free her or stop her heart from aching when he turned to another. Besides, Coll had allowed his stomach to overrule his judgement. He was only a dog after all. She had to stop relying on him. 'I had help. A task like this is easier when you have many hands.'

'The women suddenly seem less sullen. Your doing, I presume?'

'They wanted to know if you were like your brother and sacrificed women to the gods. I told them absolutely not.'

He tilted his head to one side. 'How do you know that?'

'I saw your face at the grove. You are no murderer of women. It makes you different from Thorbin and his ilk.'

'Your voice holds echoes of my mother. She used to say—it is the little things that show your true intentions.'

Her gaze caught his and she tumbled in. She was the first to look away. Caring about this man would only lead to complications.

'Her words of wisdom sound like my mother's,' she said with a hiccupping laugh. 'It is the little things people notice.'

'Perhaps...' He cleared his throat and everyone turned towards him. 'I have given orders. The bodies which were hanging will be properly buried. We have no need of that sort of magic when my sword arm will protect this island.'

The women clapped their hands and their faces

shone. Several straightened up and adjusted their gowns.

'We will be sure to wear our best gowns and put flowers in our hair,' the large-bosomed maid called.

'I am sure my men will appreciate it.'

Liddy ducked her head and her heart gave a little pang. There would obviously be a competition to catch the new jaarl's eye.

'I suspect it will be much easier to keep this hall clean,' Liddy said in an undertone, pushing the jealous thought away. Sigurd would never be hers. She had to focus on the important things like finding the gold and becoming free, rather than wishing for something impossible.

Sigurd return her smile. 'I suspect you are right, but that is not why I did it.'

'Thorbin's last mistress…' Liddy began to get the conversation away from dangerous things like her attraction to him.

He held up his hand, stopping her. 'I know about her. She vanished along with all her things a little under three months ago. According to Gorm, her mother has no idea where she is.'

'And you don't find it odd?'

'Why?'

'If Thorbin felt she had stolen from him, he would have destroyed her family. Look at what he attempted to do to my family simply because Malcolm didn't address him in the right manner.'

Sigurd nodded. 'True.'

'Thorbin knew where she went, you mean.' Liddy's stomach roiled. 'You mean she is dead… in that grove. Have you searched it?'

'Not the grove. It has been checked. And the priest values his life.' Sigurd's face became hard. 'He found reason to show me where each was sacrificed. There have been no sacrifices in the grove for six months.'

'Someone will know what happened to her, but they may not know that they know. If we can find out what happened to her, we may find the gold.'

'Little things again.'

'It always is. I mean to find the gold. I have no desire to remain a slave.'

'You are impressive, Lady Eilidith, king's daughter.'

The way he said it, it was not exactly a term of endearment.

Liddy made a cutting gesture. 'Please, the title ended a long time ago. And my father was a very minor king.'

'Once the daughter of a king, always one, in my experience.'

She thought then of his mother as the shadows appeared in his eyes. Had being a king's daughter been the one thing she'd clung to? Certainly her son was arrogant. Liddy corrected her thoughts—not arrogant, because he fulfilled his promises. But he moved with a certain assurance and he had played his half-brother with finesse. She had to hope that the islanders realised their new lord was not as lazy as the old one. She also hoped he was wrong and they did not have to fear any more Northern incursions.

Liddy pinched the bridge of her nose. There was little point in trying to dissuade him.

'Where do you expect me to sleep? We have our agreement after all. I would hardly like to deprive you of such a place. I've kept the servants out in case it still needed to be searched.'

'You sleep where I sleep.'

Her heart clunked against her chest. It would be too much to hope for that he wouldn't sleep there for two nights in a row. 'But...'

'It suits my purpose. Do I have to explain everything? If you like, I will carry you out of the hall when your bedtime comes. Or you may walk. But you will end up where I want you to be.'

One of his men called to him about the possible finding of an iron-bound chest in a barn. He moved rapidly away without a backwards glance, leaving her to stare open-mouthed in his wake while several of the giggling maids nudged each other.

Liddy clenched her fists. Two could play at this game. 'I will walk. I retain the use of my limbs and we shall see who can sleep in that chamber.'

The other women nudged each other and hastily pretended to be doing something else.

'Is there a problem?'

'You are right,' Mhairi said. 'He is nothing like Thorbin.'

The great hall rang with the sounds of men laughing and telling tales in front of a roaring fire. The women were busy serving food and ale and exchanging banter with his men.

Sigurd closed his eyes and savoured the moment. His hall and his men. It was a far cry from the day when he'd run barefoot from the baying mob with only a short sword and bow. He'd made this happen and it was all the sweeter for having vanquished Thorbin. He would keep it. Ketil would approve his jaarlship and he could think about his next conquest. Islay was merely a stepping stone. He would hold his course and steer true towards his destiny.

Tomorrow would bring the remainder of his men and the takeover would be complete. The youth who had lived with the pigs was the jaarl of all he surveyed. But there was something hollow in the victory. He had rarely felt as alone. The men were joking and laying foolish wagers about their strength, but the enormous weight of responsibility lay on his shoulders.

Sigurd glanced towards where Liddy had just returned to the hall. All evening she had flitted here and there, rarely standing still like the butterfly she sported on her face. He frowned. The vivacious woman of two days ago had become a pale grey ghost. Weariness was etched on her brow. Not so much butterfly as wilting flower. He motioned to her.

As if she had been watching out for him, she came over with a jug of mead. 'Your cup is empty. That should not be happening, not at this feast.'

He laughed. 'What is so special about this feast?'

She ducked her head. 'It is only what I would do for any honoured guest in my household. You asked me to behave as if I ran this household and I have.'

He covered her hand with his and felt it tremble beneath his. For someone who had sparred with Thorbin, she appeared remarkably ill at ease. 'But I appreciate the care. It has been a long time since someone cared enough to pay attention to my mead.'

'I will bear that in mind. I had best go.' Her gold wrist shackle caught his sleeve and sent the mead flying. She gave a soft curse.

All the noise stopped and everyone turned their heads towards them, expecting him to explode. It was as if the entire room held its breath.

'Stay.'

Sigurd calmly reached for the goblet, righted it and poured himself another glass. The noise rose again.

She checked her movement and peered up at him. Despite the weariness of her face, her eyes blazed. 'A command? From master to slave?'

'A request. I share the blame. Any other warrior, well...who knows how they would react.' He patted to the bench beside him. 'Sit beside me. You are a puzzle, Liddy.'

'Liddy is for my friends. You are now my master.'

'*Fithrildi*, then.'

She rested her hand on her chin. 'I don't know the word.'

'Butterfly.' He leant forward and removed her hand from her face. 'Like the mark you keep trying to cover up.'

'It is ugly.'

'I don't find butterflies ugly, do you?'

She looked at him from under her lashes with

blazing storm-sea eyes. 'You may call me Liddy after all. Once you get to know me, you will see that I am not the butterfly type. I am more like the humble ant. Useful rather than pretty to look at.'

'You do yourself a disservice.' He tugged at her hand and she tumbled into his lap. 'You will sit. I command it.'

She hurriedly scrambled off his lap as his men started cheering. Coll gave a loud howl from where he sat contentedly munching a bone under the table.

'Please.'

'Very well, sit beside me. Let someone else worry about the mead.'

Liddy gratefully sank down next to him. Fighting him no longer seemed so important. Her back ached and her arms were tired. She hadn't slept properly since the news of her father's arrest.

Around her the room buzzed, cocooning her, and the warmth of the bodies had increased the temperature from earlier. Her eyelids began to close. She leant a little towards Sigurd's chest. Sigurd said something and a wave of coarse laughter rippled around the table. The sound was enough to jerk her awake.

Everyone stared at her. She covered her mouth and wondered briefly if she'd snored.

'I'm sorry. I wasn't paying attention.' She auto-

matically pasted on a smile and reached for the
jug of mead. It trembled in her hand. Some of the
liquid spilt on the table. She gave a soft curse and
tried to clean it up.

'That is enough, Liddy.' He took the jug from
her fingers and placed it on the table. 'You are no
good to me like that.'

The brush of his fingers sent a jolt through her.
She narrowed her eyes. 'Like how?'

The last thing she wanted was to be attracted
to this man. She was going to win their wager.
He might think that she would fall into his arms,
but she was made of stronger stuff. She knew that
type of man, intimately—all soft words and teasing until you were under his power.

Brandon had been like that, so sure and certain that all of womankind would fall at his feet
if he so much as crooked a finger. And yet he'd
had little regard for his lawful wife's feelings.
She was supposed to understand that she was the
mother of his children and his wife. All the other
women meant nothing to him. And the boat had
capsized, the boat which Brandon swore would
never capsize. After that, he had not bothered to
hide his contempt.

'You go now. Off to my chamber. I will join
you there later.'

All her tiredness vanished. 'I… I…am fine.'

'I dislike it when my dinner companions fall asleep in their food. It tends to mean they are exhausted and not fit for the purpose.' He made a little shooing motion. 'Coll is ready for his new sleeping quarters. Humour me.'

Coll gave a thump of his tail.

'I have found somewhere else to sleep, more convenient for me as I am to be supervising the refurbishment of the hall,' she said concentrating on the jug. She knew her face had flushed crimson. She only hoped that Sigurd would think it had to do with the heat in the hall, rather than the image of them sharing a bedchamber and what could happen there or rather what wouldn't happen there.

He banged his palm on the table. 'Go to my bed.'

'Is this how Northmen behave? Changing their minds when it suits them? I thought you were a man of honour,' she said, glaring back at him.

His eyes darkened. 'Are you afraid to be alone with me? It says little for your resolve.'

She lifted her chin, but inwardly she seethed. 'My resolve remains as it ever was.'

The shadowy dimple returned, playing on the corner of his mouth. 'I see.'

'You understand nothing.' Liddy didn't know who she was more irritated with—herself for being attracted to him or him for guessing. And it didn't matter where she slept. He'd promised not to use force. She would remain unwilling, except the incessant rebellious part called her liar. That part wanted to explore the kiss they had shared and it seemed to be growing with every passing breath.

His voice lowered to a deep purr. 'Or would you prefer that I carried you? A demonstration for the other women that I am taken?'

His voice slid down her spine, doing strange things to her insides. 'When you put it like that, who am I to argue? I'll leave immediately.'

'Who are you indeed?' He turned back towards one of his men and began a conversation about the state of the harbour.

Giving small thanks for a reprieve, Liddy beat a hasty retreat.

The small chamber was no more inviting now than it had been when she left it this early morning. Last night she had hunkered down in a corner, waiting for Sigurd who never came. Tonight, she needed to be more positive.

There was a distinct smell of damp about the bedding and there was no way she could sleep on that. She tore the bedding off the bed and put it out of the door. A large cloud of dust rose making her sneeze.

'I am not sleeping in that bed. Fleas,' Liddy muttered. 'That's my story and I am sticking to it.'

She made a nest on the cold flags with her cloak and overgown. She laid her belt and eating knife to one side before she carefully did her hair into a loose plait. Little familiar routines which somehow took on a new significance. Coll whined slightly and nudged her arm. She put an arm about him and tried to ignore the golden shackles glinting in the faint light.

'This is only temporary, Coll. I will regain my freedom. He can do what he likes to me. I did obey him by going to his bedchamber. But we do have an agreement—no kisses unless I specifically ask for them. I will demonstrate that I am less easily won than he seems to think. As if I'm supposed to melt because he calls me something ridiculous like butterfly.'

She cupped her hand over the birthmark which suddenly did not seem as big as it had done. 'Maybe he is right. Maybe I have been making too much of it.'

Coll gave a deep woof of agreement and she wished that she had as much confidence in her abilities as Coll seemed to.

Chapter Seven

Sigurd knew the dream the instant it began. He had experienced it a thousand times, but usually not with such vivid clarity.

Warm luscious curves pressing against him and long limbs wrapped about his body. His mouth covering hers, drawing substance from her lips. Her body responding to his, welcoming him.

He knew the dream and relaxed into its pleasure, all the while knowing that no one yet had matched his dream woman. In all the time he had been dreaming it, he had never once seen her face. At first he didn't want to, fearing it might prove to be Beyla's, but now he was past caring. He accepted the mysterious woman. However, this time a gold light infused the dream and the woman half-turned to him. Her blue-green eyes were heavy with passion.

In the dim light, he could see a butterfly perched just below her lower lip.

Recognition thudded through him. Liddy.

A small cry shocked him out of the dream. His body thrummed with unspent desire.

The real Liddy, not the dream one, lay several feet from him on the hard stone. She cried again in her sleep and her hands flailed against the thin cloak. In the dim light, her cheeks sparkled with silent tears. Something tightened deep in Sigurd's gut. He wanted to take them away.

At his movement, Coll gave a small whine.

'It's all right, boy,' Sigurd said softly. 'I have this one.'

He heaved himself up from the roll of blankets he'd been sleeping on. He retrieved the fur-lined cloak that he'd earlier spread over her and tucked it more firmly about her body.

Instantly her thrashing stopped and her lips curved up into tiny smile.

'Sweet dreams,' he whispered.

Liddy woke with a start on the cold floor with her cheek resting on Coll. Sunlight streamed in from the narrow slit in the wall, hitting her eyes. Earlier she knew she had been dreaming of the day when the boat had overturned, throwing both Keita and Gilbreath into the water. She had worked hard to save both them and the nursemaid, but this time they kept slipping from her grasp.

The dream had been getting worse and worse as the coldness of the loch seeped into her and started to drag her down. Suddenly she had been covered in a great warmth and a thousand butterflies enveloped her. Keita and Gilbreath waved at her and faded as the butterflies bore her up, freeing her from the ice-cold tomb. Warm arms reached out to embrace her. Liddy woke with a start.

It took a few heartbeats before recent events flooded back. The fight. Her father's betrayal. Her slavery. And this—sleeping in the same room with a Northman who once he discovered what she was truly like would destroy her.

Sweat drenched her body. A thin grey light filled the room. She lay there for a moment, trying to come back to earth and to forget the dream she had just had.

There was no hope for it. Sigurd had started to invade her dreams. And when he invaded her bed, she knew any foolish hope of romance or love with Sigurd would end.

The dream about Brandon had been a warning. She, too, had thought him wonderful. His kisses were sweet and then the wedding night happened and nothing she could do would please him. It had turned out to be a lie so that he could get her dower lands with the trees to fashion his unsinkable boats.

Someone had spread a heavy cloak over her in the middle of the night. A faint but not unpleasant masculine scent rose from it and held her in its embrace.

She hugged her knees to her chest. The shackles were less heavy this morning. She twisted one, noticing its intricate design.

'You are awake. Finally.' Sigurd's voice rolled over her and made her body tingle anew.

She turned her head. In the dull light she could make out his shape. He occupied a bedroll close to where she had collapsed earlier. He sat up and the fur cloak slid off of him, revealing his chest. A silver cross on a chain rested on his naked muscle.

'You wear a cross?'

'In memory of my mother.' He gave a soft laugh. 'Interesting that you noticed.'

Liddy gulped hard and hurriedly looked away. Her hand curled and she could almost feel the warm muscles of his chest sliding under her fingertips.

'You didn't sleep on the bed.' Her voice came out more breathless than she intended.

'I spotted the flea-ridden bundle you had

placed outside the door. A wise precaution.' There was a faint shuffling noise and she hoped it meant that he was covering up. Cowardly she kept her gaze away from him. 'I've slept in worse places than on a stone floor.'

'I left you the bed frame and a blanket,' she said, trying to concentrate on the wall, rather than glancing at his chest again, but she knew she faced a losing battle.

'When I sleep on a frame, I prefer to have feather bedding and furs and a distinct lack of fleas.' He stretched and his torso rippled. 'It adds to the comfort. When my trunks arrive, you will discover the difference.'

Her mind conjured the image of Sigurd, leaning back against the soft fur, naked, inviting her to join him. Her mouth went dry. She hastily swallowed. Simply because she was physically attracted to the man did not mean she had to do anything about it. Or that it would happen. She hastily touched her birthmark.

'I will take your word for it.'

'Have you ever slept on furs, Liddy?'

'I'm not in the habit of discussing my bed arrangements with strange men.'

'I will take it as a no.' He lowered his voice to a velvet purr. 'Given that we have spent several nights together, I would hardly call us strangers.'

'We are not lovers,' she said and instantly regretted it. 'I mean…friends.'

Sigurd instantly sobered. 'I consider you a friend, Liddy, despite what you think, despite what anyone thinks. But we will be lovers—soon.'

'You are so arrogant.'

'No, I keep my promises. There is a difference.'

Liddy reached for her gown. 'Much remains to be done to make this place habitable.'

He mouthed *coward*, but his eyes gleamed.

'You should have woken me earlier.' She pulled her gown over her head and attempted to breathe normally. The sooner she was away from him, the sooner her mind would clear and she'd go back to being level-headed and practical. Passion happened to other women.

Once enveloped in the folds of the gown, she scrambled to her feet and made a pretence of trying to find her belt. However her body was acutely aware of every move he made and every breath he took.

'Lord Thorbin left this hall in a terrible state,' she said to cover the silence. 'I did small things yesterday, but it will take a good deal of effort to make it truly comfortable…and there is always the possibility of finding the gold.'

At the end of her speech she turned to face him with a bright smile.

'I will allow you to retreat this time, but the battle is not yet over, Liddy.'

'Which battle?'

'You know the battle I mean—the one between the ice-cold shield you use and the warm woman underneath.'

Liddy regarded her hands. It was pointless to argue with him, even if a part of her did enjoy it. For so long, she had kept her voice low, kept her movements quiet and pretended that she was unimportant, trying to make sure people forgot she was there. 'Coll needs his breakfast.'

'I would hate for my new friend to go hungry.' Sigurd stroked her dog under the chin. Coll looked at him with adoring eyes.

'And afterwards...I will make sure the storerooms are attended to.'

'Afterwards, you will sit and rest. You will need your strength later.'

Her heart thumped against her chest. 'Later? What happens later?'

He inclined his head. 'My men will be bringing my household effects here today. I want this place inhabitable. We shall stay for a few weeks before we visit the next fort. I trust you are well versed in moving households from one fort to another.'

Liddy rubbed her hands along her arms. He en-

joyed teasing her. He wanted her for her housekeeping abilities.

'Have you found the gold?'

He shook his head. 'It isn't here. Thorbin knew
the fort would be searched. He also had to know
that he would be sent off to Ketil. He will have
hidden it well. The trouble is knowing where.
Once his death becomes known, Ivar the Boneless will try to take advantage of the situation.
And if you thought Thorbin was bad for this island, Ivar will be a thousand times worse.'

'Thorbin stayed here and required the food
and tribute be brought to him over the past few
months,' she said, trying not think about the
leader of the Dubh Linn Northmen and what he
could do. 'He must have had a reason. I think the
gold is near.'

He raised a hand, stopping her words. 'I am not
my half-brother. I know how important it is for the
overlord to be seen. Tribute has a way of falling
when the overlord is remote. My household is too
large for this fort to support us all year round. If
you wish to rule, you must be prepared to travel—
something Ketil said to me years ago and I have
held it in my mind, waiting for my time to come.'

'You never doubted it would.'

'I made my vow on the dying embers of my

parents' funeral pyre.' A muscle jumped in his jaw. 'I intend to rule well.'

She nodded. When she was small, they had lived in several halls. After the Northmen came, her father only managed to save one hall, but he still visited every one of his tenants every week. Brandon had been the same when he was at home—visiting his tenants. But she had never been aware of Thorbin moving from the fort on the headland. But she could understand why Sigurd needed a woman to manage the household more than he needed a mistress. It was a fine art, knowing when to stay and when to move on. It was dictated by the seasons and the weather, but there were other factors. 'I can do as you ask.'

'Good.' He tilted his head to one side. 'Is there something else?'

Liddy swallowed hard. She should leave the room, but her feet were reluctant to go. This man had shown confidence in her and her abilities. He made her think that her past did not have to define her completely.

'You were kind to me last night,' she said, bowing her head before she lost her courage. 'You put that cloak over me. It was…unexpected. It eased my sleep.'

'I've no reason to cheat on our agreement,' he said quietly. 'Not like that anyway.'

'I know that,' she said, backing away from him. The room suddenly seemed too small for them. Her eyes kept returning to the great expanse of his chest. 'I appreciate it. My feelings haven't changed.'

She stopped at the sound of his laughter.

'Go on, my lady fair. You have your battle armour on now.'

Liddy ran out of the room before she was tempted to do something stupid like kiss him. Behind her, his laughter echoed.

Liddy kept going until she reached the busy kitchen. Only then did she pause for a breath. 'I'm immune from him, Coll. I just made a strategic retreat because…because so much needs to be done and I may yet find the gold. Hope—that's what is important.'

Coll cocked his head to one side and gave her a significant look before going off to investigate a pile of kitchen scraps.

'It's fair perishing,' Mhairi said, wiping her hand across her forehead. 'But what a difference. These new tapestries are certainly fine.'

Liddy regarded the gold-shot tapestries. Sigurd must have acquired them in the east. He might need the missing tribute to keep his jaarlship, but he was definitely a wealthy man in his own right. 'Now that they are up, there is little left to do today.'

'Good, even you are running out of ideas,' Mhairi said with a laugh. 'Not that we mind. It is good to feel that we can do something rather than sitting around, wondering which one would be next for the hanging. You worked a wonder with Lord Sigurd, getting him to say that he'd ended that practice.'

The others made noises of agreement.

'What do you suggest we do?' Liddy asked, stretching out the kink that had developed in her back. The women considered her lucky and no one seemed to be staring overlong at her birthmark. They were quite natural about it and thought her being there was a good thing.

Mhairi gave a conspiratorial wink. 'We can bathe and wash away the dirt.'

'Where?'

'Down by the loch. The men will be at training. No one will know. Besides, it is when we always go on days like this. How many times does the sun beat down on Islay? The weather is fair begging for a cool dip in the loch.'

'What would the priest say?'

Mhairi looked serious. 'He would rail against us and call us Jezebels, but he does anyway and we are under the Northmen's protection. They expect us to smell sweet between the sheets.'

The other maids echoed Mhairi's words.

'And there is a whole new crop of warriors arrived. We want to look our best. It can make all the difference. Not all of us grace the jaarl's bedchamber, but there are other warriors...'

'Paddling my feet would be permissible,' Liddy said, putting her hands in the middle of her back. It was not as if she was sailing. The thought of cold water did sound better than staying in this overwarm hall. A memory of splashing her feet with Keita and Gilbreath hit her—Keita's excitement as she tried to catch the water between her hands and how Gilbreath had stomped with both his feet, trying to make the biggest splash. They had adored the sea. It did not make her heart ache as much as she thought it would. Perhaps the hole in her heart had begun to heal after three years. 'Just this once.'

Mhairi smiled. 'I knew you were one of us!'

The cold water lapped against Liddy's feet. She had to admit that it felt wonderful.

'Come further in, Eilidith!' Mhairi called. Mhairi and the rest of the women had discarded their clothes and were now bathing in the cold water. 'You will love it once you try.'

Liddy balanced precariously on a rock. 'This is far enough.'

Coll bounded up with a bark. He lifted a paw and unbalanced her. Liddy whirled her arms to try to regain her balance, but tumbled backwards, landing in the lake with a loud splash. Her kerchief slipped off and the few remaining pins which held her hair in place fell out, disappearing into the lake's mud.

'Oh, Coll, what have you done? I'm soaked,' she cried.

'Making sure you had a good wash, I expect,' a voice behind her said.

The women further out in the lake froze like statues, their faces showing panic.

Liddy gritted her teeth. 'We have finished the hall.'

Sigurd stood, with his blond hair gleaming in the sun. The dark blue of his tunic perfectly complemented his eyes. And Liddy knew what a sodden mess she must look. 'I saw what happened. Coll was merely trying to help.'

'Don't blame the women, blame me.'

'I will take that under advisement.' Sigurd gave a nod. The other women climbed out of the lake, grabbed their bundles of clothes and fled.

'They meant no harm.'

'I'm far from being angry. I expect my men

will enjoy the spectacle.' His voice was a low purr. 'Shall we speak of something else? Something far more enjoyable?'

If she reached her hand out, she could touch his chest. Liddy was aware that she was dressed only in her damp shift that had moulded to her body and that her hair fell in disarray about her shoulders. Sigurd stood between her and her outer gown. She should move, but her feet were rooted to the spot. 'The day is getting away from me. There is the feast tonight.'

'All in good time.' He lifted her hair from her shoulder and ran it through his fingers. She fought how to breathe. What came next, in or out? All she could think about was the shape of his mouth and how strong his arms appeared. 'We are speaking about opportunities and what you do with them.'

Coll nosed her hand and broke the spell. She heaved a sigh of relief. She had nearly given in and touched Sigurd.

She stepped around him and rescued her outer gown. Liddy rapidly put it on and tied her belt with fumbling fingers.

'You shouldn't have done that. We have a bargain. No touching until I ask.'

He tilted his head to one side. 'We never specified the rules but if memory serves—the bargain was no kissing until you begged.'

She put her hand on her hip. 'Do I look like I was begging?'

His thumb brushed her birthmark, sending a series of warm pulses radiating outwards. 'Are you?'

Liddy drew a steadying breath. 'No, I'm specifying the rules now. No touching at all. It isn't seemly.'

'I always have had trouble following complex rules.'

His breath interlaced with hers. She forced her head down and concentrated on retying the belt. 'Try.'

'Your hair is like the sunrise.' The soft words curled about her insides. 'Such a shame to keep it confined the way you do. You should wear it down.'

'It would get in the way. Think about what the priests would say, as my mother always told me.'

'The ones here or from the North?'

Liddy tilted her chin upwards and met his dancing eyes. She longed to wipe the smile off his face. 'Both!'

'I will try to remember that, but anyone who says you should cover up your hair is wrong. Humour me and keep it uncovered.'

Liddy pressed her lips together. Why did he have to pay her compliments? Very few people ever said anything pleasant to her.

'My hair has nothing to recommend it.' She

ticked the points off on her fingers. 'It is red, not golden or black. Bards don't sing about such things and I get freckles across my nose every summer. Ordinary, rather than a stunning beauty, made worse by my birthmark.'

A smile twitched on his lips. She paused in her tirade. 'You are laughing at me!'

'Trying very hard not to.' With a great effort he sobered. 'Allow people to reach their own conclusions, Liddy, rather than telling them what to think. They might surprise you.'

'When I need your advice, I will ask for it.'

'I am merely seeking to do you a favour.'

'When I need a favour or a compliment from you, I will ask for it.'

'Another of your rules?'

'It might be.'

He gave a very low bow. 'You appear to delight in them.'

She caught the twinkle in his eye as he stood up. Somehow that made it worse. He had anticipated her reaction. In seeking to prove to him that he didn't matter, she had alerted him to the fact that he and his opinion did. And she knew how Brandon had used that, how he and his mistresses had delighted in tormenting her, knowing she would not complain. How could she? She'd been the one to beg her father and mother for the marriage, insisting on it despite her mother's clear reservations. And she had had too much pride to explain to her mother how right she'd been to be wary. By then, she was married and Brandon had thoroughly charmed her mother with little gifts and seemingly thoughtful gestures.

She ground her teeth. 'I will ensure a feast to be remembered.'

'But I doubt you will give me what I truly want from you.'

'Do you want it, or merely think you do because I have refused to fall in with your plans?' she said back over her shoulder as she walked away from him.

The shout of laughter echoed over the lake. Keeping herself aloof from him was going to prove much harder than she had previously considered. And she strongly suspected he knew and that he wouldn't play fair.

'Redouble my efforts, Coll. That is the only hope. Or otherwise he will steal my heart away.'

Coll gave a short sharp bark and looked back at the lake with great big eyes.

'Traitor,' she said with a fond smile and gave his ears a stroke.

'Are you going to stop now? You have already made us practice far longer than normal. The sun is starting to set.'

The red mist cleared from Sigurd's eyes. His opponent was down on the ground. Sigurd reached out a hand and pulled him up. In the end he'd sent Hring instead of Gorm to the North lands to fetch Beyla and another of his men to inform Ketil of his victory and Thorbin's demise. It remained to be seen if Gorm was to be trusted.

Sigurd jabbed forward with his sword, grazing the man's belly. 'You are unfit, Gorm. All of Thorbin's men are unfit. What happens if Ivar the Boneless does conduct a raid? What if the Gaels decide to rebel?'

'You didn't seem overly worried about that a few days ago when you decided to taunt one of their warriors.'

'What are you talking about?'

Gorm seemed unperturbed. 'Aedan mac Connall, king of cennell Loairn and laird of Kintra, will see it as an insult, you taking his brother's widow as a slave. We barely contained him last summer. You should be considering that rather than worrying about Ivar the Boneless.'

'Eilidith had returned to her father's. If he had a quarrel with the sale, he should attack the seller, not the buyer.'

'Have you encountered Aedan? He already bears a grudge against the Northmen, something to do with his aunt.'

'Ancient history.'

Gorm narrowed his eyes. 'Here I thought I was reckless, but I'm a new babe compared to you. You enjoy stirring up wasp nests.'

Sigurd parried Gorm's blow. 'I want a quiet life.'

'Then send her back before you bed her. Aedan mac Connall may forgive you.'

'How do you know I haven't bedded her?' Sigurd sent the wooden sword flying from Gorm for the third time that day.

'Everyone knows Eilidith of Cennell Fergusa sleeps in your chamber, but you are out here, hounding us to death. It does not take a genius to work out why. You have an itch you want to scratch and you haven't scratched it yet. Plough the woman and be done with it or release her and save us trouble when the king of cennell Loairn comes to call.'

Sigurd wiped the sweat from his brow, irritated that he was easy to read. Gorm probably spoke the truth about Aedan mac Connall, but he was doing it to see if he could get under his skin, rather than any real concern about the Gael. 'Now will you fight properly this time?'

'I reckoned I was.' The large warrior stroked his chin. 'Ever since you went down to the lake the other day, you have been working us far too hard. I understand her bottom looked quite delectable in the shift.'

Sigurd slammed his sword against the shield, breaking it into two pieces. He tossed it away in disgust. 'My relationship with Eilidith is none of your business. Now we start again. This time, actually attack me. Put your back into it rather than your mouth.'

Gorm rubbed his jaw. 'Still, I will feel better when you have.'

Chapter Eight

~~~~~~~~

Liddy stared at the mountain of furs which now made up Sigurd's bed. Combined with the tapestries, the bedchamber had been transformed from a cold place to one of warmth, one where a person might want to linger. She was impressed with the richness of the tapestries and the deepness of the furs once they were finally unpacked.

The various other maids had sighed and exclaimed as the furs were brought out, giving her jealous looks. Liddy held back the words explaining that she still slept on the floor, next to Coll. Since the incident at the lake where she'd nearly kissed him, she had redoubled her efforts to become exhausted. However, he increasingly invaded her dreams.

In the end she had chased them from the room, saying she preferred to make up the bed herself. The women gave her knowing glances, but departed.

'There goes my excuse,' she muttered as she plumped up the pillows one last time before she went to the great hall to face the main meal. 'I will have to find somewhere else to sleep.'

'Did you say something?' Sigurd asked from the doorway. 'You appear to be most elusive these days.'

Liddy's heart beat a little faster. 'I was just commenting to Coll about the space in the room. You won't want a dog sleeping in here, not with these furs on the floor.'

'Coll and I are friends. I see no reason to change his sleeping quarters.'

She grabbed a pillow and held it in front of her like a shield. 'There are things I should be doing. The women will be down bathing again if I am not careful.'

Sigurd came over and took the pillow from her slack hands. He tossed it towards the bed. 'That goes on the bed.'

Liddy smoothed her hands on her apron. He was so close that if she stretched out, she could touch him. Her body started to sway towards him. Liddy pivoted too quickly and stumbled backwards, falling on to the bed, landing beside the pillow.

'Oh!'

Sigurd's eyes creased at the corners. 'A dive for your shield? Or an invitation to join you?'

'An unplanned tumble.' Her voice was far too breathless. Liddy rolled off the bed, painfully aware that she displayed far too much leg as she did so.

'Well, I have much to be getting on with,' she said into the sudden silence.

'Don't let me delay you.' He went over to one of his iron-bound trunks. 'I only came back for my one remaining practice shield. The other one splintered on the training ground.'

Something sank a little inside Liddy. He hadn't come back to tease her. 'I see.'

Instead of a shield, he took a game board out of the trunk and placed it on the bed. 'Later, though, I intend to play *tafl* with you to decide who sleeps where.'

'*Tafl*? I've never heard of it.'

'A strategy game.' Sigurd withdrew a leather pouch and spilled the counters on the bed. He gave her a speculative glance. 'It keeps my mind occupied. I am guessing you will be a formidable opponent if you are given the chance.'

'A compliment, I think.' Liddy bit her lip. A reprieve of sorts, but it felt like she was falling back into the old ways. 'I must warn you: once I learn the rules, I intend to win.'

'It is what I like about you Liddy, you never give in.'

'A compliment?'

'An observation.' The corners of his mouth lifted. 'But you may take it as a compliment.'

He began to explain the game. Her heart sank slightly. She was no good at flirtation. He might proclaim that he expected her to win, but he really wanted her to lose. It was how Brandon had been—willing to play until she was better than him. Brandon hated losing to a woman, unless he had planned it. 'Is something wrong?'

'It sounds very like a game my husband used to enjoy playing.'

'With you?'

She shook her head. 'With his brother and... others.'

'Which others?'

'People.' Liddy plucked at her skirt. There was no way she could confess about how, after the marriage, he had thrown temper tantrums when he lost to her and refused to play again. 'Kintra is a large estate and Brandon was often absent, fighting the Northmen. It left little time for frivolity.'

'And you were always too busy to play.'

'Yes.' She forced a smile as a glimmer of hope burgeoned within her. An avenue of escape appeared. 'It is amazing what needs to be done in a hall. Even now…there are things which should be attended to. I should go.'

He came over to her and grabbed her elbow, preventing her from moving. She was aware of the way his chest rose and fell and how his hair skimmed his shoulders. 'You sit now. Study the board.'

'Why?'

His eyes crinkled at the corners. 'Because you use your busyness as a shield and my men will be glad of the respite.'

Her tongue moistened her suddenly dry lips. 'You are wrong about that. I keep busy because then I don't have to think about my captivity.'

'It is how I see it.'

His fingers captured her chin, forcing her to look into his eyes. Her mouth ached anew. Her body trembled. He was going to kiss her. She parted her lips, ready to give in, but he let her go and stepped away.

'My opinion is the only one which counts here.' He gestured to a stool. 'Sit and play. Let's see how quick you really are. Indulge me.'

'As if I have a choice,' Liddy muttered, concentrating on the board.

'What shall you ask for when you win?'

'Not a kiss,' she retorted. 'Otherwise you'd contrive to lose.'

He burst out laughing and covered her hand with his. 'Ah, Liddy, you are good for me.'

She allowed her hand to rest in his for a heart-beat longer than she should have, then she reached for a counter. 'Shall we play, then?'

The first game she lost badly, but the second one she began to get the hang of it. With the third, she managed to win. Liddy clapped her hands. 'You see. I can do it.'

Sigurd stared at the board in disbelief.

'Impossible. I haven't lost in years. You have to believe I was trying.'

'Why?'

'Because I know how it feels when people let you win.'

A bubble of pleasure went through her. She had done it and he wasn't cross with her. She had to wonder if Brandon's reaction had been because he was spoilt.

And if he was wrong about that, what else had he been wrong about? Her curse? The boat not being able to capsize? The cause of Keita's and Gilbreath's deaths being an accident, and not her fault? asked a little voice in the back of her mind.

Liddy silenced it as she hurriedly set the board up again.

'We could have another game unless you have other things to attend to,' she said.

A frown line appeared between his eyes. 'I shall have to change my tactics.'

Liddy pressed her lips together. 'Perhaps you make allowances for my inexperience.'

'I shall have to try harder and ignore the distractions.'

'Distractions?'

'You know what I mean. Distractions.' He gave a half-smile and reached out to smooth an errant lock of hair from her cheek. 'I am pleased you wear your hair uncovered.'

A warm pulse throbbed through her at the touch. She forced her eyes to focus on the counters. Pleasurable distraction? The man enjoyed teasing her.

'Unintentional, I assure you.' Liddy moved her first counter. 'You were the one who commanded my hair be worn down.'

'Shall we make it interesting and play for a small prize?'

Liddy's hand trembled on her counter. She could well imagine what he would ask for. Even now the bed piled high with its luxurious furs kept drawing her gaze. She could all too easily imagine the feel of the soft fur against her bare skin. She gulped hard and bade the image to be gone. Sigurd would want something else. Besides, she wasn't going to lose. She had the hang of this game now.

'What sort of a prize? I thought we were playing for the right to choose where to sleep?'

'Such a woman. Your mind always turns towards the bed.' He countered her move. 'No, it would not be fair to put that sort of pressure on you…yet. We play for something else.'

'I will win and then decide,' she said, banging the counter down and making the other pieces jump.

'That is the sort of attitude I like.' He covered her hand again briefly. 'Let the battle begin and I do expect a fight, Liddy.'

'You reek with over-confidence. This will be easy.'

The contest was hard fought with Sigurd taking the early advantage, but just when she thought all was lost, she saw a way to win. Liddy rapidly moved her remaining counter and captured Sigurd's king piece.

'This time you will have to admit it was not a fluke.'

'What are you going to claim as your prize?' His low voice slid over her skin as he watched her with hooded eyes.

It was on the tip of her tongue to ask for the

long-promised kiss. Her entire body tingled with awareness of him.

'A walk outside the compound with Coll,' she said quickly before her tongue had other ideas. 'I want to feel the sun on my face and the wind at my back.'

'I am at your disposal.' He stood and made a very correct bow.

'Both of us?' she cried. 'We are both going outside the fort?'

He tilted his head to one side. 'Do you think I would allow you to go on your own? What if you strayed too near the sacred grove? I must insist.'

'I gave my promise. I will return. A little bit of freedom.' Liddy hated the pleading in her voice. 'And you promised no more bodies.'

'They have been buried,' Sigurd confirmed. 'The soothsayer was whining about it earlier. I allowed one of your priests to say a few prayers over the women. The sacred grove is empty, but it remains sacred. My men have a right to their religion.'

'I wouldn't go near it.'

'If only it was that simple…' He brushed her face with his hand. It took her all of her will-power not to turn her face towards his palm. 'I was taught to mistrust, Liddy. I won't change a habit of a lifetime, not even for you. You go outside the fort with me or not at all.'

The woods were dappled in sunshine and filled with birdsong. In front of them, a butterfly flitted from one wildflower to the next. Liddy walked slowly, breathing deeply, enjoying the fresh air and appreciating the silence. Sigurd was right. It was good not to have to do anything.

Coll bounded alongside them until he caught the scent of a rabbit and went off to investigate. Lately, if Sigurd was with Liddy, Coll seemed content to wander off on his own.

'It feels wrong somehow,' Liddy said, determined to ignore her growing awareness of the man beside her. She had thought that being outside would banish the intimate feeling she had in the bedchamber.

'Why?'

'You wanted me to supervise the women. They will find excuses to go to the loch and bathe.'

'They always seem busy to me.'

'They hope to catch your eye and warm your bed.'

He put his hands on her shoulders and spun her around. 'And that bothers you?'

'No,' she lied. 'I'm fine with it. They are welcome to it. I would hardly like to be churlish.'

'Truly? You are a very poor liar.' He touched her cheek. 'Your eyes appear ready to spit fire at the mere thought of another in that room. I heard you were determined to do the room on your own.'

She tilted her head upwards and met his dark gaze. Every particle of her was aware of him. Her heart raced quickly. 'One last check for the missing gold. I desire my freedom above all things.'

His thumb traced the line of her mouth. 'I do think you protest overmuch.'

Her mouth tingled, but moving away was beyond her. 'You are not playing fair.'

'Who ever said I did?' His mouth was a breath away from hers. 'Is there something you want, Eilidith? Something you truly desire?'

She knew she should move away from the temptation of his mouth, but her feet seemed to have turned to stone. All the reasons not to kiss him which had seemed sensible only a short time ago faded into nothingness and all she knew was that she wanted to, because she could—out here in the green wood where they were not master and slave, but a man and a woman.

She raised her mouth and brushed her lips against his. 'Kiss me. Kiss me now.'

He lifted a brow. 'Is it what you truly desire?'

'Yes,' she whispered against his mouth.

His arms went around her instantly, crushing her against him. Her body thrilled in his nearness. She drank from his mouth, revelling in its clean taste. His tongue tangled with hers, teasing and probing deeper. Her body arched closer, meeting the hard planes of his chest.

His hand roamed down her back and pulled her closer still. The evidence of his desire for her pressed into her belly.

'I did wait,' he murmured against her ear. His breath did strange things to her insides. 'But I took pity on you. I didn't make you beg.'

His mouth trailed a line down her throat. Each new touch sent the fire burning inside her a little higher and she knew she wanted more.

She tugged at his shirt, wanting…no, needing to feel his skin against hers. He seemed to understand what she wanted and immediately divested himself of the garment. His skin gleamed gold in the late summer sun. She touched the pale scars which criss-crossed his skin with a gentle finger and then, giving in to impulse, she traced the lines with her mouth. They were smooth to her touch.

'You've suffered greatly,' she whispered.

'Time heals most things. Makes you stronger than before.'

'I hope you are right.'

He captured her hand and raised it to his lips.

'Unless you want to continue, stop. If we go much further, I cannot guarantee I will have the strength to pull back.'

She stared at him. He was giving her the option. It was her choice about what was going to happen here. She could pull back and pretend that it wasn't what she wanted. But she was finished with pretending. She wanted to explore this fire which was burning inside her. She wanted to see if it had been truly her who had been as cold and unfeeling as Brandon had accused her. Right now her body burnt, teetering on the edge. Her stomach knotted. 'Do you think I want to stop?'

He took a half-step backwards. There was a vulnerability about his look that she hadn't noticed before. 'Do you?'

'I want this. I have dreamt about it. You've been invading my dreams,' she cried before she gave in to her memories of how everything went wrong with Brandon. Sigurd wasn't her late husband.

'I have dreamt about it as well.'

She gave a shaky laugh. 'I hope I live up to the dream.'

'More than.'

Instantly his hands returned to her body, holding her as though she was special. He recaptured her mouth, swooping down. This time his tongue probed and stroked, penetrating deeper than he had before, feasting on her. Her body arched towards him and she felt his rampant arousal press into her middle. She rubbed her body against him, seeking relief from this burgeoning feeling which kept growing inside her.

He quickly undid her cloak and it fell on to a bed of ferns.

He slid his hand down her shoulder, capturing her breast under her gown and teasing the nipple until it became a hardened point. It rubbed against her shift, sending fresh waves of heat through her. She whimpered and tugged at his head.

He raised his eyes and gave a very masculine smile as he proceeded to play with the other nipple, teasing it until it, too, ached.

Her hands pushed at his trousers as the heat within her became unbearable. He pushed them away and undid them. His rampant erection emerged. Giving in to temptation, she curled her hand about his steely strength and felt him grow and pulse under her fingers.

'I can't wait any longer,' he rumbled in her ear as he eased her down on to her discarded cloak. She parted her legs and pushed up her skirts.

She was more than ready for him. Her body opened as he entered, enveloping him. She matched his thrusts with answering arches of her body. Faster and faster until the world was made new.

And she knew then that she'd been wrong about the act of joining. It could be wonderful and magical if it was with the right person.

Sigurd drifted slowly back to earth. He had taken her far too quickly and not how he had planned at all.

Liddy had fallen asleep in his arms. He watched her chest rise and fall and the way her bare legs were entangled with his. The gold of the shackles contrasted with the whiteness of her skin and seemed to rebuke him. Had this woman truly had a choice?

She was the most exquisite creature he had ever seen. Her hair only hinted at the depths of passion she possessed and he knew he wanted to explore it and wring every last drop out of her.

What he and Liddy had shared had been indescribable. His only regret was that they were lying on a hard bed of ferns, rather than on the furs he'd carefully arranged on the bed. She was still dressed in her shift and gown, which was less than ideal. He wanted to explore every inch of her body.

A surge of protective feelings ran through him. He gathered her close. He wasn't ready to give her up yet. She would remain his. He struggled to remember the last time he had felt this much at peace.

She murmured softly in her sleep.

He pressed a kiss against her temple. 'Time to go.'

Instantly she was awake and straightening her skirts, hiding her gorgeous legs.

'It is getting late,' he said with a smile. 'And the next time, I want to experience you in that new bed of mine.'

'There will be a next time?'

He silently cursed her husband. What had he done to her? 'Of course—did you think I'd tire of you that quickly?'

The irony of his words was not lost on him. Unlike the other women he'd bedded in recent years, Liddy was more than a warm body in the night. He'd been a fool to consider that simply bedding her would ease his desire for her. He wanted to expose every part of her. More than he wanted to possess her mind.

'I had no idea. I have no expectations.'

He placed a kiss against her temple and tried to ignore the sudden tightening in his gut. She was thinking about her late husband and he wanted to erase all memory of him. 'Stop judging me by your husband's actions.'

She stood up and smoothed down her skirts.

'We need to return. People will come searching for us.'

'People will wait. They will be glad of a respite, rather than having me press them again on the latest shield technique.'

His body ached with the stirrings of renewed passion. He had not drunk his fill of her. All their joining had done was to make him want her more. But on a bed with soft fur and pillows instead of the hard ground. He wanted to spend the entire night exploring her depths.

Her cheeks flamed and she made a little moue with her mouth. 'I would hardly like them gossiping about me.'

'They already do. Your mouth appears thoroughly kissed.'

She scrubbed her knuckles against her lips. 'You are teasing me.'

He leant over and plucked a wisp of fern from her hair. 'Maybe a little,' he admitted. 'The men were teasing me earlier about training too hard and taking too much pleasure in defeating them because I desired this. I suspect I shall be a little kinder. They will be grateful to you.'

Desired it, but no longer? A shiver went down Liddy's spine. What was between them was purely physical on his part and she knew how brief such things were. Brandon had shown her that. She snapped her fingers and Coll, who had been investigating a rabbit hole close by, bounded over. 'Still, I want to get back.'

Sigurd watched them walk away, uncomfortably aware that he had wanted to linger. He wanted to lose himself in her again. Tonight, he promised silently. Tonight he would unlock more of her secrets and show her that she had nothing to be frightened about. He would free the passionate woman from the prison she had kept herself in.

Chapter Nine

The sounds of the feast echoed through the bed-chamber. Liddy paced the room. She had pleaded a headache when they returned and Sigurd had accepted it without a murmur, explaining he had other business to attend to. He had other things to do. Coll had even chosen to tag along with him, instead of staying with her. Even her dog was deserting her now.

She clenched her fists. It might have been a mistake to quit the field, but she could clearly remember what a naïve fool she'd been with Brandon and how she'd had to endure his flirting with anything in a skirt. He'd laugh and say that she was over-sensitive. However, she had learnt the hard way that every woman he flirted with, he bedded.

She wasn't ready for that with Sigurd. She'd seen his easy way with women. How he could charm them with very few words. All the women in the fort would sigh as he went by.

She wanted to think she was special for a little while longer. She'd been a coward to hide here, but she wasn't ready. The bed seemed to loom larger each time she passed it. Should she get in and wait for him, or what if he chose not to come like Brandon had done? This time she wasn't going to ask more than Sigurd was prepared to give. What had happened out in the woods was a pleasant idle moment, a time out of mind. She mustn't hope too much. Brandon had certainly been in no hurry after their marriage night. But then his lovemaking had been rough and crude compared with what she had experienced with Sigurd.

She sighed. She might as well be truthful. Brandon had been surprised at her tears. He had never cared for her pleasure at all.

Her body thrummed at the memory of Sigurd's lovemaking. She began to plait her hair. The sooner she restored herself to how she used to be, the sooner this madness would end.

A noise made her pause. Sigurd stood in the door, a quizzical expression on his face. Her heart leapt. She ruthlessly dampened it down. 'You failed to appear at the meal.'

'My head is better.' Liddy straightened her

apron. She could do this and get through the practicalities. She would act as though he had come for another reason. This sort of subterfuge had worked with Brandon—feigning ignorance and assuming he had come on mundane tasks. 'I take it the ale casket is empty and someone has forgotten where I put the key to the storeroom.'

He didn't move from where he stood in the doorway. 'If the key was lost, I would simply order the door broken down. You and I have unfinished business.'

She fingered her birthmark and nodded miserably. For a little while, Sigurd had made her believe that she could be attractive. 'We need to discuss our new rules, you mean? Only I don't think there are really any rules… If you will excuse me… I need to find Coll and make sure that he isn't into any mischief.'

She pointedly moved to go past him, but he snaked out an arm and caught her elbow. 'Don't…' he said.

Her entire body burnt from his touch. She wanted to lean into him. She kept her back straight, but her heart hammered so loudly she thought he must hear it. 'Don't what?'

'You have no need of that shield, after what we shared this afternoon. Put it aside and speak the truth. Why have you been hiding in here?'

'You are talking nonsense.' She twisted her belt about her fingers.

He touched her jaw and her flesh trembled under the onslaught. 'Am I? Maybe, but you are required here. The kitchen has other servants. Coll is happy with the bone I gave him. You serve me and me alone.'

'Yes, by looking after your hall,' Liddy said slowly, hating the way her treacherous heart turned over.

He shook his head. 'All the while I was in the great hall, listening to the men feasting and singing songs, I kept thinking about you and hoping that this was a feint.'

Her breath hitched in her throat. 'A what?'

'A feint to give me an excuse to leave early because I wanted to do this.'

He took her face between his hands and kissed her. Long and slow. Insistent, but also persuasive as if he wasn't sure what her reaction would be. It amazed her that he could be so gentle.

Liddy's body responded instantly and the kiss became more passionate in its intensity. Then he let her go. She stumbled backwards, putting out an arm to steady herself. Her mouth tasted of ale, but mostly of him.

'Tell me that there is something more important to be done elsewhere,' he said, watching her with hooded eyes.

She pressed her hands together to stop them trembling. 'That would be lying. Why would I lie about something like that?'

'Good, you are learning. You have much to learn.' He gathered her into his arms. 'I hope you will be a most attentive pupil.'

'I will do my best.' She scarcely recognised the husky rasp as her own.

Impatient but gentle fingers undid the plait in her hair and it fell about her shoulders.

'Silken fire,' he murmured. 'Wear it down. It makes you look as you are—untamed and passionate.'

A small fire grew within her. He considered her passionate, not cold. She would have scoffed at being called that this morning, but now she wanted to be. 'Untamed? Are you sure you have the right woman?'

'You underestimate your charms.' He inclined his head towards where the bed covered in furs stood. 'This time, we have a bed and time. Let me show you what can happen in a bed.'

The bed loomed larger in the torchlight, reminding her of her failures. The burgeoning fire flickered and began to fade.

'Liddy?' he said with his breath tickling her ear, fanning the flames again.

'I had a good time this afternoon,' she spoke to the floor. 'Better than I thought possible.'

'It will have nothing on tonight.' He smoothed the hair back from her face in a gesture which made her heart turn over. There were so many reasons why she shouldn't allow her heart to become involved, but every time she encountered him, he stole a little more of her.

'Let me see all of you,' he whispered against her ear.

Liddy froze. All of her? Naked? Her heart sunk. The memory of how Brandon had turned from her after the twins were born sliced through her. 'All of me? Why?'

'Because I want to explore every bit of you.'

Her heart wanted to believe him, but her brain kept hammering on about how Brandon had been repulsed after she had given birth. His shuddering look remained seared on her brain. She knew how the pregnancy had scarred her belly. She shook her head and took a step backwards. 'I'm not ready. My late husband understood—darkness is best. We should never have…not in the daylight. My body…'

She hated how her voice shook. He tilted his

head to one side as if he was assessing a very nervous horse.

'You've seen my body with its scars,' he said softly. 'It adds to my pleasure to see your face when we couple.'

Seeing her face—a reminder that he had coupled with many women. It was about desire for him and that always faded. She wanted something more and that was impossible. When he turned from her, it was going to hurt and she didn't want to go back to that hollow feeling.

She started to back away, but his hands held her shoulders gently, pinning her in place. 'Please. It is but a little thing. The priests used to say that this sort of thing was forbidden.'

He ran his hands down her arms, sending little tongues of fire lapping through her, sapping at her will to resist. She swayed towards him.

'Very well, then we wait until you are ready.' He lifted her hair from her body and placed a kiss at the junction where her neck met her shoulder. He went over and doused the torches one by one until one small lamp remained. 'We go at your pace, Eilidith. No lights.'

Liddy closed her eyes. Sigurd was taking his time and he seemed to consider they would be together for longer than one night. 'Thank you.'

He put his hands on her shoulders and held her

away from him. 'Did your husband treat you well? I want the truth, Liddy. I want you to look me in the eye and say what happened to you.'

'I ran the house and he ran his estate. Everyone said that we were well matched in that.' The half-lies nearly stuck in her throat, but what choice did she have? To admit the full truth would mean more explaining about how Keita and Gilbreath had died because of her incompetence and in their deaths, the true ugliness of her marriage had been exposed. Brandon's damning words lingered in her mind. How he had only wanted the land she brought as a dowry rather than her. The soft words he'd used during their courtship had been lies. He'd never felt anything for her as a person and she'd been unable to fulfil him for even one night. How she had extinguished the only brightness in their marriage through her careless arrogance.

Sigurd laced his fingers through hers and brought her back. 'You answered a different question.'

'He treated me as well as could be expected.' She took a step backwards. 'Is that Coll barking? I should go to him.'

'You are more nervous than a maiden on her first night. What did your husband do to you? Did he hurt you? Is that why Coll rarely leaves your side?' His voice hardened. 'I'm not your late husband, Liddy. Coll senses that. It is why he trusts you with me.'

'It is in the past, Sigurd.'

'Did he hurt you?'

'He never beat me.'

'There are other ways to hurt a woman.'

Liddy wrapped her hands about her waist and knew she had to give him something. It was wrong of her to hope. He would find out eventually and then his look would turn to disgust.

'He disliked my birthmark. He called me cursed and blamed me for all that went wrong in his life.'

'He was a blind fool and a weak man. To blame his failures on someone else. A man makes his own luck.' His thumb brushed her chin. 'It reminds me of a butterfly, wanting to taste the sweetness of your lips.'

A tiny bubble of pleasure exploded within her, but she tried to dampen it down. 'You don't know me very well.'

He lifted her chin and his eyes loomed large in the torchlight. 'I searched out the rumours about you and your husband, Liddy, after this afternoon. Your husband had many women, didn't he? But he didn't know how to treat a woman.'

'Why do you say that?'

He stroked her hair and gave a long sigh. 'I can

feel the passion in you, but you are too nervous to enjoy it. I won't hurt you. I took you too swiftly this afternoon and apologise for that. Give me another chance.'

Her heart thumped far too loudly. He deserved to know about Keita and Gilbreath and her part in their deaths. Telling him about them might end this and she selfishly wanted it continue. She wanted to be in this dream world for a while longer. 'Then you know everything about me. Soon I will have no secrets left.'

'There are some things I am waiting for you to tell me.' He rubbed his thumb across her lips. 'I wanted to let you know that I only have one woman at a time. When we are done, I won't humiliate you. I will provide for any children we have.'

Children. The very word sent a chill down her spine. She moved away from him and wrapped her arms about her waist. She'd fallen pregnant so quickly the last time. And Brandon had used her pregnancy as an excuse to abandon her bed.

'Children may never happen,' she whispered, hating that a sudden hope sprang in her breast. A second chance. 'There is no guarantee.'

'I wanted you to know that I take my responsibilities seriously. The world will consider them free-born, not slaves.'

She knew he was being more than generous, but it didn't dispel her fear or the pain. Soon his eyes, like Brandon's, would look on her with disgust or, worse still, pity. 'You do me much honour,' she said around the ashes in her mouth.

He dragged his hand through his hair. 'Shall I leave? Was this a mistake?'

She knew if she let him walk out of this chamber, she would lose her chance. She focused on his mouth and knew what she had to do. When she was in his arms, all doubt vanished.

She raised herself up on her tiptoes. 'Later, we can speak of what happens when we part in the future. Right now this is what I want.'

In the morning she would confess to Sigurd and explain why the thought of children excited her and terrified her. She would explain about Keita and Gilbreath. In the morning she'd watch his desire shrivel and turn to horror, but tonight she wanted to feel beautiful.

'Later,' she murmured again, looping her arms about his neck and pulling his face closer.

He claimed her mouth. The passion that was deep within her sprang to life. Her hands slipped under his fine linen shirt to his warm skin. She trailed up his chest until she encountered his nipples. She rolled them between her fingers, feeling them harden against the pads of her fingertips.

He growled in the back of his throat. Suddenly he scooped her up and tossed her on the bed.

Down, down she went into the soft fur, every bit as silky as she had imagined. Then he leant over and blew out the small lamp so the room was plunged into darkness. Within a blink of an eye, Sigurd had divested her garments and she lay naked. The air was cool against her skin. She stretched, enjoying the freedom of the darkness. Her body tingled with anticipation of what was to come. She struggled to stay still.

'I want to know all of you, even if you will allow me only to learn by touch.' He ran a hand down her flank. The touch caused warm pulses to shoot through her. Her body arched.

'I'm sorry,' she whispered. 'I know I am supposed to keep still. My husband used to get cross.'

He laughed. 'What is there to be sorry about? If your late husband was such a blind fool that he had no idea how to pleasure his wife, that was his loss. You are better off without him.'

Liddy blinked twice. Was he saying that Brandon had borne most of the responsibility for her failure in the marriage bed? 'You want me to move?'

'To move, to cry out and most of all to tell me what you like and what you don't.' His teeth nibbled her ear.

Liddy gave a soft sigh as her body arched upwards to encounter his bulk. 'I definitely like that.'

'By the night's end, we shall have discovered a few other things that give you pleasure.'

'Oh, I hope so.'

He gave a throaty laugh. 'We are well matched. But fair is fair, if I can touch, you must also touch me. But see the light has no fears for me. Undress me.'

Emboldened, she tugged at his shirt and helped him to shed all his clothes.

She traced the raised lines of his scars as they snaked across his chest. The metal from the cross he wore was warm under the pads of her fingers.

Her hand strayed to his groin and she was left in no doubt of his desire for her. Giving in to temptation, she wrapped her hand around his shaft, marvelling at its strength beneath the silky smoothness.

He groaned. 'If you keep this up, it will be over before it has properly begun. Tonight is about taking our time and enjoying. Giving you pleasure makes it more enjoyable, too, for me.'

He lowered his mouth and paid homage to her breasts. Taking each one in turn, suckling and nuzzling until the growing heat within her made her arch and then he traced a line down her belly to the apex of her thighs.

Then he positioned his mouth over her core. She had never been touched that intimately before. Her world exploded about her. She tugged at his shoulders and he understood her wordless plea for more.

He drove his shaft inward and her body opened, enveloping him fully. He rolled over so that she was on top and then he grasped her hips.

'Ride me. You set the pace.'

She began to move her hips, driving him deeper into her until he was completely sheathed. Her body expanded, allowing the length of him. And there was no pain.

It was even better than out in the woods because she was able to match his rhythm. And she knew he wanted her. He wanted this as much as she did.

Their cries filled the room.

Sigurd lay in bed with Liddy next to him. He struggled to remember when he had last felt this content. He ran his hand down her flank and knew he wanted her again. But he wanted all of her. His hand strayed to her stomach. Suddenly he noticed little telltale marks that in his passion, he'd missed earlier.

Sudden anger swept through him—at her, at the situation and his own blindness for not noticing before and for not thinking about why people had dropped their eyes and mumbled about Liddy and the curse.

'When were you going to tell me?' he asked, curling his fingers about her belly and dragging her back against him.

'Tell you what?'

'That you have children.' He raised himself up on one elbow. 'How could you abandon them to try to save your father and brother? Surely your first duty was to them.'

She struggled against his arm and he allowed her to break free.

'Because I don't have them.'

Sigurd struggled to control his anger—at her, at himself for not guessing earlier, for not paying more attention to the rumours about her. No one had mentioned children. He had made her a slave and her children had lost a mother. 'Your belly has a network of little indents, scars. I traced the indentations with my fingers. I don't believe you've ever been in battle. I ask again—where have you hidden your child? Why have you kept the child hidden from me?'

'On a hillside overlooking Kintra bay. There is nothing I can do for them now. The angels watch over them.'

All of Sigurd's anger evaporated. Something

clenched inside him. He had never considered the possibility. Her child was dead. It was why she considered herself cursed. 'Your child is dead?'

'Two—twins,' she said, sitting up and hiding her face with her hair. 'Keita and Gilbreath. I became pregnant shortly after my marriage. Possibly even the night of my marriage. They were the light in my life and then they died in the second spring after their birth. It is why I never go on the sea. I had taken them and the nurse on a picnic on a small island. In those days, I sailed and I even swam. It was the only thing Brandon admired about me—my skill at sailing. I sailed too close to the wind and the boat which Brandon had designed capsized. I thought I had saved them all, but Keita died of secondary drowning hours later and Gilbreath caught a fever from the chill he suffered. He died a week later.'

The stark words hit him in the stomach. 'And the nursemaid?'

'She, too, caught a chill and nearly died, but survived and tells a different story to mine.' She gathered her knees to her chest. 'Now you see why I am cursed. Brandon swore that the boat would never capsize. He swore it in church at their funeral. The nursemaid said that I was behaving recklessly, pushing the boat to go faster. Of course she had reason to lie—she was enthralled with my husband.'

'And you planned on keeping your children and their horrible death a secret?' he asked, trying to puzzle it out. Liddy had acted heroically in attempting to save the children and the servant. And accidents happened with boats. He'd seen many men die. He silently cursed her husband for heaping the guilt on her when she was obviously grieving.

'They are in the past. No matter what I do, I can't bring them back. I've accepted that. Talking about them makes my heart ache far too much.' She made a hopeless gesture. 'I planned to confess this morning, but I wanted one night of feeling special before you regarded me with horror.'

Sigurd's chest tightened. This woman's past should not mean anything to him, but it did. He hated that she had experienced a moment of pain. Here he'd taken her and had never considered what her life had been before. He had never thought to ask about children. And he knew in his heart of hearts that it wouldn't have made a difference. He would have wanted her still, but he wouldn't have made her his slave. He had thought for a heartbeat that he'd have to let her go back to that child, but selfishly he was glad, he would be able to keep her for a while longer.

'How was the accident your fault?' Sigurd asked, trying to understand.

'I was angry at Brandon. The nursemaid said something about him and I knew he was sleeping with her. I sailed too close to the wind and the boat turned over. It should never have done that. Brandon swore that I did it deliberately as he designed the boat so it wouldn't tip.'

Sigurd wished he could murder Liddy's late husband for his selfishness. The man had been a pig of the highest order. He turned her over and drew her unresisting into the circle of his arms. 'You would never have done that deliberately. What actually happened?'

She gave a sad smile. 'There was a sudden wave and the boat went over despite what the nurse said. But Brandon was right—I should never have set sail. I wanted to be out on the sea, feeling the wind in my hair, feeling alive and then this happened.'

Sigurd tightened his hold of her. 'Freak waves have been known to happen. In the right condition, any boat can capsize.'

'Kintra bay is normally as smooth as a freshly hammered sword.'

Sigurd thought about how his father had died after he had fallen from a cart and how he'd been blamed when his only crime was that he was the nearest person to him. 'Sometimes, there is no one to blame. It is just an accident and somehow that makes it harder, but hate eats you up.'

Liddy wriggled out of his arms. 'You were right about one thing earlier—Brandon blamed me for being cold in bed. He never returned to my bed after the twins were born. Perhaps in time he would have, but…it was easier to let him find solace in the arms of other women. Before he died, he suggested that I go into a convent. He'd gone to Ireland to find a suitable one. He said that we would both be happier. The thought of travelling by sea terrified me then and it still does.'

'Brandon was a fool,' he said, reaching out for her.

'He was well respected.' She shook her head. 'Everyone loved him. He was the life of every gathering. His boat-building skills were famous. That design had never capsized…except for the one time when I was at the helm.'

'How do you know?'

'He swore this in church at their funeral. He offered to carry hot iron to prove the truth of it. The priest accepted his word and pronounced me cursed.'

'He was still a fool. He didn't know how to look after his wife and blamed her for his faults.' He smoothed the hair from her forehead. He knew he had to get the words right and he often made mistakes. And just because he wanted to make things better for Liddy, it didn't mean he cared for her. He was doing this for selfish reasons—he wanted a responsive partner. 'He had everything he could want in a woman and more and chose to ignore it. His fault, not yours. He wanted to blame someone for a tragedy. Again his fault, not yours. It is not your fault if your late husband made mistakes and blamed you for them. It is your fault if you decide you are cursed and refuse to live. One tragedy does not mean the rest of your life is cursed. Would your children have wanted that for you?'

'You know how to make me feel special.' She laid her head against his chest. 'I could almost believe you.'

'That is because you are special. Passionate and giving. And you have brought luck into my life.'

Sigurd gathered her to his chest and held her until the trembling stopped. All the while he kept thinking about how right she felt there and how much that frightened him. After all this time his heart seemed to be waking up. His mother had died because of his false declaration of love for Beyla. He was never going to make that mistake again.

He found with Liddy in his arms, he didn't want to think about the future, he simply wanted to exist in the present.

Liddy allowed her face to rest against Sigurd's chest for another heartbeat. It was all too easy to believe that he might care. For the first time she wanted to believe that it had all been a terrible tragedy and that she should not bear all the responsibility.

One kind gesture and she was ready to believe it was love. How pathetic. She should have learnt by now. In time Sigurd would discover that he needed another woman, someone who could advance his career. He had no heart, he'd proclaimed. She could not expect any kindness from him and yet she had found it. She pushed against his chest and his arms fell away.

'It is fine. I've accepted it. I just wanted to let you know why I don't speak of it. Why I prefer it to be dark.'

'Do you visit your children's graves often?'

Liddy hated how her throat tightened again. The hardest thing for her had been leaving those two graves, knowing that no one would tend them. Aedan only saw his brother as a hero to worship and took Brandon's side in blaming her for the accident. It had hurt because she had considered him her friend before. It had been easier to go than to face him and his judgements after she learned of Brandon's death.

'Hardly ever,' she said, focusing on a spot behind Sigurd's shoulder. 'My brother-in-law inherited the hall when Brandon died. It is best for all of us that I stay away. My curse...'

'Some day I will take you there. Aedan mac Connall will be made to see you have been wronged. You should be able to visit the graves whenever you wish.'

'Northmen do not go to Kintra.'

He thumped his fists against the bedstead. 'Is Kintra not part of this island?'

'Kintra is on a headland with a very narrow strip of land connecting it to the island,' Liddy tried to explain. The last thing she wanted was Sigurd fighting Aedan. It was a battle neither would win and totally unnecessary. 'It is easy to defend. Ketil saw fit to pay for the service of my husband and now my brother-in-law, rather than trying to conquer them. Thorbin honoured the arrangement.'

'You are counselling against the move?' His low voice held a note of barely suppressed anger. 'Do you doubt my sword arm?'

Liddy winced and tried to move away from his encircling arm, but the arm had become like iron. 'My brother-in-law is away in Ireland, fighting the

Northmen who follow Ivar the Boneless and who raided his farms earlier this spring. There will be nothing there. You don't want to give him an excuse to break the truce when he returns.'

'He fails to worry me.'

'Still, Kintra holds nothing for me. My life has started afresh.'

'Nothing except your children's untended graves and they have been denied to you for too long.' He caught her hand and raised it to his lips. Her heart did a flip. It would be easy to care about him and to start believing that he cared about her.

'They will be there for a long time, looking out to the bay.'

'You should visit. Soon. I will make it happen.'

'You will let me go on my own?'

He laughed. 'You will have proper protection, something the men in your life should have given you long before now. You will be allowed to visit those graves whenever you desire when I am finished.' His breath tickled her ear. 'And some day you will see that there is nothing to be ashamed about. You will let me gaze on your body.'

'I can't see that happening.'

'And until then, I will wait.'

Liddy lay completely still. It bothered her that he could play her body like a harp. But she wasn't ready to allow him to see her fully. It was one thing for him to imagine. Another for him to actually see. Brandon's look of disgust remained seared on her soul. What she had shared with Sigurd was too new and precious. She didn't want to take any risks with it.

Chapter Ten

Sigurd surveyed the men with their petitions and requests for delays. Nothing out of the ordinary. He'd been surprised to hear how lax Thorbin had been about demanding proof, but everyone did comment how poor the growing season was.

'This man insists on seeing you.' One of the guards dragged Liddy's brother forward. 'He wasn't polite about it.

Sigurd snapped his fingers. 'Release him.'

Malcolm adjusted his cloak. 'Thank you.'

'You should be helping your father. There remains tribute to be paid and from what I understand the season is not a good one.'

A soft leather pouch landed at Sigurd's feet. Sigurd left the pouch where it was. 'You should learn some manners.'

'Go on, pick it up,' Malcolm jeered. 'See what it contains.'

'I can guess. The balance of the tribute.' He leant forward. 'Why the drama? Why wait until all could see you?'

Malcolm lifted his chin. 'More than that!'

'So you can pay. Interesting.'

Malcolm's face went red. 'Aedan has returned. He wants Liddy free. He provided the gold. You let her go. The full tribute will be paid.'

Sigurd stared at the leather pouch like it was a venomous snake. If he accepted the gold, he'd never see Liddy again. She'd be out of his life and he wasn't ready for that.

'Eilidith is not a hostage. She is my slave.' Sigurd looked at Malcolm. 'Why would Aedan mac Connall do that?'

'He dislikes the thought of any of his family being a slave. He has the gold from his summer in Ireland. He wants to buy her for the same price you paid for her.'

Sigurd struggled to contain his temper at Malcolm and the brother-in-law, the one who had stood by while Liddy had been abused. The brother-in-law who intended to send Liddy to a convent in Ireland simply because he was doing her late husband's bidding. Liddy had made her choice when she left Kintra to return to her family. And he would not give Aedan, the so-called king of cennell Loairn, power over her.

'It was your father who offered her up for sale. I merely bought her, rather than allowing her to go on the open market. Or did you give him a different version of events?'

Malcolm flushed scarlet. 'I told him that. He refused to believe me. He says that she must be a hostage and therefore a ransom can be paid.'

'Aedan mac Connall should come to me, rather than sending you to do his dirty work. He would learn from me that I do not sell my slaves. Ever.' Sigurd gestured to the pouch. 'Pick it up. Take it back to him and tell him that the lady is not for sale.'

'Are you going to release her? Free her?'

Sigurd shook his head. If he released her, she would go and he'd never see her again. Her family would ensure that. And the passion between them was growing rather than diminishing. But when it was finished, he would not be releasing her back into the custody of people who had abused her in the past. She would belong to no one but herself. The tension eased in his shoulders. When the right time came, he'd ensure she was free, but until then he protected her and his heart.

'Your sister is my slave. It is up to me to decide her fate.' He gestured towards the pouch. 'Now take that away from here.'

Malcolm picked up the leather pouch and

backed away. 'Fa predicted you would say something like that. It is why he sold her to you.'

Sigurd stared at the man. 'Your father said what?'

Malcolm straightened his shoulders. 'My *fa* advised me not to waste my breath. You didn't look like the sort of man who'd sell a woman, particularly a woman like our Liddy. He'd made a mistake with her once, but this time he knew he had it right. Personally I think my father's wits went when he was imprisoned.'

'Did he say this?' Sigurd frowned. There was more to Liddy's father than he had first considered. The man had had no intention of selling Liddy to anyone else. Sigurd ground his teeth, hating that his desire had been that obvious.

'I reckoned it was a try.' Malcolm shrugged. 'May I see her? Alone?'

'You may see her with me.'

'I want to see her alone.'

Sigurd shook his head. He couldn't take the risk. 'Impossible.'

'As I was leaving, Fa advised me to ask if I neglected to mention Aedan's offer to Liddy and your refusal, would you see clear to let the rest of this year's tribute go?'

Sigurd ground his teeth. Did they think he'd be swayed by blackmail? He had planned on let-

ting Liddy know about the offer and that he was
not prepared to release her into the custody of a
man who thought her cursed. 'Your father is in-
corrigible, but I want the tribute paid on time. I'd
hardly like to be accused of playing favourites.'

Malcolm touched the side of his nose. 'I will
keep it between us. Liddy's temper can be incan-
descent.'

'Stay there. I will send for her.'

Malcolm's face became like a scared rabbit's.
'No, no. I can't tell her any good news. It is best
that I don't give her false hope that she will be
freed any time soon.'

'She is freer with me than she ever would be
with Aedan mac Connall.' Sigurd leant forward.
'You can inform him of that from me.'

The feast was in full swing. One of the men
had had too much to drink and had challenged
Sigurd to an arm-wrestling competition. He accepted without blinking an eye and Liddy made
her excuses, rather than staying to watch. Sigurd
was in a strange mood tonight. Far jumpier than
she'd seen him before.

She'd experienced enough of those sorts of
fights when she was Brandon's wife. She gave
the excuse of fetching more ale and escaped.

Liddy drank in the fresh air. She gathered from

the shouts that Sigurd had won in short order. She shook her head. Men. Her husband had been the same—picking a fight at every opportunity.

A sharp pebble caught her shoulder.

'Hey!' she cried, rubbing herself. 'Have a care!'

Another pebble was tossed from the shadows. Liddy's heart thumped. There was only one person who would do something like that.

'Malcolm?' She shook the jug of ale under his nose. 'What are you playing at?'

Malcolm took the jug from her hand and peered in. He wrinkled his nose as he realised that it was empty. 'Liddy, if you keep up that racket, you will have the entire fort down on me. I was supposed to leave earlier, but I couldn't go without seeing you alone. You needn't worry. I brought some of Fa's gold as a bribe. There is nothing these Northmen love more.'

Liddy went over to the shadows where she barely made out her brother's form. 'You are supposed to be at home with Fa.'

Malcolm twisted his cap. 'Fa gave me permission. Someone had to let you know. I'm working on it. I thought I had the solution today, but you won't have to remain under the Northman's control for much longer.'

A prickle went down Liddy's back. Over the years she had had enough experience of Malcolm's schemes to know that they had a habit of going disastrously wrong. 'Working on what?'

'Working on getting you out, getting you away from this place and that man.'

'You mean Sigurd Sigmundson.'

'It isn't right. I had a think about that as we left here the other day. You being a slave and me being free.'

'I can rescue myself. Plans are in hand. I didn't save you just to have you toss your life away.' She hated the way her stomach knotted, but Malcolm was courting disaster by being here. And she had no idea how Sigurd would react. She wasn't ready to end this affair she and Sigurd had started. Malcolm would not understand how alive she felt, how life had begun to be worth living again. 'You have taken a terrible risk for nothing. You are needed at home. Fa needs to stop sending money to Kells to pray for souls which are not in danger.'

'That's the trouble with you, my girl, never letting anyone help you. Letting things eat you up from the inside like Fa says.' He shrugged.

'When I need your advice I shall ask for it.' Liddy tapped her foot on the ground. She didn't bother mentioning the missing gold and Sigurd's promise to free her if she found it. The last thing she needed was Malcolm causing more problems and getting himself in trouble again. He would not know anything about it or the woman, Shona, who had disappeared. 'Let me be.'

'Indeed, but some day you will see beyond the shape of his lips. He will discard you or sell you on to someone else when he marries.'

'Sigurd is going to marry?'

Malcolm rolled his eyes. 'Don't you pay attention to the gossip? Of course he is. He needs a wealthy bride, not some Hibernian slave who used to be a king's daughter but no longer has any gold. It is what their kind do—marry wealthy women with land and gold.'

Liddy pressed her lips together. 'You mustn't believe everything you hear.'

Malcolm's eyes narrowed. 'You've changed, Liddy. You look less pinched. You have stopped covering your head! Are you Sigurd's mistress in truth? If you knew what the priests have been saying about you!'

'Does it matter? Fa has the land. And they would have said such things if I had been a hostage or a slave.' She glanced over her shoulder towards where light streamed through. Sounds of laughter filtered out on the night air. 'It may sound strange to you, but I enjoy having the freedom to talk loudly or wear my hair differently or even paddle in the loch with my bare feet without priests crying shame.'

'I'm trying to help you to escape. You are supposed to be miserable.' He ran his hand through his hair. 'I was a fool to let you do this. I should have demanded that I take your place.'

Liddy rolled her eyes. As if Sigurd would have paid as much for him... Malcolm always did have an exaggerated sense of his self-worth. 'You think he would have paid the same price for you? Somehow I don't think you are the right sex to hold his interest.'

Malcolm gulped twice. 'It still isn't right. Some day you will see that. You should escape when you have the chance.'

'I'm not one for breaking my solemn word.' Liddy put her face close to Malcolm's. 'Fa would send me back. He was right. He does have a duty to the people who live on our lands.'

Malcolm hung his head. 'Fa is one of the details I'm still trying to work out. You need to have a bit of faith. Know you have friends. You aren't alone. I know what it is like to be held prisoner, Liddy. I should have protected you. I failed. Maybe Brandon was right and your mark is cursed.'

'I make my own luck.' Liddy pressed her hands together and tried to control her anger. Shouting at Malcolm was not going to do any good. 'I have every faith that you and Fa will get a decent harvest. Once that is in, then we can discuss more.

Keep Fa from sending more gold to Kells. The estate can't afford it.'

'I think you are being harsh on Fa. He seems to know what he is on about.'

'He is the one who sold me.'

'You are angry about that.' Malcolm nodded. 'I understand. I really do. But what choice did Fa have? You should have stayed at home.'

Liddy clenched her fists and struggled to keep her temper. Little over a sennight and Malcolm had already started to change history to suit his own purpose. 'Had I not come for you, you would have been the one to be sold! You were the one who took the cabbages to the fort in the first place.'

'There were reasons for that.'

'Truly?' Liddy tapped her foot against the dirt. 'I am waiting. It was supposed to be easy silver for the taking. The answer to all our problems. What happened—did you get drunk?'

'I thought I saw…never mind about that.' Malcolm ran his hand through his hair. 'This is what I should have said—Aedan returned early. He knows about your enslavement. He sent gold to buy you, but your lord refused to take it.'

'Aedan sent gold?' Liddy stared at her brother in astonishment. 'You should have told me that right away.'

'Your Northman refused it. He said he wouldn't sell you, not to someone like him.'

'Did Aedan say where I would go if you were successful?'

'He has arranged a place in a convent in Ireland. Where you were to go when Brandon died.'

Liddy gritted her teeth. Aedan had returned and was still as arrogant as ever. There was no way she would go to that convent. She was not going to do Brandon's bidding and go over any water. But Aedan's return explained Malcolm's sudden attack of remorse. After Aedan stopped several other men from bullying Malcolm three Christmases ago, Malcolm had been convinced the man was all powerful.

The only thing which was surprising was that Aedan wasn't there, challenging Sigurd. *No kinswoman of his a slave ever again,* was his proud boast. She had to wonder if her father had considered the consequences when he offered her up. 'Do I look like I am despairing?'

'It would be more seemly if you were.' Malcolm reached out and put his hands on her shoulders. 'They say you are the new lord's mistress. Aedan discounts that. He said you are far too... too strong-willed to give in like that.'

She could well imagine what Aedan had said about her looks or her temperament.

'Too strong-willed or too cold? I know the lies Brandon spread about me.'

'How do you know they are lies?'

Liddy lifted her chin and glared back at her brother. 'Because I know the truth.'

'You know what Aedan is like. He worshipped Brandon. He never believed your story about how the twins died. Brandon's boats don't just capsize, even I know that. It is a big thing to ask, but you are his sister-in-law and your predicament reflects badly on him.'

Liddy twisted away. How like Aedan. Any pity he felt for her would be down to slights to his honour rather than actual caring about her welfare. 'I spoke the truth. The boat capsized. It was a tragic accident, nothing to do with my birthmark despite Brandon swearing differently in church. He endangered his immortal soul, not me.'

'You remain bitter.'

'You tell Aedan that if I need rescuing, I will ask for it. And when I do, I will not be going to a convent over the water.' She put her hands on Malcolm's shoulders and gave him a little shake. 'Promise me you will tell him that. Tell him not to act unless he has my direct order. I will refuse to come.'

Malcolm looked dubious. 'He won't like it.'

'He can do as I say for a change. Tell him that

Coll likes Sigurd and that dog is the best judge of character I have ever encountered.'

'Liddy, do you have deep feelings for this Northman?'

Liddy drew away. Her heart beat far too fast. What she shared with Sigurd was purely physical. It was not going to last. She'd suffered enough hurt for a lifetime. They were friends after a fashion...that was all. 'What? Absolutely not.'

A shuffling noise echoed about the courtyard. Liddy froze. A Northman stumbled from the great hall with an arm about a giggling serving girl. She dragged Malcolm further into the shadows. The couple stopped for a passionate kiss just in front of them.

Sweat trickled down her back. Thankfully the couple went past and Liddy was able to breathe again. What was between Sigurd and her had nothing to do with finer feelings and everything to do with her first proper experience of passion properly for the first time.

'Disgraceful, that,' Malcolm commented.

'I didn't see him forcing her.'

'That woman is a Gael. She should have more pride. She should be resisting him. She should prefer death.'

'Sometimes it is not that simple.'

'Says the woman who chooses to be a slave!'

Liddy pointed towards the darkened gate. 'You go home to Fa. You plough that field and tend to the corn and barley. You stay out of whatever is happening here, whatever Aedan has planned. I'm no longer your concern or Aedan's.'

'That would be spitting in the wind. He takes it as a personal insult that you are here. He has sworn before the priest that he will see you in Ireland or he will see you dead.'

Liddy went rigid.

'Aedan is thinking of himself and his reputation rather than about me.' Liddy lay a hand on Malcolm's arm. 'You know me. Can you see me in a convent, even if I wasn't afraid of travelling on the sea?'

'Not unless you were running it and even then...no, you are right, I can't see you in a convent. Unlike our mother, you are not always at your prayer beads.'

'I shall take that as a compliment.' Liddy tightened her grip. 'Allow me to do it my way without unasked-for interference. I saved your worthless hide, remember?'

'Eilidith!'

'Your master calls,' Malcolm said.

'I only left to get more ale.' She held up the jug. 'I did have a purpose in leaving the feast.'

'One day this land will be free of the Northmen who boss us about. All of them.'

'Or they may become part of this land,' Liddy retorted.

But Malcolm didn't answer. He had slipped away into the shadows.

Liddy hurried back into the hall after getting some more ale, hoping that Malcolm had done as he promised and had left. What was the point of her sacrifice, if he was going to throw his life away? And Aedan would have to wait. She was not going back to being the woman who believed she was cursed.

Sigurd gave her a pointed look and beckoned her over. 'You were gone longer than I expected.'

'It wasn't immediately obvious where the open ale cask was,' she explained with her heart knocking so hard against her chest she thought he must have heard it. 'And then the cook had a few questions. You know how it goes.'

Sigurd wiped a hand across his face. Liddy's eyes were darting everywhere except on him. She was hiding something. He hated the pain it caused, knowing she lied to him. It was like his time with Beyla all over again.

'You finished the wrestling match,' she said.

'I won,' he corrected her.

There was little point in telling her that he'd been worried about her. For the first time in for ever, he had looked for someone to share the moment. Caring made him vulnerable and if he was vulnerable he could not protect anyone.

Halfway through the match, Sven, one of his hand-picked warriors, had made a laughing remark about Liddy. Sigurd had put the Dane on the floor in less than ten heartbeats. He had barely managed to keep from beating him within an inch of his life. And after that, Liddy lied to him. Did she think he wasn't aware of what happened in his fort?

Right now, he'd wager her brother was attempting to depart through the gate. Sigurd had left orders with Gorm to allow him through with a token bribe. But he was patient man. He'd wait and see if she chose to tell him the truth before the cock crowed.

'Very well, you won the match.'

'I won because the day I lose is the day I begin to lose their respect.'

'That is good to know.' Her voice sounded strained.

Sigurd draped an arm about her and pulled her close. She relaxed against him, but then she stiffened.

'Is that a noise? Do you think there is trouble outside?'

'Next time,' he said, giving in to his impatience, 'ask your brother in. Earlier he didn't stay long enough in the hall for me to summon you. I presumed he would make contact.'

Her mouth dropped opened. 'How...how did you know?'

'A wise ruler knows what is happening in his hall and on his lands. Your brother-in-law has returned. Did Malcolm bring you that news? He threw a pouch of gold at my feet. However, you are not for sale, certainly not to a man who believes you cursed.'

'You will let Malcolm go.' She grabbed his arm and her eyes held an element of fear. Something inside him twisted. 'Let him return to my family. Please.'

'Does he mean me any harm?'

She quickly shook her head. 'He worries about me. I've reassured him. But he must be allowed to go back and tell my family that. Will your warriors stop him at the gate?'

'Gorm is on guard duty. He is under orders to let him through with a token bribe.'

Her lips turned up and a tiny laugh escaped. 'Here Malcolm was bragging how easy it was. Serves him right.'

Sigurd inclined his head. 'Next time ask him in. He might accept the invitation to dine from you.'

She tucked her head into her neck. 'I was going to tell you.'

One short visit from her brother and she'd become bothered about her mark again. She was keeping something back. Something to do with the brother-in-law, he had no doubt. It was the reason why Malcolm had made a show of departing and had doubled back. He had a private message to deliver. He caught a wisp of her hair between his fingers. He refused to allow anyone else to dictate her future.

He wanted her to stay with him of her own free will, but until he was certain of it, certain that no one in her family would force her to do things against her will, then he would keep her.

'I know you were.'

Liddy stood in the centre of their chamber, dressed only in her shift. The light from the torches threw strange shadows on the tapestries which now lined the walls. Sigurd had gone to give his night-time orders, with Coll tagging along. It was a routine they had worked out to give her time to get into bed without having to make a scene every time. Only tonight was different.

She chewed the back of her knuckle, watching the shifting shadows. Everything had changed with the news Aedan had returned. She could see that she was still behaving as though Brandon was around, allowing him to dictate her every move. She should have confessed to Sigurd instantly about Malcolm and now it appeared that she didn't trust Sigurd.

She had to hope Malcolm would deliver her message to Aedan and Aedan would heed the words.

She touched her mark. It was a butterfly, not a curse. She had changed and she was not going back to the woman she'd been before. Letting Brandon influence her life stopped now. All she had to do was to keep the light on.

'You are not in bed.' Sigurd stepped into the room with Coll at his heels. Coll swiftly settled in front of the door, guarding.

'You have a talent for stating the obvious.'

'What brought this on? Are you worried about your brother? Gorm reports he made it out of the fort and is now riding towards home.' Sigurd put the gold necklace down on a chest. 'Gorm has seen fit to give you this necklace.'

'Malcolm will be fine. He always is.'

Sigurd's face creased with concern. 'Then what is it?'

'I'm tired of the darkness. I want to be able to see your face.' Liddy held out her hands. 'I want you to see my face when you pleasure me.'

He crossed over to her and gathered her hands

within his. His brow knitted with concern. 'Why are you doing this?'

Liddy bit her lip. She had thought Sigurd would be overjoyed, but he seemed saddened and perplexed.

'Because I thought you wanted to see me,' she said finally. 'Because it is time I stopped living in the past.'

'You look fiercely determined.' He stroked her face. 'I know every inch of you by touch. It is enough. You don't have to do it to please me.'

She pulled away from him. 'I want to do this. I want to see you. I am tired of hiding in the shadows, tired of hiding. Brandon called me ugly and you are not him.'

He laughed softly. 'Shadows or sunshine, as long as you are in my arms and as long as you are not doing it to please me.'

'This is about me living in the here and now. I can only control today. I refuse to have the past define me.'

'You think too much.' His mouth descended, taking her breath away.

She held him off with her hand. 'Then you approve?'

'You couldn't disappoint me,' he murmured as he placed playful kisses on her lips. 'I know you by touch. You are supremely desirable.'

She tore her mouth away. 'I'm being serious.'

His nimble fingers loosened her shift and pushed it from her shoulders. 'You are being delightful and now that I know the reason for the light, I'm happy to obey.'

His mouth trailed down her skin to where the material skimmed the tops of her breast. Her back arched, inviting him to sink deep.

Slowly he lapped at the material, turning it translucent so that the dusky pink colour of her nipples shone through. Round and round he lapped. Then slowly he pushed the material further down until it was gathered about her hips.

The cool air made a pleasing contrast to the heat from his mouth.

'Beautiful,' he whispered against her skin.

Her body shivered in anticipation. 'Truly?'

He pushed the last bit of material from her, causing it to pool at her feet. Her hands instinctively went to cover the apex of her thighs but he gently moved them. He gave a crooked smile. 'Truly, but you are not completely naked.'

'What are you talking about?'

He reached into his pouch and withdrew the slender gold key. With a click, he undid the shackles and allowed them to drop to the floor. The pile of gold glinted up at her. Her wrists and ankles felt feather-light.

'Why are you doing that?'

'Because I wanted to see you completely un-adorned. Much better this way.' He placed a kiss on the underside of her wrist. 'Don't you think?'

He scooped up the shackles and put them in a trunk.

She tilted her head, trying to assess his mood. 'You are the master here.'

'See how much I want you before you find fault.'

He quickly took off his clothes. Her breath caught at the magnificence of him. His skin was golden, but covered with a network of silver scars. She traced the longest down to where his member stood proud from its nest of curls. He was so beautiful that it made her lungs hurt.

She snaked her arm about his neck and pulled him down on to her. 'We shall have to see what we can do about this, then.'

He laughed and fell to the bed, pulling her on top of him. 'It is your turn to call the rhythm. Ride me. Let me see your pleasure.'

Slowly, slowly Liddy came back to earth. The torches were flickering and beginning to go out.

She leant down and brushed her lips against Sigurd's. There had been a new depth to their joining, something that she wasn't willing to put into words yet.

'Shall I put the shackles back on?' she asked, rising up on one elbow.

He shook his head. 'No need. Everyone knows who you are.'

'And who am I?'

'The woman who shares my bed. The woman who makes all men envy me. My butterfly. You give me hope.'

'You make it sound like I flit from here to there, never resting.'

He laced his hands through her hair. 'As long as you come back to me.'

Liddy drew a shuddering breath. This was the nearest Sigurd had come to saying that he cared about her. Her heart beat far too fast. She wanted to think that he might care for her. 'Thank you. You made me feel beautiful.'

He nipped her chin. 'That is because you are beautiful. In fact, like this and in my arms, I would say you are the most beautiful woman in the world.'

'I have imperfections. My nose isn't straight and my hair never does what it is supposed to. And then there are the scars from carrying my children...and my birthmark.'

He put two fingers over her mouth, silencing her. 'They enhance your beauty. Never let anyone tell you differently. They are what make you,

you. Who wants bland perfection when you can have true character?'

Liddy laid her head on his chest and hoped that he was right. If Malcolm was right, then Sigurd would have to marry a wealthy North woman and this affair would have to end. She would have to find a way to escape, even if it broke her heart. She could never do to another woman what Brandon's mistresses had done to her. Maybe Brandon was right, maybe she was cursed and would always lose those she loved. She drew a deep breath. Over-thinking again. She made her own luck. Her butterfly mark was a symbol of hope, not fear. 'I will try to remember that.'

Chapter Eleven

'Here I find you in this different fort rather than the old fetid one. Sharpening a sword, rather than drilling the men. I take it you have bedded our little saviour.'

'Hring! I didn't expect you back so quickly.' Sigurd glanced up from the sword he was cleaning. The move further down the island had proceeded peacefully. The new quarters were more spacious and commanded a better view of the strait between the island and Jura where most of the shipping traffic passed. And he and Liddy had settled into some of the best sex of his life. Except it was no longer just passion, there was a deeper meaning to it which Sigurd did not want to think overly much about.

'I see you have acquired her dog,' Hring said as the wolfhound bounded forward to greet him. 'Is Lady Eilidith still about, then? You haven't sent her back to her family. From what they say your women last less than a month before you move on.'

Sigurd nodded. The charge was a fair one. Until Liddy, boredom had set in very quickly and he moved on. Liddy was different. 'Liddy remains in my care.'

'I heard your mother's story. My daughter reminded me about it when I visited her. Ragnhild has a good memory for details.' Hring tugged at the neck of his shirt. 'I guess I owe you an apology.'

'Your daughter knows about my mother?' Sigurd asked in astonishment.

'My late wife was a cousin of your father's—I thought you knew. She could not stand his wife. She would have wanted me to assist you.'

Sigurd bowed his head. He had not ever truly considered who his father might be related to. Or that some might wish to take his side. 'I had no idea that we were kinsmen. Rather than looking to the past and family connections, I have allowed my sword arm to carve my place.'

'You need friends, Sigurd. Friends who can smooth matters over.'

Coll padded back and settled down at Sigurd's feet. If Liddy was busy supervising the household chores, the dog seemed to prefer to be with him. Sigurd made sure that he always had plenty of dried meat or hard cheese for him. 'It is amazing how quickly people will move out of my way.'

Hring nodded. 'And when you are surrounded, what will happen to Liddy?'

'How was the North country?' Sigurd asked, choosing to ignore the tiny spark of fear. What had Hring heard?

'No room for anyone who disagrees with the King.' Hring rubbed the back of his neck. 'My daughter will be joining me here. It is well past time that she was married, whatever Ragnhild thinks of it. She needs a warrior to tame her ways.'

'I am sure she will find a mate,' Sigurd said carefully. Hring was a valuable ally, but he would not be marrying his daughter. 'But personally I've no intention of marrying.'

'You travel alone.'

'That's correct.'

'Have you found the missing tribute?'

'It is somewhere on this island. I can feel it in my bones.'

'Ketil will require more than a feeling. He will demand payment. You exceeded your orders. Can you provide the gold? Even you are not that wealthy. You need a wealthy wife to provide the amount.'

The tension eased slightly in Sigurd's shoulders. Hring was definitely angling for an alliance through marriage. It showed that the grizzled warrior felt Sigurd would be confirmed as jaarl, provided he gave Ketil the missing tribute. 'There is no need to speak of an alliance. I have no plans to change my current situation.'

'So you do have feelings for that woman.' Hring shook his head. 'You are a great warrior, Sigurd, but you are thinking with the wrong part of your anatomy. Use your brain.'

'And Beyla?' Sigurd asked between gritted teeth. 'Did you find her and deliver the news to her? I want every detail, no matter how small.'

'Beyla swears she knew nothing of Thorbin's scheme. She collapsed in a dead faint when I told her. Her father and Ketil fought together many years ago. I gathered her influence contributed to Thorbin's rise. She expressed her disbelief that Thorbin could betray Ketil in that fashion, though.'

'Beyla refused to come with you? She has no interest in this island?' Sigurd frowned. Had he been mistaken? It was his last gamble—Thorbin would have confided in Beyla and Beyla would be unable to resist claiming the gold. It was his final plan if other schemes failed. Had Thorbin been telling the truth and had the murder of Ketil's envoy been a terrible accident? 'I need to know!'

'I can't make her out. A very cold fish. She made

it very clear that you were childhood sweethearts, but she was forced to marry Thorbin.' Hring bared his pointed teeth. 'That is a lady with an eye to the main chance, if you catch my meaning. She is coming, since it is you who defeated Thorbin. That is a woman with matrimony on her mind.'

Sigurd pressed his lips together. Forced to marry was not how he would put it. Beyla had made her choice and made sure Sigurd had discovered it in the worst possible manner. He would have defended her to the death, but she wanted something more than a strong arm and a willing heart.

He concentrated on the patterns etched into the sword. Beyla had taken the bait. She cared nothing for him and he had left her betrayal behind years ago.

'Perhaps her first marriage was not a happy one.'

Hring laughed. 'An understatement. She has no thought for vengeance. On the contrary, she seems delighted that Thorbin is dead. He had humiliated her once too often. She declared as much when I told her the news. And she will make her own way. She wants you to understand what she can offer.'

'I know what she has to offer.'

'She inherited men and ships from her father.

She has kept them separate from Thorbin. Apparently.' Hring shook his head.

Sigurd tapped his fingers together. There was far more to this than it appeared on the surface. Beyla might speak of humiliation, but she had never divorced Thorbin. If she had been truly unhappy, she could have gone and with no shame. Unlike the Gaels, in the North Country women could divorce.

Beyla was not coming for some pretended emotion, but because she could scent gold. It was why she wanted control of her ships and men. His instinct was correct—Thorbin had confided in her. She was coming, not with marriage on her mind but gold and conquest.

Until he sprung the trap, Beyla had to remain in ignorance. She had to think that he remembered her fondly and might contemplate marriage to her. Even the faintest whisper of the contrary could spook her.

'I want her here and then I will decide what to do with her. Is she as beautiful as she once was?'

'I've no idea what she looked like as a young girl, but Beyla could rival Sif in her beauty,' Hring said, naming Thor's wife, a goddess fabled for her golden beauty. 'She can lay a claim to Thorbin's holdings in her son's name, Sigurd. Have you considered that?'

'His holdings are forfeit. They belong to me as the victor of the battle.' Sigurd concentrated on his sword. Even Beyla was not so lacking in feeling that she would harm her son, a boy who could be his, but belonged in every way to Thorbin. He should not be concerned for the lad. He hated that a small part of him hoped she'd bring the boy. 'But I am pleased she is travelling here. It will be an end to it. Have quarters prepared for her. The best. I want no complaints.'

'I like to call it stating the probabilities.'

Sigurd pointedly began sharpening his sword.

'You may be experienced in war, Sigurd, but you have little experience with women. Beyla is a determined woman. Eilidith...'

Sigurd gestured to the door. 'Get out, I have better things to do than listen to you prattle about my women.'

Hring left in a hurry.

Sigurd threw the sword down in disgust. Hring had no business speaking to him like that. And he wasn't dishonouring Liddy. If he freed her, she might not choose to stay with him and he couldn't lose her, not yet. She was the best thing to have happened to him in a long time.

He glanced at where Coll sat resting on the floor. The dog gave a little growl in the back of his throat.

'What is your problem? Your mistress and I are good together. She is happy here. Nothing is going to change because Beyla is coming. They are two separate problems.'

The dog covered his nose with his paws.

Sigurd shook his head. 'I know what I am doing. And that includes not getting married.'

'Where are you going with that bedding?' Liddy asked, stopping Mhairi. She'd spent most of the day in the still room, supervising the preserving of the fish for the winter. Her hair hung in damp ringlets, but she was quietly proud of what she accomplished.

The woman gave a perfunctory curtsy. 'A ship is expected on the next few tides, my *lady*. Hring has asked for a set of chambers to be made up for our expected guests. There is a rumour that they will include at least one Northern lady. Wagering has started on which one our lord will marry.'

'Since when does Hring give orders? Why wasn't I told?' Liddy wiped her hands on the apron. Northern ladies with marriage on their mind. The tribute remained missing. Sigurd needed to find gold from somewhere. The vague dream she had of continuing on with him tumbled down at her feet. Her mouth tasted like ash. She'd allowed her dreams to overrule her judgement. Of course Sigurd would marry.

'Lord Sigurd gave his approval. He didn't want you disturbed for something as trivial as this, according to Hring.'

'Anyone we should know?'

'The ship is coming from the North land. I heard that it might be the late jaarl's lady, Beyla. Oh, she is supposed to be a right witch, but beautiful.'

Beyla, the woman Sigurd had been in love with, the woman who had held his heart. Liddy recalled his words about why he could never feel anything just after he purchased her from her father. She fingered her birthmark. How could she compete against a lady like that?

'Why didn't Hring say anything to me?' Liddy wondered out loud, more to Coll than to the servant.

Mhairi plucked at her gown. 'Perhaps he thought it was better that you didn't know. It is how Lord Thorbin was before he changed mistresses. All secretive. I remember Shona complaining about it before she disappeared. How the signs were clear if one cared to look.'

Liddy shook her head, trying to get rid of the buzzing sound. 'Sigurd isn't his brother. He had the women buried.'

'It is the way of it. Women buzz about a jaarl

like flies around a honey pot. You might want to think about going in case your lord turns out to be like his brother.' Mhairi tapped a finger against her nose. 'Aye, I can see you are not wearing your gold any more, but it doesn't make you any less a slave. It just makes you an ordinary one, not Sigurd's special property.'

'You know nothing about my relationship with Sigurd.'

'Northmen don't marry slaves, they bed them. They marry women with large dowries who can help their career. It is the way of the world. Get used to it.'

Liddy clenched her fists. It took all of her self-control not to react to the woman. One of the lessons she'd learnt during her marriage was that responding to such taunts only made them worse. But Mhairi was right. This was the beginning of the end. Neither she nor Sigurd had discovered the missing tribute. He would have to find the gold from somewhere to pay Ketil if he wished to remain jaarl. Marrying an heiress, particularly one he still had feelings for, was the simplest way. Silently she vowed that she would not be around when he did.

Liddy's heart knocked in her chest. She wanted to laugh at the irony of it. A few weeks ago, she would have been thrilled at the news, but now she didn't want her time with Sigurd to end. She had half-thought that they would drift on and on in this dream bubble. But of course, he had responsibilities and Ketil would want him married.

'Of course, I had forgotten Sigurd's bride would be arriving. So much on my mind,' she said around the ash in her mouth.

Liddy stopped. She couldn't have deep feelings for Sigurd. It was supposed to be about passion, not feelings. Something she knew was going to end. And yet she cared about him.

She clenched her hands. She had forgotten the hard lessons she'd learned during her marriage. She needed to get back to the person she was before Sigurd. And she knew where to start.

'Where is Lord Sigurd?'

'He is about to go to Kintra by sea. I thought you knew, lady.'

Liddy closed her eyes. The day was getting worse. Sigurd knew she hated travelling by sea. He was going without her. He was going to arrange her future without her. She would see about that. No one decided her future but her. She was through with men dictating her life.

Liddy burst into the training area with her kerchief and apron slightly askew. Her butterfly mark was dark against the paleness of her face.

Sigurd dropped his sword. His heart thumped far harder than it should do. Had Liddy heard the rumours about Beyla and the possibility he had played a part in the making of her son? He had been witless to think he could keep such news a secret. But she had to understand—he was going to look after her. The boy's future meant nothing to him after what Thorbin had tried to do to him. She needed to trust him.

'Is there something wrong?' He braced himself for a stream of insults. Her eyes were too large for her face and bore an anguished look. He wanted to run through the person who had caused her any heartbeat of pain.

'You said that you would take me to Kintra when you went and you are planning to go without me. You are going to go by sea. Can I no longer trust your word?' Her words cut deep into his soul.

'I am here, not in Kintra,' Sigurd pointed out. There was little point in explaining that he wanted to make it clear to Aedan that Liddy was not for sale before he took her there to visit the graves. Away from the hall, he could explain about his plan to ensnare Beyla and why Liddy needed to be somewhere safe.

'But you are going. Soon.'

'It needs to be done. Aedan mac Connall's men

have been fishing where they shouldn't be. He needs to understand where the limits lie.' The half-truth made his guts churn, but too many people could hear. There had been an incident yesterday, but that was an excuse. The king of cennell Loairn wanted to speak to him.

'Pure provocation. Ignore it. He is simply annoyed you refused his offer of gold.'

'I will not have him encroaching on my territory. He needs to learn a lesson.' He rubbed the back of his neck. 'I thought you had no desire to go there. You said as much the other night. I want to go quickly.'

'I have the right to change my mind. Now that you are actually going.' She drew her upper lip between her teeth. 'Now that things are changing.'

Sigurd's heart twisted. He wanted to take that terrible sadness away. He'd hurt her and it pained him worse than he thought it would.

He motioned to his men who disappeared, leaving them alone.

He pushed the hair from her forehead. 'Tell me the truth. What made you change your mind? Tell me that and I will let you go to Kintra with me, but I want the truth.'

She broke away from him. 'I understand we are preparing for a guest who will arrive on the next tide.'

'Which guest?'

Liddy hid her face in her shoulder. 'Beyla, your first love. The woman you are planning on marrying. The woman you were involved with when your father died.'

Sigurd silently cursed. He never considered that Liddy would believe the rumours or would take them seriously. 'Hring has been spreading rumours. Don't you think I would know if I was planning to marry? He also proposed an alliance with his daughter, Ragnhild. Did you hear that rumour as well? Who else is in the running?'

She gave a hollow laugh. 'You would know that better than me. Apparently your brother was like this when his eye began to roam.'

Sigurd winced as the barb hit home. 'I didn't think it important. I am content with the woman I have.'

'You should have told me about Beyla's expected arrival. I deserved to know. You sent for her. You kept her hidden. Why?'

Her words struck him harder than any blow from a sword. It was his way to keep things contained and separate. He realised that he wanted Liddy in every part of his life, but he also wanted to protect her. Liddy would play no part in his scheme to expose Thorbin's treachery through his wife. She'd done enough. 'Beyla deserved to know of the manner of her husband's death.'

'You intend to marry her. They say she is beautiful.'

He reached out and gathered her to his chest. She stood stiffly rather than melting against him. 'You do me a disservice. Beyla belongs to my long-past youth. My mother had hopes for our marriage, but they never happened. Beyla chose someone else. I have a new life.'

'Then you don't deny it?'

Sigurd winced. He knew unless he gave something, he'd lose her and a world without Liddy at the moment was unthinkable. It also frightened him that he could even think that. 'I'm not my brother, Liddy.'

'What is that supposed to mean?' Her anger was palpable.

'Whatever happens between us, I will see you safe and protected. I have never sacrificed my mistresses to the gods and I am not about to start with you.'

Her face became like thunder and he knew he had not said it right. His feelings for Liddy were far too new and raw. He cared for her more than he'd cared for any other woman, but he had no idea about her feelings for him.

'What is Beyla to you exactly? I deserve that.'

Sigurd stared at the ground for a long time. He owed Liddy something. He had shut her out, hoping to keep his heart whole, but he didn't want that.

'Beyla and I once were lovers. We had dreams,' he said, choosing his words with care. 'I offered to marry her, but she chose a safer option. I have spent the last seven years hating her. I've no wish to marry her, let alone bed her. She has a son which Thorbin claimed could have been mine.'

Instead of clearing, Liddy's face became paler. 'You had best tell me the full story. What precisely is this woman to you?'

Sigurd rapidly began to relate the tale of how he had fallen for Beyla, the only child of the jaarl in the next estate. His mother had seen them together and had encouraged the match. Beyla seemed to return his feelings. He had asked her to come away with him and make a new life. She kept giving excuses and reasons why they should stay. His mother counselled patience as Beyla's love could be seen in her face.

On the night his father died, Sigurd had discovered Thorbin and Beyla together, locked in an intimate embrace. Beyla had attempted to make excuses, but Sigurd had known what passed between them.

His mother continued to believe that Beyla

would follow her heart. She agreed to be sacrificed on the condition that Sigurd be allowed to have his inheritance. She had died, believing that true love would out. Then Sigurd had received a summons from Beyla to their secret place, only to be confronted by Thorbin and his followers who beat him up. Beyla found him and led him to safety. Later he discovered she had left him food, his father's second sword and a bow and arrow.

'Beyla made her choice. She wanted riches and an easy life. Any child she has will be tied to Thorbin's fate, not mine.'

'Even if this child is innocent?'

'It is the way of my people.'

'Perhaps that way should be changed.'

Sigurd slammed the door on the memory. However, the terrible ache that had always been there when he thought of that time had vanished to next to nothing. It was more a ghost from the past. 'I vowed the next time I saw her again—I would be a great warrior. My fame would eclipse both Thorbin's and my father's.'

Liddy's eyes grew thoughtful. 'Did you invite her?'

'In a manner of speaking,' Sigurd admitted.

'You don't know women very well, do you?'

'Normally I am busy with other things.' Sigurd rubbed a hand across his face. 'You are the first woman I'd consider a friend since Beyla tore at my heart.'

'A friend? Only a friend.' Liddy broke away from him. Her chest heaved as she bowed her head.

'What would you call us?' he asked, perplexed. He had just admitted that he cared about her.

'Lovers, for a start.'

Sigurd inwardly winced. 'You are more than a bed-mate.'

The tension in Liddy's face eased slightly. 'I see.'

Sigurd ran his hand through his hair. He hoped she did.

'Do you still want to go to Kintra? Or were you merely trying to escape from Beyla?'

'I'm through with allowing Brandon or Aedan to dictate my moves.' Liddy straightened her shoulders and lifted her head. 'I will travel on the sea. I can do it. Aedan needs to understand that I am wise to his tricks. He means to make you another offer for me.'

Sigurd wanted to take her in his arms and whisper that he was frightened of losing her, but that would have revealed too much. 'Why would I accept it?'

'Good.' She raised her chin and stuck out her hand. 'Now will you give me your word?'

'My word for what?'

'That you will keep the peace and will not provoke a fight with Aedan. Let me speak with him first. I can stop him from doing something that everyone will regret.'

The muscles in his shoulders tightened. 'What sort of man is Aedan?'

'He was kind to me once. He made sure Coll could stay with me when I first married, when Brandon would have sent him away.' She gave a half-shrug. 'He is a man of honour, but he can be reckless. He will have done this to get your attention. He wants you to meet him, but the people of Kintra can't afford a war with you.'

He stroked his chin and beat back the twinge of jealousy. Despite how they had treated her, Liddy remained loyal to Kintra and its people.

'For the gift of the dog, I will not provoke him and I will hope that I do not have to raise my sword.'

She did not answer his smile. 'I pray you don't as well.'

Sigurd fought against the urge to enfold her in his arms and beg her not to go. He had a bad feeling about this, the same sort of feeling he had had before his mother died...for nothing but an empty dream.

Chapter Twelve

'Are you sure that boat is safe?' A knot had developed in the pit of her stomach. It was one thing to agree to go by boat and another to actually do it. The breeze had whipped the normally still loch into white-capped waves. She couldn't help remembering how the boat had rocked just before it tumbled over. 'The sea appears rough today. Is there another way?'

'It is the quickest way. And I had not expected you to go.'

'I want to go.' Liddy swallowed hard. 'But is it the right way? Are you just playing into Aedan's hands?'

'What do you suggest?'

'We could walk—less confrontational. Aedan will have his men in place for a sea battle.' Liddy waited, her heart thumping. But more than that the success of her plan needed her to be outside where she could see Aedan and stop any problems before they started.

Sigurd shook his head. 'Impossible. I want to go across to the island at a quicker pace.'

She clamped her hands together and regarded the sea once more. 'I haven't been in a boat since Keita and Gilbreath died. Somehow it doesn't feel right to use one to visit their graves. I thought I could, but I can't. I am begging you not to leave me behind.'

Sigurd lowered his brows. 'Do you always argue back?'

'One of my worst faults. What can I say? I like getting the last word in.' Liddy breathed a little easier.

'But why walk? You can ride with me. You have done that before.'

Liddy examined the ground. 'I am not sure what my brother-in-law's reaction to that would be.'

'It is hardly a secret that you are now my mistress. Are you becoming shy suddenly? Do you actually care about what Aedan thinks of you?'

Liddy shook her head. She did want a little more time of being close to Sigurd, but confessing that she knew their time was ending was impossible. As long as there was the slimmest chance, they could be together, she wanted to forget about what the future might bring. 'As it is the best way to get there, I accept your offer.'

He burst out laughing.

Liddy pressed her lips together. 'What is wrong? What have I done to amuse you?'

'The joke is on me. I thought perhaps the offer to ride with me would offend you. I love to see your eyes flash. It is getting harder.'

Love—the word made her heart turn over. She loved Sigurd and she had no idea of his true feelings for her.

'Once it would have,' Liddy admitted. 'But if it is the next quickest way after sailing, then I will take it. It will be intriguing.'

'You are unlike any woman I have ever met.'

'A compliment, I think. Then shall we share a horse?'

'Much as I might like it, I have a better idea as I have no wish to offend your brother-in-law. And I've no wish to overtax Floki.'

'A better one?'

'I have a horse, a sturdy mare, for you if you can ride.' He motioned to one of his men who went to the stable and returned with a sweet-faced mare.

The horse was sturdy and definitely not as high spirited as the stallion Sigurd favoured, but Liddy loved her instantly. Liddy held out her hand and the mare's ears twitched forward as she nuzzled it.

'Next time,' Liddy quietly promised her, 'I will bring you a bit of carrot to munch on.'

The mare lowered her head slightly.

'Does she have a name?'

'You can name her. I purchased her earlier for you.'

Liddy tilted her head to one side. 'To keep?'

'You will need a horse to ride if we are to travel the island together. I had remembered about you being wary of boats.' He gave a crooked smile. 'I was going to give her to you when I returned from Kintra.'

Liddy threw her arms about Sigurd, burying her face against his shoulder and breathing in his masculine scent. She made a memory.

'What's the matter?'

When she trusted her voice, she raised her head and discovered that he was regarding her with such tenderness that she wondered how she'd ever doubted that he had a heart.

'It has been a long time since anyone has given me such a wonderful gift. I shall treasure her always.' She gave the mare another stroke. 'I will name her Hope, because it is always good to have hope in your life.'

He frowned. 'Where is Coll?'

'I left him in our chamber with a bone. He doesn't feel the need to be my shadow so much these days.' She put her arms about her waist. If Coll wasn't there, Aedan would be more inclined to let her return with Sigurd. He knew her fondness for the dog.

Sigurd gave a little smile. 'Perhaps he trusts me to look after you.'

'Perhaps.' She smiled. It was a pity dogs, even wolfhounds, had no real concept of the realities of life. Coll might trust Sigurd, but Sigurd needed a wife with a dowry if he failed to find the missing gold. 'They say you never forget how to ride.

'My men and I are at your disposal.'

'Your men?' Liddy concentrated on the ground, all the pleasure in her new gift vanishing. The way Sigurd said it, he made it sound like an invasion force. 'How many are you bringing?'

'Enough. Aedan mac Connall needs to understand that while I may not be ruthless like Thorbin, I am far from weak. He caught my attention this once, he should not do so again. You will remain my woman. I protect my own.'

Liddy's heart thudded. Sigurd had called her his woman. She had to be careful. It wasn't a declaration of love or marriage. 'Your woman?'

'It is what others call you. I want to banish those clouds from your eyes, Liddy.'

She blinked rapidly. Her heart wanted to believe that he had feelings for her but her head kept saying that she'd been wrong once. 'You already have.'

Shortly before they arrived on Kintra's lands, Sigurd stopped his horse and slid off. The seven bodyguards did the same.

'Is there a problem?' she asked, pulling Hope to a halt. The horse was sturdy, she moved well and Liddy had found it easy to keep up.

Her feelings of foreboding had grown throughout the journey. She had tried to talk to Sigurd, but he seemed distracted. She couldn't help thinking that he had another motive for going out to Kintra, something that was linked to Beyla's expected arrival.

'You may get down now. We will all walk. It will be safer that way.'

He held out his hands and she slid into them. The strong arms enfolded her for an instant. She stepped away.

Liddy gave him a grateful glance. 'Thank you.'

'For what? It is easier to fight if I am off the horse.'

'It won't come to that. Aedan will understand that I want to visit my children's graves. He told me that I always could. You can speak to him about the incursion after that. Once he meets you, he will understand.'

Liddy stared at the small plume of smoke which rose from Kintra's hall. The way Aedan had said it when they parted had shown that it was more out of duty than out of any real expectation that she would. The things they had said to each other probably could not be unsaid. There was little point in explaining this to Sigurd, though, as he would only get defensive.

Sigurd inclined his head. 'I shall be interested to see if he is a man of his word.'

Liddy put her hand on his sleeve. 'Allow me to speak to Aedan before you start making threats. He reacts badly to threats. I swear he has a worse temper than his brother.'

'I never threaten. I deliver on my promises. And no one will be allowed to insult you.'

Liddy's stomach tightened. The last thing she wanted to be was a pretext for war. 'Allow me to speak first. Let Aedan prove that he is a man of honour. He won't know you can speak Gaelic. You can listen and learn the measure of the man.'

Sigurd gave a half-smile. 'I'm sure everyone knows by now. There is no such thing as a secret on this island.'

'Aedan will discount it. It is the way he is. He thinks all Northmen are brutes who steal women and hang them when they have no further use for them.'

'Too proud to believe that someone could learn his language? Is it any wonder that the Gaels failed?'

'If you wish to lose your advantage, it is up to you.' Liddy patted Hope's neck. She'd been right to come. 'I'm trying to help.'

'Very well, Liddy, who am I to deny you? You may speak first as you know your brother-in-law, but remember I can understand what you are saying as well.'

Liddy's heart did a little leap. He had faith in her and her abilities.

Kintra's great hall was bathed in a rosy light. The fresh tang of sea air and grass pervaded her senses. This had been one of the things she had loved about living there, but it also reminded her of the bad times she'd experienced there.

Liddy wished she felt better about this. In her panic about the imminent arrival of Beyla, it had seemed the best thing—a way to escape and to keep Sigurd with her for a little while longer. Except now that she was in the bay's shadow, the enormity of being here with a host of Northmen warriors weighed on her.

As they approached the farmhouse, a host of

Gaelic warriors appeared, blocking their way. Sigurd signalled discreetly to his men.

'Tell your master the Northern jaarl is here to see him on business of great importance,' she said, spying the oldest of Aedan's retainers.

'My master recognises no jaarl,' came the spirited answer. 'We will defend what is ours without assistance or interference. If the Northmen want anything, they will have to pay for it in their blood. You have wasted our time and your breath, *Lady* Eilidith, if you thought any different.'

Aedan's men banged their swords against their shields at the end of the speech.

'These men behind me are not your enemy.'

'They are from the North and therefore they are not our friends.' The man gestured to a basket and said loudly in Gaelic. 'These are the mackerel we pulled from the sea today. We fish where we please.'

'Aedan should have a care. This lord is half-Gaelic. He understands our ways better than most,' Liddy said in an undertone.

'If it is a battle they want, I am prepared to give it,' Sigurd said.

'Give me more time.' She glanced over her shoulder. Sigurd's bodyguard had drawn their swords. 'Please. Aedan simply wants to demonstrate that he won't be cowed.'

Sigurd's face became grim. 'Then they should keep the peace.'

Liddy turned to face Aedan's men. Many of them had been Brandon's. She resisted the temptation to hunch her shoulders and hide her mark. She had nothing to be ashamed of. She was not cursed. Sigurd had shown her that. She made her own luck.

'Fetch Aedan and refrain from this madness. I know he is here and he is not one to skulk behind warriors like a toothless old woman. He wanted Sigurd here on account of me,' Liddy said, holding out her hands. 'I beg you. You know me from the time I was lady here. Do you want me to curse this place?'

'It is fine, Aleric, I am here. I can defend this place. Lady Eilidith speaks true. The jaarl Sigurd is here at my instigation.' Aedan strode out of the hall, wearing his battle armour. A priest Liddy particularly disliked followed three paces behind him with his eyes piously lowered.

'Sister, you have returned to us.' Aedan bowed low, completely ignoring Sigurd. His blue eyes flashed in his wind-burnt face. 'Will you be staying long? Do you wish sanctuary?'

Liddy squared her shoulders and resisted the temptation to hide her chin. 'I wish to visit my children's graves.'

'When have I tried to stop you?'

She quickly glanced at Sigurd. 'You gave me reason to think I would be unwelcome.'

'You misinterpreted my words.' He pressed his lips together. 'Why are you here, Northman?'

'Lady Eilidith desires to spend time at her children's graves.' Sigurd inclined his head. 'I wish to ensure my property remains safe.'

Aedan's eyebrows rose. 'Your property?'

'My lady certainly is not yours. Nor is she for sale. I wanted to make sure the message is understood and we have no more incidents over...fishing rights.'

Liddy quickly glanced at Sigurd. The pair were certainly as stubborn as the other. 'Please, Aedan, I want to visit my children. You know who caused me to lose my freedom and it was not a Northman.'

'Your father and I have had words.' Aedan clashed his fists together. 'It is never right to sell your children.'

'You cannot unmake the past.'

Aedan winced. 'Totally unnecessary. You should have enlisted my aid. When we last spoke, I informed you that you could always count on it.'

Liddy bit back harsh words. Aedan had accused her of being cursed, an accusation she'd been too ready to believe. 'I will bear it in mind for the next time.'

Aedan's cheeks became rosy pink. 'I would see you properly settled. I still consider you part of my family. There are things we need to discuss.'

Liddy shook her head. She wasn't going back to the woman she'd been, and she wasn't going to abandon the island she loved to go to a convent in Ireland where they'd beat the curse out of her as Brandon had threatened. 'In the past, Aedan. We have little to say to each other now. Allow me to visit the graves. Then we will depart. Keeping the peace is important. We must keep the truce which was negotiated.'

As he continued to stand there, blocking her way, Liddy held out her hands. 'They were my children. I've not visited them since I left here.'

'Will you allow Lady Eilidith to visit the graves?' Sigurd stroked the hilt of his sword. 'You are vulnerable here. There is but a narrow strip of land.'

Aedan drew his sword half out of its scabbard. 'Easy enough to defend.'

Behind him, his men beat their swords against their shields again.

'Easy enough to starve,' Sigurd retorted. At his signal, his men gave a cheer.

'Do not underestimate my little ships.'

'They are no match for my longships.'

Liddy's blood ran cold. They were nearly at each other's throats. She coughed and they both turned to stare at her.

'We are here because I wanted to visit the graves, not because there was a fight to be had.'

Sigurd bowed low. 'Of course. I am trying to ensure it happens without incident.'

Liddy put her hands on her hip. 'I will not have this used as an excuse for bloodshed.'

Aedan was the first to blink. 'Very well, you may go, but to the graveyard, no further.'

Sigurd gave the briefest of nods. 'It is good that you have seen sense.'

'Wait!' the priest thundered. 'I will not have pagans defiling that sacred space! Aedan, have you not heeded my sermons?'

Aedan gave an apologetic look. 'Lady Eilidith is hardly a pagan, Father Columba. You gave her mass many times when she lived at Kintra.'

The elderly priest gave her a long look up and down as if he were undressing her. Liddy fought the urge to pull her cloak tighter about her. Finally, Father Columba sniffed. 'She consorts with one. Her cursed mark has brought shame on this place again.'

Liddy clenched her fists. She had never cared for that priest. He had always turned a blind eye to anything Brandon had done. She tensed, but the old feelings of inadequacy did not wash over her. Instead a deep-seated rage filled her.

'You wrong me,' she cried. 'I have never shamed this place.'

The words hung in the air. Everyone was looking at her.

The colour drained from Aedan's face. 'You have overstepped, Father. Apologise.'

Liddy stared at Aedan, astonished. He had taken her side. He had made a concession. It was so different from their last conversation, the one where she had stammered and kept giving mumbling apologies until she had slunk off.

The priest mumbled something inaudible.

'Lady Eilidith may go to the graveyard on her own.' Aedan bowed low. 'Northman, I pledge my word no harm will come to her and she will return.'

'She had better,' Sigurd growled.

'I will return. I give my word. I don't want anyone dying on my account.' She stared at both of them. 'On either side.'

'I will take your word,' Sigurd said. 'It is but a little thing. I will keep my temper until you return.'

The priest made noises about showing her the way, but Liddy glared at him and he backed away.

'I go alone.'

* * *

When she arrived at the windswept graveyard, her eyes widened and her steps faltered. A large stone cross stood guard over the two tiny graves. She went over and traced her children's names. The cross was carved with a profusion of birds and animals, including a dog which could have been Coll. In the centre was a mother cradling two children. The entire scene swam before her eyes. She had had no idea that it was there. Why had Aedan done this? Why had he put up such a fine cross? And why had he forced the priest to apologise?

She stood, taking it in, holding the scene in her heart.

'Eilidith is out of earshot,' Sigurd remarked, clinging on to his temper. He wanted to tear the Gael from limb to limb for being disrespectful to Liddy. He'd been about to after the priest gave his speech, but the man had changed his mind. 'Explain why you broke the truce. Be quick about it and I may be merciful.'

Aedan mac Connall asked, 'Why did you come by land?'

'Does it matter why?'

'I believe it does. Humour me. We have time.' Aedan's lips turned up into a slight smile. 'You gave Eilidith your word.'

Sigurd ground his teeth. 'Lady Eilidith was determined to come, but she still fears the water so we came by land.'

Aedan's brow creased. 'A pity. I hadn't realised she still fears it.'

'She blames herself for the accident. Your brother—'

'I will not speak ill of the dead.' Aedan's hand went to his sword. 'There are things which need to be said, but I intend to say them first to Eilidith, not to the man who enslaved her.'

Sigurd ground his teeth, regretting his promise to Liddy. 'We speak of fish, then. You stole from me.'

'Are you going to continue the alliance Thorbin had with Ivar the Boneless? His men have driven us from our fishing grounds. We have no choice. Either that or starve.'

Sigurd stared at the warrior. Those vague rumours were true. Thorbin did have an alliance, but it sounded more like he had taken gold rather had been given it.

'I know of no alliance. Ivar and his Vikings from Dubh Linn remain Ketil's enemies.'

'Even so…they fish and they raid. Until it ends, we fish where we like.'

Sigurd choked back his anger. Aedan the so-called king of cennell Loairn and laird of Kintra, needed to learn a lesson about manners. 'If it is as you say…then steps will be taken. Ivar is no friend of mine.'

Aedan shrugged. 'It is your problem, not mine.'

'Malcolm returned the gold,' Sigurd said, changing the subject to the true reason why Aedan was behaving in this fashion.

'I've had your message and I know why you made her your mistress.'

'Do you?' Sigurd crossed his arms. 'Enlighten me.'

'To provoke and humiliate me.'

Sigurd stared at the man, dumbfounded. 'You are joking? I bedded Liddy because she is passionate and fights for what she believes in. She is also a highly attractive woman. Believe me when I say you and your kin played no part in my bedding of her.'

Aedan opened and closed his mouth like a fish. 'You made her your mistress because you desired her?'

'What other reason is there?' Sigurd shook his head. 'It is hardly my fault if you are blind to it.'

Aedan's colour rose. 'I had never thought of her in that way. She was my brother's wife and I know why he married her.'

'We obviously know very different women, but

then her dog trusts me with her. Did he ever trust her with your brother?'

'My brother disliked that dog, but recognised its virtues. It saved Eilidith from raiders once.' Aedan's jaw jutted out. 'A dog's devotion is easily purchased with a bit of meat and a space beside the fire. Is that how you accomplished it?'

Sigurd reined in his temper. If he had not given his word to Liddy, he would start a fight with this man. 'You should know that Liddy is not for sale. Nor will she be going to a convent here or in Ireland. She will not be forced to travel on the sea until she is ready.'

'As long as she remains with you, I will work to free her.'

'She wants to stay with me.'

'Oh, you have given her a choice?' Aedan crossed his arms. 'The Eilidith I know is concerned with propriety. She will be dying on the inside. Do you have plans to marry her?'

'I have no plans to marry.'

'These things change.' Aedan gave a derisory laugh. 'Rumours have reached here, and since when do Northern jaarls ever marry their slaves? Who will you honour—your mistress or your wife?'

Sigurd ground his teeth. He shouldn't be surprised that Aedan had already heard the rumour.

'Your spy network is to be congratulated. No doubt you know before I do the name of the bride and her nature. Why should you care? You were the one who called Liddy cursed.'

Aedan scuffed a line in the dirt. 'I don't want Liddy hurt again. That's all. She left on bad terms and I mean to make it right. Brandon implied some things about her which were untrue. I discovered my mistake this summer and vowed to make things right.'

'It is Liddy you need to speak to, not me. Now, I will get my woman and go.'

'Wait, give me time to speak with her.'

'Will you fish according to the treaty?'

'You drive a hard bargain. I will see what can be done.'

'I'm pleased Father Columba had the idea of not allowing your master in,' Aedan said, breaking the graveyard's peace. 'You and I need to talk.'

'Who put this up?' she asked, keeping her eyes on the cross. Faint praise from Aedan was not required. And the last thing she needed was a lecture from him or Father Columba.

'I did.'

'Unexpected. What do you hope to accomplish with it?'

Aedan's cheeks reddened. 'I owe you an apology. This goes some way towards it.'

Liddy crossed her arms. 'For what?'

'Brandon lied.' Aedan began to pace up and down. 'That boat design of his has a major flaw—it capsizes easily when people are shifting about in the bottom. It goes upside down with barely a breath's notice.'

The stone carving dug into her palm, but she knew she couldn't let go. Brandon had lied about the boat. He bore some of the blame. 'The boat I used, the one he swore in front of the priest could not capsize in a little wave?'

'The very same. Five good men drowned earlier this year because I listened to his advice. They had no chance to escape.'

'How does this change things?'

'When I returned I spoke to Aline, the nursemaid. She and the twins were having a game of sliding about on the bottom when the wave hit. They were not sitting still as she told Brandon.' He put his hand on her shoulder. 'You did your best, Liddy, to save them. You nearly did. You got them all breathing back to shore. Then Brandon arrived. He was more concerned with the boat than the children. He threatened Aline if she said anything. You are not cursed. The one who was cursed was Brandon.'

Liddy traced the intricate carvings on the cross. Once it would have mattered, but now she felt sorry for Brandon's wasted life and self-serving lies. She silently gave thanks for Sigurd's belief in her. That had been what had saved her.

'Whatever you say, it won't bring my children back, but I've spent far too long hating and not living. It has been three years since Keita and Gilbreath died. And I've learned that it isn't important how others view me, but how I view myself.'

'Then the cross was worth the trouble it took to bring it over here. I'm pleased it opened your heart. Father Columba thought it might.'

The mention of the priest caused a red mist to form in front of Liddy's eyes. 'It has nothing to do with the cross and everything to do with that pagan as you called him.'

Aedan's mouth flew open. 'How could you have feelings for one of them? He will destroy you. He believes things totally different from us.'

'Not so very different. Underneath, it is the person who matters and he is a better person than you think.'

'If you say so…but I must say I am dubious.' Aedan held out his hands. 'You have a home here. Always. Not a convent over the water, but some place near your children.'

'I used to think my whole heart was buried

there, but I know now it was only part of my heart.' Liddy stared out to sea rather than taking his hands. 'I don't belong here.'

His arms fell to his side. 'I beg to differ. Let me show you that I can put things right. I can right some of the wrong Brandon did to you. You don't have to be a slave for ever, Liddy. But I think you are right—your Northman cares for you in his own fashion.'

Liddy ran her hand down the carved stone cross. Perhaps Aedan was right. They had both made mistakes. Arguing about it was not going to bring her children back. Just as arguing about why she'd been made a slave was not going to change that either. 'Thank you for placing this here, but my mind is made up.'

'My pleasure.' He bowed slightly. 'Now, will you tell me why you are here? I know why he is here, but not you.'

'I wanted to see the graves and to make sure you had received my message.' She turned to the sea. She could hardly confess about Beyla's imminent arrival and her fears. 'Sigurd will free me in time. I'm sure of it. He is a man of his word.'

'He is a Northman.'

'Northmen can be honourable.'

'He should marry you if he is honourable.'

Liddy focused on the waves coming into the

shore and the screech of the seagulls rising up from the day. 'It is complicated. He will need to marry a woman who is worthy of ruling this island.'

'And you are not? What more could he want?'

'A woman from the North with a dowry. Several are coming. I know he will need a wife and I will not have done to her what was done to me.'

'I can rescue you and keep you safe from all Northmen.' Aedan pressed an intricately carved pendant into her hand. 'Send this to me when you need me. It belonged to my aunt, the one whom the Northmen kidnapped. She would approve of it being used like this.'

Liddy closed her fingers about the carved pendant. The woman's passing, over twenty-five years ago, had nearly destroyed the family. It was one of the reasons Brandon had hated the Northmen. But no one knew what had ultimately happened to her. Liddy hoped that she had found some measure of happiness.

'And what about the people left behind? If I run away, Sigurd would be in his rights to take revenge on my family.' Liddy shook her head. 'I won't have that happen.'

'This should be on your father's head.'

Liddy shook her head. 'Allow me to deal with

this in my own way. I will not die a slave. I give you that promise.'

'It isn't that simple. I have a duty towards you.'

She hugged her arms about her waist. This was the problem with Aedan—he thought women were to be protected, rather than letting them contribute fully. Women in his world were delicate creatures who did not have any sense. She might not be able to wield a broad sword for any length of time, but she certainly knew how to protect herself. 'That duty finished when I left here as a widow.

'No more messages, Liddy, except the one I want to hear. You don't have to do this alone. That is part of what the fish were about—a message to that overgrown lump that there will be consequences if he tries to harm you.'

Liddy closed her eyes. She should have known that he would not listen to the message she sent. When she had control of her temper, she looked directly at her former brother-in-law. 'He had the women in the grove properly buried. Did you know that? He doesn't sacrifice women. He is different. He is honourable. I promise you.'

'When you are ready to see sense, send the pendant.' He bowed low. 'We may have our differences, but you are family. No family member of mine stays a slave if I can help it.'

Chapter Thirteen

Sigurd waited until they had left Kintra's lands with its graveyard far behind them. His heart had skipped a beat when Liddy returned with the sunlight turning her hair red-gold and had readily agreed to Aedan's suggestion that this was the start of a new era.

He'd not realised how worried he'd been that she'd just disappear. He should have known that Liddy would keep her word. His mother would have loved her and he could think of no higher praise.

She had passed the test. And it frightened him. Had she only returned because he owned her?

If he freed her, would she stay? Or did she want something more from life? Hring was right. Once he'd found the gold, then he could marry her and offer a secure future. His gamble with Beyla would work. She would lead him to it.

However, the spark faded from Liddy's eyes as they soon as they left Kintra behind.

'How did you find the graves?' he asked, trying to discern what was wrong. 'Neglected?'

He waited as Liddy studied the ears of her mare for a long while.

'Aedan apologised to me. He no longer believes I am cursed. He knows it was Brandon's invention to cover up the defects of his boat. He lied in church about me being cursed.'

'The utter swine. It's a pity he is dead. I would have loved to challenge him.'

Her mouth turned up. He found lately that he was striving more for her little smiles, the ones which lit up her eyes like the sun peeking from behind the clouds after a morning's rain shower. 'You would have defeated him as well, I'm sure of it.'

'Will you need to return there?'

She slowly shook her head. 'There is nothing for me there. I've said my goodbyes. It is a lovely spot, though, overlooking the bay. Peaceful. Aedan commissioned the most beautiful cross. Part of his apology. He offered me sanctuary if I wished to escape...'

'You wish to escape.' Something tightened in his chest. He half-wanted her to say yes. It would make things easier. His mother had died because of him. He did not want Liddy being used against him.

She turned in her saddle, eyes blazing. 'Do you think so little of me? Or would you like me to go?'

'Will you take his offer?'

Quickly masked pain and hurt crossed her face and Sigurd knew he had said the wrong thing. He hadn't explained it well enough.

'Are you giving me my freedom?' Her voice shook. 'Are you saying that our time is at an end? How long have you been plotting this? Did you arrange it with Hring and Mhairi so that I would demand to come?'

Sigurd regarded the rugged landscape. The words about loving her and being frightened to be without her stuck in his throat. The last time he thought he'd loved someone, it had ended badly. All he could see was Liddy slipping away from him.

'It was a mistake to come here.'

A mixture of emotions fluttered across her face. 'I see.'

'I hope you do.' The words about how much he dreaded losing her wouldn't come out. But equally he dreaded having her stay only because she was bound to him. Aedan's words taunted him. 'I hope you do. When you want to go back to Kintra, you tell me and I will arrange it. I will make sure you are looked after. But I want you to stay with me because you want to be with me, not because your father sold you. You are now a free woman. You belong to no one except yourself.'

A lump formed in Liddy's throat and the carved pendant Aedan had given her felt heavy in her pouch. He'd just done the unthinkable and had offered her her freedom. He knew that the gold was lost for ever and he'd have to marry a wealthy woman to make up the missing tribute.

She had been prepared for the end, but not so suddenly. She doubted if she could bear it— watching him with a new woman. While it might not be Beyla, the entire experience showed that she could take nothing for granted. Sigurd needed a wife with a dowry. With Brandon she had had some rights, with Sigurd she had none and yet she'd been freer with Sigurd than she had ever been with Brandon.

Freedom did not have the same feeling that she thought it would. 'We are going a different way back. We should have taken the left fork in the track.'

'You wish to return with me?'

'Coll would be cross if I left him.'

Sigurd's face broke into a wreath of smiles. She wanted to savour the moment and pack it away so that she could bring it out when she was old and grey and Sigurd had long departed from her life. A moment of perfect understanding that needs no words. 'Of course Coll. He depends on the both of us.'

'He is at home with you. We should get back.' Once they had returned and she had picked up the threads of her life, this unsettled feeling would go. Sigurd was going to be part of her life for a little time yet. She wanted to savour each moment.

'There is no hurry. I want to inspect more of the island.' Sigurd leant down and patted the side of his horse. 'A good lord knows his lands and his people. I have time. We are in no hurry that I know of.'

Liddy concentrated on the twitching of Hope's ears. 'Was this always your plan?'

'Before you invited yourself along? No, but there are reasons why I wanted you to have a horse.' He smiled and her heart turned over. 'Allow me my secrets, Liddy. Allow me to give you surprises.'

'And you don't want to be there when Beyla arrives? Won't that make her upset?'

He tilted his head to one side. 'You seem far more worried about giving offence than I am. Beyla will wait on my pleasure, not the other way around. Hring can entertain her. It may well be that she decides to remain in the North.'

Liddy concentrated on the path ahead of them. They were following the coastline as the island looped around to Loch Indaal. 'Why are we going to my father's?'

'Don't you want to see your family?' he asked with deceptive quietness. 'You should make peace with them. Do you remain angry with your father?'

'It depends.' She tightened her grip on the reins. Some day she might be able to forgive her father to his face. He was going to be insufferable. 'I thought we were friends.'

He gave a half-smile. 'Lovers, you said.'

'Both,' she admitted. 'I have changed my view. Lovers can be friends. Very good friends.'

He gave a very satisfied smile. 'I am honoured. There is something I learnt at Kintra. A theory I want to test.'

'Sail on the loch!' one of the bodyguards shouted.

Sigurd instantly straightened in his saddle and turned his head towards where the bodyguard pointed. First one longboat and then another appeared, their sails billowing in the breeze.

Sigurd let loose a volley of curses which Liddy barely understood.

'Ivar the Boneless's. It appears Aedan told the truth.'

Liddy watched the sails flutter in the wind as the men brought them down. 'Then it is true, he did make common cause with Thorbin.'

'He will find out that he picked the wrong warrior to antagonise.' Sigurd thumped his hand against the saddle. 'Sometimes the fates are with us and they are today. You see how you bring me good fortune, Liddy?'

'I'd hardly call a fleet of hostile Northmen good fortune.'

'Ah, but the element of surprise is on our side.'

'What are you going to do?'

'For now I watch and wait. If he does nothing, then I do nothing, but he will do something. He didn't come all this way for a pleasant sail. We will be ready for him.'

'But…but…'

'They will have to come ashore somewhere, probably not close to a settlement. I do know how raids are carried out. The most important element is surprise.' He motioned to one of his men. 'You will return to the fort with Sven. He has a decent sword arm now.'

Liddy shook her head. 'We are near to my father's lands. I have to know that they are all right. Please, Sigurd, I will stay out of danger. And I trust your sword arm before anyone else's. I've seen you fight.'

He had to agree. Explaining that she worried about him was not an option. She waited for the longest breath of her life.

Sigurd finally nodded. 'Fine. But if there is trouble, stay way back.'

'I hardly have a death wish! I have a lot to live for.' She started in surprise and knew her words were true. She did have a lot to live for. The graves on the hillside were in her past. Joining them would not bring her children closer. She did have a lot of living left to do and she wanted to spend as much of it as she could with Sigurd.

He laughed at that and then sobered. 'We follow them and see where they make landfall. It may be they can be reasoned with, but if not, they will feel the point of my sword.'

'I know the area around here well, as it is between my family's lands and Kintra. What sort of landfall are they looking for?'

'A quiet stream where they can pull up their boats and which gives reasonable access.'

Liddy concentrated on her mare's twitching ears and tried not think about all the innocent people she knew—the farmers, their wives and children, people who would be rich pickings for a band of raiders. These boats had to be stopped before any more disappeared. 'They have already passed three such places. Do you think they could be headed somewhere specific, somewhere it was easy to raid?'

'You mean your father's farm? It is on the headland, isn't it?' Sigurd's face became determined. 'I don't know. It is a possibility. I doubt they are travelling to enquire about the state of fishing in these waters. Is there a place near your father's hall?'

'We should warn them. Give them a chance to hide.' She bit her lip. 'We should also inform Aedan. One of the reasons he returned early was to protect his people.'

'What would he do?'

'He could send men to help. His warriors are far closer than your men. They could be here before nightfall. The raiders like to strike in the dark. We could strike first. The element of surprise would be with us.'

Sigurd shook his head. 'He won't come.'

Liddy took the pendant from her pouch. She had to use it now and save everyone. If Sigurd went in alone, he would be outnumbered. 'He will come, if you give him this. He promised me that.'

Sigurd's eyes widened and he turned it over and over in his hand. 'When did you get this?'

'Aedan gave it to me today. It is…for emergencies.'

'And you took it without asking me?'

'It seemed best.' Liddy concentrated on Hope's ears. Her stomach knotted. Explaining now why she'd taken it would only delay things. Later after the battle was won, she'd confess her fears. 'It was a peace offering. Use it now. Summon him. Ask him to come where you think they will make landfall.'

Sigurd motioned to two of his men. 'You ride and tell all the estates under our protection and Kintra about the danger. They must make up their own mind about what they will do. Then come find us. Does that satisfy you, Liddy?'

The men took off at a gallop. The tension flowed out of Liddy. They would arrive long before the raiders, particularly if Sigurd was right and the raiders would take their time. Her mother had a long-established routine of what to do if raiders should appear.

They rode on a little until they came to a sheltered cove.

'Here!'

'How can you be so sure?'

'It has been used before.' Sigurd pointed to a shallow indentation. 'They had a fire here and you can see how the shoreline has been disturbed in the past, if you know how to look.'

'But we have had no problems with raiders,' Liddy protested.

'Your brother-in-law has. It is why he went to Ireland. It is why he took those fish.' Sigurd stroked his chin. 'Interesting, yes?'

Sigurd directed his remaining men on how they should position themselves.

Liddy watched in fascination. Now that Sigurd had pointed out what she should be looking for, it made sense that they had made landfall here.

'It amazes me that they never raided my father's estate, it's no distance away,' Liddy said as she came to stand beside him. 'He will appreciate you being here. Thorbin would never have done that. He rarely came out here this way.'

'Rarely, not never.' Sigurd paused in his preparations. 'When was the last time?'

'Is it important?'

Sigurd nodded. 'It could be. I have taken both the forts apart as well as the sacred grove. There is no way the missing gold was there. But it exists. I believe the islanders when they say that they paid. He will have hidden it somewhere.'

'Why? Why are you so certain?'

'Because I have done as you suggested on that first day. I have shown faith in the islanders. They have started to pay the tributes. Slowly and with grumbling, but they are paying. Islay is a productive place. And the shipping alone makes it profitable.'

'And no one has seen Shona, his last mistress. She disappeared about the time he sent Ketil's man back in a barrel.'

'She will be buried with the treasure so that her spirit guards it. The question is where?'

Liddy tried to remember precisely when Thorbin had visited the estate. 'The last time was earlier this year. My mother commented on it. It was after that he became paranoid and started issuing decrees.'

'Before or after your brother attacked him?' Sigurd's voice held a note of barely suppressed excitement.

'Before. I returned from Kintra just after that. My father encountered him and his entourage hunting in the woods and invited them for a meal. My mother was very upset at the thought of such a man dining with us. However, Thorbin refused. I can't remember if they had a woman with them.' Liddy shook her head, trying to work out why Sigurd might be interested in such a thing. 'After that he significantly increased the tribute. My mother blamed my father, saying that he had made too many extravagant promises and Lord Thorbin must have considered that we had more gold than we knew what to do with.'

'Is that when your brother decided to attack Thorbin?'

'Malcolm went to the fort to take the first portion of the tribute. There was a field of winter cabbage. He had heard that they wanted fresh vegetables. Fa had been laid up or otherwise he'd have gone.' Liddy studied the ground. 'I never thought Malcolm would do such a thing. My father was astonished.'

'Do you know what the fight was about? Did Malcolm confide in you?'

'Why is this important now? What does it have to do with these Northmen?'

Sigurd looked out to where the ships were slowly moving up the loch. The cries of the men could be heard as they stroked their oars in time. 'It may have great bearing. This lot are making no pretence at silence. They have been here before.'

'It was out of character for Malcolm. He is a farmer, not a fighter. He cares about the soil and making things grow.'

'Youth can be hot-headed. Your brother does have a quick temper.' Sigurd gave a soft laugh. 'It runs in the family.'

'We are not talking about me.' Liddy shielded her eyes against the sun's glare. The boats were coming ever closer. 'I don't see how discussing what Thorbin did will help us defeat those Northmen. Perhaps we should make for my father's hall.'

'Is there a bay near this cabbage field?'

'What?'

'I suspect your brother saw something or Thorbin thought he did.' Sigurd slammed his fists together. 'I should have seen it before. He made an example of Malcolm when there was no need to do it. He also made sure that I knew Malcolm for a troublemaker and malcontent.'

'You mean as if the cabbages were a secret sign.' Liddy trembled. 'The gold. Do you think he might have hidden it around here? And that Malcolm was attempting to blackmail him.'

'Precisely.'

'Why here? Why in this area?'

'It is reasonably close to his fort, but nowhere that any of Ketil's men would look, particularly as your father is well known to be loyal.' Sigurd leant forward. 'And Gorm was wrong. Thorbin did not pay Ivar anything. Ivar paid him. He had to keep the gold away from his men and that meant secreting it somewhere where his men would not suspect.'

'But he arrested my father and brother.'

'I suspect Thorbin felt he could manage the situation better than he did. He expected to return if he was sent to Ketil. Then he felt threatened.'

Liddy thought hard. 'There is a small inlet. It is

not often used. You could land a boat or two there. But these Northmen are landing here.'

'Thorbin will not have trusted them.' At her questioning glance, he added, 'I feel it deep in my gut. It is the same sort of feeling I get before battle.'

Liddy gave a soft laugh. The love he felt for her threatened to overwhelm him. 'And you are asking me to trust your gut.'

'We have this one chance to stop them, so, yes, I am asking you to trust me. Can you lead me there after this is all over?'

'Yes, but there will be nothing there.'

'There will be and I will find it.' He put his hands on her shoulders, willing her to understand what he wanted to do and why. 'I have this one last chance to find this gold and I will.'

'I believe in you.' She put her hand to her eyes. 'They seem to be turning around. Do you think they will just go away?'

'They are waiting for the tide to turn. It is easier to beach your ships when the tide is with you.'

'What do we do now?'

'We wait and we give them a welcome that they will not soon forget!'

The boats remained offshore, not doing anything, but the water had begun to lap in earnest at the shoreline. Sigurd had arranged his remaining men in position. Half of her hoped that nothing would happen, but the other half wanted Sigurd to be right. She wanted to believe that the Northmen from Dubh Linn could be defeated here.

The first warrior had returned without her father or brother. They were busy securing the hall, but would come to help if circumstances permitted. Liddy pressed her lips together. Typical.

'Can you see the boats?' Sigurd asked.

Liddy's stomach clenched. The lead boat had turned and was heading straight for the bay. She had had such hopes. 'We have run out of time. The tide has turned.'

'Go, Liddy. Go to your father and keep safe. You have your freedom. You can then go where you will.' He gave her a little shove. 'No one else will be coming. Aedan mac Connall will be like your father. We have run out of time.'

Liddy crossed her arms and refused to move. 'No.'

'No?'

'Either I will be safe here with you or Ivar the Boneless's men will overrun everywhere. You asked me to trust your sword arm and I have.' Her throat worked up and down. 'You can dismiss me if you like, but I will find a way to stay.

If you have given me my freedom, then I am free to make up my mind. I stay with you, Sigurd. You and I, we make our own luck.'

Sigurd's eyes widened. 'You have more grit in your little finger than your brother or father.'

'Someone has to.'

Liddy counted the warriors again. No matter how many times she counted, she still came to the same conclusion. They were outnumbered. She knew she should flee, but she was reluctant to leave Sigurd. Somewhere deep in her heart she knew if they parted, it would be the last time she saw him. 'Will you have enough men?'

'You only know that when the battle is done. Sometimes one man is enough, sometimes you can have a thousand and still lose,' Sigurd said, giving a half-truth. He had the advantage of surprise and that was about all. 'We will manage with what we have.'

The tiny frown relaxed between her eyes. Sigurd heaved a sigh of relief. Liddy didn't realise the peril they faced. If the gods and fate were with him, he could win, but if not, he would lose and lose badly.

'That makes sense.' She stiffened. 'I hear horses. Aedan will be coming to our aid. I knew he couldn't resist the chance to fight Northmen.'

'Just the wind.' Sigurd cocked his head to one

side. 'You tried, Liddy, but Aedan has his own concerns.'

'You have more men,' Aedan called out as he rode into view. 'My scouts spotted the ships just after you left and I summoned my men. I will admit to thinking you had double-crossed me. Thinking to attack after mouthing peace, however, I met your messenger on the road and he explained.'

Sigurd bowed. 'I am grateful you decided to join in the fight.'

Aedan bowed towards Liddy and handed her the cross. 'I would have come with or without this, but it made my decision easier. One way or another you will be free. You have requested sanctuary.'

Liddy tore her arm from Aedan's grip. 'It is not why I sent for your help. It is time you did more than proclaim your opposition to men from Dubh Linn. Time to start fighting for your land!'

'Your men are most welcome,' Sigurd said, putting a restraining hand on Liddy's shoulder. 'Liddy, he is here to help. We have enough enemies without making more.'

He rapidly explained his plan to Aedan, who seemed to grasp the rudiments and asked pertinent questions. Sigurd's respect for the warrior grew. It was easy to understand why he had been able to gain control of the headland.

Liddy linked her arm with his. The simple touch did much to steady him. She smiled. 'What do you want me to do?'

'Stay hidden. Keep out of the way,' Aedan retorted. 'I can't believe you allowed her to be here, Sigurd. She should be in hiding.'

'Liddy made her own choice.' Sigurd gave Liddy's hand a squeeze before stepping away from her. 'Keep back from the fighting, Liddy. If you see the tide turning against us, use your horse and ride far away from here. We agreed on this.'

She stood proud with her red hair flowing free. 'I believe in your sword arm, Sigurd. I have seen it in action. I stay.'

Sigurd gave Aedan a look. 'Eilidith is a woman who knows her own mind. If you had had more warriors with her spirit, you would have not lost this island.'

'I wish that my father...' Liddy pressed her lips together. 'He will not fight.'

'But his son will,' her brother said, coming out from the shadows. 'Don't worry, Liddy, Fa has taken Ma off, but I figure we need to make a stand.' He motioned to the group of men who stood behind him. Most of the islanders had hoes and scythes, but the priest held a smouldering torch.

'What is that for?' Sigurd asked, nodding towards the priest.

'I figured that we might be able to burn their heathen boats, the same way they have burnt us in the past.' The priest glared back. 'I want to do more than bind wounds afterwards.'

'I am grateful for any help.'

'First boat coming this way,' one of his men shouted out. 'It looks like you were right, Sigurd. They will make landfall here.'

Sigurd raised his right hand. 'Wait until they are in the water. It is when they are most vulnerable.'

'How do you know they mean harm?' one of his men asked.

'They haven't come calling the usual way.' Sigurd beat his sword against his shield. 'Will you follow me?'

The men gave a ragged cheer and then were silent.

Sigurd's nerves tightened. This was the part he normally loved best about any battle—the tension and anticipation before the start, but today, all he could think about was keeping Liddy safe. He wished she was a thousand miles from harm, but he was also pleased she was there, with him. He glanced over his shoulder to where she stood, by the horses. She gave him an encouraging nod. Then he turned his gaze towards the sun-dappled bay.

The lead longboat slid into the shallow waters with its shields down. Its warriors started to get out, more intent on getting the boat ashore than noticing their surroundings. The second boat slid alongside them and the third had just started its manoeuvre. The warriors were definitely from Ivar the Boneless, and they had no idea that they were being watched.

Sigurd lowered his arm. 'At them.'

His warriors rushed forward, shouting. The priest tossed his torch, sending it arching in the sky until it connected with the sail cloth where it caught fire. Plumes of smoke issued from one boat.

The would-be raiders took one look and started running back for the boat. One climbed the mast to put the fire out, but an arrow felled him.

Sigurd grabbed their leader by the arm, recognised him as one of Ivar the Boneless's most loyal warriors. 'Not so fast. This is my land and you need to ask my permission.'

'Never.' He tried to knee Sigurd in the groin.

'Then you face the consequences.'

Sigurd pivoted and landed a blow on the man's back. The man screamed in agony.

The battle was fast and furious and the blue

water of the bay turned a dull red from the blood. But when it was done, Sigurd counted two dead from his band and more than twenty from the opposing side. The remaining Northmen rapidly surrendered.

Chapter Fourteen

Liddy picked her way around the smouldering wreckage of the longboat and the other debris from the brief battle. A group of Northmen from Dubh Linn sat on the beach with their arms tied. After the noise and fury of the battle, the sudden stillness hurt her ears.

Just when she had nearly given up hope of spotting Sigurd, she saw him sitting on an up-turned rock, speaking to Aedan and Malcolm. Anger swept through her. Here she'd been worried about him and he was laughing and joking.

She marched up to the group. 'You might have told me that it was over. I thought something must have happened to you. I worried that I might not see you again.'

The instant they heard her voice, the discussion stopped. Sigurd went over to her and enfolded her in his arms. She laid her head against his chest and listened to the steady thumping of his heart. He was alive.

She touched his face and felt the soft bristles of his stubble against her hand. 'I was so worried. Is it over?'

'Wait here. Once you see this, you will understand.' Sigurd loosened his arms and let her go. He went over to where he'd been sitting and retrieved a large sword which he handed to her with a flourish. 'The leader of this particular *felag*'s appetite for battle vanished once he realised that this was not going to be an easy raid. He attempted to run, but misjudged it. One boat got clean away. Another burns, but the third I claim as bounty.'

Liddy raised herself up on tiptoes and tried to peer around his bulk. 'Will they return?'

'They will not be able to use this place again to launch their raids on my people. I will keep a guard on it,' Aedan declared.

'We both will,' Sigurd said, holding out his hand.

Aedan reluctantly took it. 'I never thought I'd be grateful to have a Northman on my side, but I am.'

Liddy awkwardly held the sword. A large part of her wanted Sigurd to enfold her in his arms again. As it was she kept looking to see if he was injured, but he appeared unhurt except for some minor bruising. Aedan had a cut to his cheek and his hand bore a nasty gash.

'But where have they gone? Will they regroup? Bring back more men?'

'Last seen, heading towards Ireland,' Aedan commented. 'It did me good to see Northmen turn tail and run. We may have differences, your man and I, but he is as good as his word and I've never seen a better fighter.'

'The battle may be over, but they will return.' Sigurd tapped his fingers together. 'I'm not altogether convinced they were here to raid or even to fish. I think they had another quarry.'

'What other quarry could there be?' Aedan asked.

'Sigurd is convinced that Thorbin hid his gold and possibly told Ivar the Boneless where it was hidden. Or at least gave him enough of a clue.' Liddy looped her arm through Sigurd's. 'Isn't that right?'

Sigurd gave her arm a squeeze before moving away. 'Unfortunately none of those surviving has much of a clue. The leader perished in the attack. He had, however, promised them great treasure, ripe for the taking. I suspect Ivar paid Thorbin gold and this is where he collected it.'

Aedan nodded. 'Interesting. To the finder, the

gold, eh, Sigurd? If it is on my land and I find it, it is mine.'

'That is the law.' Sigurd drew his brows together. 'We need to go, Liddy.'

A clatter of hooves interrupted the preparations. Hring rode into view. 'Sigurd Sigmundson!'

'A bit late,' Sigurd remarked, going forward. 'We will discuss defence of this island later, king of Loairn and laird of Kintra.'

'I look forward to it.'

Hring saluted Sigurd. 'There has been a development. Beyla has arrived with her son.'

Liddy's stomach tightened. Was this why Sigurd had given her Hope? Was that why they journeyed towards her father's estate rather than away from it? He was planning this. Her stomach roiled. This was supposed to be goodbye. And now she had forced the issue by demanding that she stay with him and yet she knew she had to fight for him.

'She was expected, several days ago by your reckoning,' Sigurd said. 'Why the panic? She will be easy to deal with in due course.'

Hring's face became graver. 'But that is not all. Ketil has also arrived.'

'Ketil?' Sigurd stared at Hring in astonishment. Ketil Flatnose being here was absolutely the last thing he needed. After settling things with Aedan, he wanted to take Liddy somewhere quiet and explain things to her, but this had thrown his plans. 'Why is he here?'

'Beyla has outfoxed you,' Hring declared. 'She outfoxed us all. She went straight to Ketil and demanded her husband's blood price. Claimed you had no right to kill him. Claimed it was in cold blood. She had spies, Sigurd. I blame myself for not considering the option when she said that she wanted her own ships.'

Sigurd silently cursed. He had failed to consider that option as well. 'Not your fault, Hring.'

'Worse, Ketil has taken her side.' Hring pushed his helm back. 'If you remember, her father saved Ketil's life way back when. He has a soft spot for her.'

Sigurd closed his eyes. Just when he had considered the day could not get any worse. 'What blood price does she claim?'

'Ketil named a weight in gold. Far more than most jaarls would be worth.'

Sigurd winced. If he had found the missing gold, it would not have been a problem, but as it was, the amount would be difficult to raise. 'Does Ketil agree to it?'

'Ketil has come to make sure that he gets what is due him and that justice is done.' Hring gave a short laugh. 'He appears to have a liking for Beyla. There again, he always did have an eye for a well-turned ankle and a soft smile, but he always makes sure to put business before pleasure.'

'Beyla can be most persuasive,' Sigurd said, remembering how her soft words of undying devotion had nearly undone him and had lulled him into Thorbin's trap.

Hring bared his teeth. 'Are you coming? Or are you leaving in that longboat you captured? Shall I say that I couldn't find you?'

Sigurd lifted a brow. 'Do I have a choice?'

'Not really. Not if you want to live.'

Liddy slipped her hand in his. The simple touch showed him how much he stood to lose. If Beyla wanted to get to him, she'd use Liddy, just as his mother had been used all those years ago. He needed to think clearly.

'Sigurd, what is going on? What is wrong? Did your men refuse to come?'

'None of your concern, Eilidith.' He drew a breath. How could he ask Liddy to share his life with this hanging over him? She deserved much better. She deserved to stay free and to live her life in comfort. 'I will solve this, but you need to remain here where you will be safe.'

Her eyes flashed. 'You consider me safe here?

No, I am safe with you. You promised me when we first met.'

Each word was another knife in his soul. He should have considered that Beyla would act and act decisively. He had made a fundamental mistake in forgetting about her connection to Ketil. If Beyla suspected his feelings for Liddy, she'd seek to use it against him. In order to protect Liddy, he had to hurt her. He had to make her think that they were over. It tore at his soul far more than he had ever considered possible.

'Aedan offered you sanctuary. It is the best place for you. He will protect you now.' For one last time, he touched her cheek. She turned her face away. 'He knows you are far from cursed.'

'Sigurd Sigmundson, we must depart!'

'No! I won't accept that,' Liddy protested. 'We belong together.'

'You must.' He took his mother's cross and handed it to her. It had kept him safe thus far. His mother had been right—true love was worth fighting for and this time he would keep the woman he loved safe from Beyla's clutches. 'Keep this to remember me by.'

'Your mother's cross?'

Sigurd closed her fingers about the cross. 'You must accept it. It is better this way. She would have wanted you to have it.'

He hoped she'd understand its significance. He was giving her his heart and his pledge to seek her out once he defeated Beyla and any other enemy.

He nodded towards Aedan. 'Take care of her. Keep her safe. You will answer to me.'

Aedan gave him a grave nod. 'For a Northman, you are one of the good ones.'

'I hate you for leaving me here! I will never forgive you!' Liddy cried and as Sigurd forced his feet to keep on walking, he knew he'd hear those words in his dreams.

'Are you coming, Eilidith?' Aedan asked. 'Or do you have to be carried?'

Liddy stood watching where Sigurd had ridden off without a backwards glance. If she strained she could just about imagine the sound of horses' hooves. And she knew her last words to him were wrong. She had forgiven him the instant he was gone. He was trying to protect her from whatever waited for him back at the hall.

'I am a free woman, Aedan, not your slave.' She crossed her arms and glared at him. 'I belong to no man. Sigurd Sigmundson gave me my freedom in a way which my father or you never would have. I go where I please.'

Aedan examined the ground. 'You are my

sister-in-law. You should never have been a slave. I will give you sanctuary.'

'I had more freedom as a slave than I ever did as Brandon's wife,' Liddy retorted. 'Sigurd cared for me. He valued my opinions. Now he is in danger. Something needs to be done to help him.'

'That man cares for nothing but his own skin. I know his type. He won't return. He will make some arrangement with Ketil Flatnose.'

'No, you don't. You know nothing about him—who he is and what he believes in.' Liddy tightened her grip on the cross. It frightened her that he'd given his most precious possession to her. It was as if he never expected to see her again. 'But I do and I know he loves me.'

'How do you know that?'

'He has just given me this. He wore it around his neck, always.' Liddy opened her hand to show him the cross.

Aedan's eyes widened. 'His what? Your pagan Northman carries a cross? You mean…he believes in Christ?'

'His mother's cross. Sigurd's father had it made for his mother as a sign of his devotion. She always wore it until she decided to save Sigurd by agreeing to be burnt on his father's funeral pyre.' Liddy quickly put it over her head and tucked the cross down her front. The metal held a faint warmth from Sigurd's body. 'It kept him safe. Now he has given it to me.'

'Sigurd's father did that?'

'She left hers behind when her father sold her to the Northmen,' Liddy said quietly. 'I believe Sigurd's father loved his mother and she found some measure of happiness as a slave. She certainly loved her son. Everything might not be as simple as it first appears. Being Sigurd's slave was not the worst thing to happen, but the best thing.'

'I fail to see how that is possible.'

'After my children died, I was like the walking dead, willing to believe I was cursed and rightly shunned. Sigurd showed me the way back to life and that I deserve good things in my life. My enslavement ultimately has given me a reason to live. He restored my belief in my goodness.' Liddy put her hand over Aedan's. 'I know you think you are doing the best for me, but you have to allow me to go where I want to. I have a different path to follow.'

Aedan's brows drew together. 'I believe I may have wronged your man. I won't force you to return to Kintra, but you will always have a place at my hearth and I mean that. You must go somewhere and Sigurd wanted you with me.'

Malcolm rushed up. His tunic was torn and his face muddy, but other than he appeared unhurt. 'Is it true, Liddy? Sigurd left you behind? It means you have been freed!'

'There are many types of freedom,' Liddy replied. She wanted to break down and weep, but her body felt completely numb. Sigurd had thought he was doing the right thing, but she knew it was absolutely the last thing she wanted. She wanted to find a way to help him. 'I believe I have been given a life sentence.'

'It is good riddance then.'

Liddy placed a hand on her stomach. She had to hope that she would have a child to remember him by. She no longer feared having a child, but desperately wanted one to keep a piece of Sigurd with her. 'He was…no…is the best man I ever knew.'

'Then why did you let him go?' Malcolm asked. 'Why did you allow him to ride away?'

'Because he wanted it that way.' Liddy paused. Sigurd couldn't search for the missing tribute, but she could. Was that what he meant earlier when he spoke of the Northmen from Dubh Linn being familiar with this part of the coast? 'Exactly what did happen to you when you were taken prisoner?'

'I went to sell the winter cabbages.' Malcolm rubbed his head so his hair stood straight up. 'At the market I happened to see Lord Thorbin and told him that they were from that field he had been inspecting so closely. He and that woman with the red-gold shawl. She was a beauty, Liddy. All dark hair and curves. Even from a distance, I could see that. He went mad and accused me of all sorts of things.'

Liddy forgot how to breathe. Shona, the missing mistress. It had to be. Liddy tried to contain her nervous excitement. 'You never mentioned seeing a woman with a red-gold shawl.'

'I didn't think it important.' Malcolm reddened. 'They went into the trees.'

'Did you see the woman leave with him?'

'It was a moonlit night, Liddy. She could have done. I didn't stick around.' Malcolm ran his hands through his hair. 'Maybe...I am not sure. When I went back the next day, the earth had been disturbed. I figured they were doing some sort of ritual.'

'Can you show me?'

He looked at her strangely. 'You know the field, Liddy. It is the one which overlooks this bay. Strictly speaking I suppose it is your dower lands, but I didn't see any point in having it lay fallow.'

'But you saw Thorbin there,' she persisted. 'And that day he thought you were trying to blackmail him. It is why he put you in prison. You had not done anything wrong, but you could speak about what you saw.'

'What are you saying? What did I see?' Malcolm asked. 'Have you lost your wits, Liddy?'

'Malcolm, on the pain of death, you do what I say.' Liddy rocked back on her heels, all tiredness vanishing. 'You owe me your life and I am calling that debt in.'

She had this one chance to make things right. She fingered her mark—she could do it. If she could find the gold, she could make things right. She could tip the balance in Sigurd's favour, but she didn't have much time and she didn't really have a clue of where to start except a hunch.

Malcolm gave a brief nod. 'Anything for you, Liddy. You risked your life for me. I can do this thing in return.'

Sigurd rode into the fort with a heavy heart. He had done what was for the best, leaving Liddy behind and not putting up a fight for her. Aedan would look after her.

Until this mess with Beyla was sorted, he had no right to offer her anything. He certainly could not do what his father had done.

He should have known that Beyla would not have come meekly. She was one of the best *tafl* players he had ever seen, always thinking several steps ahead.

'Ah, Sigurd, at last you arrive.' The blonde

woman, waiting at the gates dressed in fine robes, inclined her head. 'I take it you received the message.'

'You want blood money for your husband's death. You are not entitled to anything.'

Her face became wreathed in deceptive innocence. 'I understand from Lord Ketil that you were supposed to arrest my husband. The charge against him had not been proved. Thorbin always paid his share on time. He knew the consequences. There has been a dreadful mistake. Ketil is here to see that justice is done.'

'Your husband died in a legitimate challenge for the leadership,' Sigurd retorted. 'No blood money needs to be paid in those circumstances. I know the law as well as you.'

Beyla put her nose in the air. 'We shall see about that. Lord Ketil may have a different conclusion once he knows the full facts. You had my husband in chains.'

Sigurd put his hands on his head. 'I am happy to have the case tried in due course, but I will be exonerated.'

An elderly man came and stood beside Beyla. With the easy familiarity that Beyla excelled in, she put her arm through his. Ketil patted her hand.

'Ah, Sigurd Sigmundson, you deign to arrive.' His voice appeared chipped from stone.

Sigurd bowed low. 'Jaarl Ketil, I regret that I was not here when you arrived but there was a little difficulty with Ivar the Boneless's men. They had taken liberties with this island. They will not do so again. I believe your envoy might have stumbled across the evidence and that was why he was murdered.'

'He lies,' Beyla said. 'The only reason that—'

Ketil waved a hand, silencing her. 'And the outcome?'

Sigurd threw the Northman's sword down at Ketil's feet. 'A victory, of course. One long-boat was burnt, one escaped, but one I claimed as bounty in your name.'

Ketil nodded and moved away from Beyla. 'And did any survive?'

'A few. Arrangements have been made for their transport here so they can be questioned.'

'No more than I would expect. Good work.'

Sigurd looked at Beyla. Two could play at this game. 'I have reason to suspect that that woman's late husband had been conspiring with Ivar. There are islanders who complain that their fishing grounds have been repeatedly violated.'

'These Gaels always find a reason to complain,' Beyla said quickly. 'My lord, for the love you bore my father, I ask that this man's claims be dismissed. Has anyone found the missing tribute? It is possible that these ruffians from Ivar the Boneless stole it. It is entirely possible that my husband was innocent.'

'We examine the charges in the morning.' Ketil opened his arms. 'For now we feast and celebrate the victory over Ivar. You do keep a good hall, Sigurd. Where is this slave, the one who enabled you to fight Thorbin? Hring has had a few words to say about her.'

'Alas, Eilidith is no longer with me.'

'She escaped? How careless of you,' Beyla drawled.

'She returned to her family,' Sigurd said between gritted teeth.

Ketil brushed an imaginary speck of his cloak. 'Pity, I could have used someone like that to run my household. I understand she is worth the largest estate's tribute.'

'You will have your share paid at the usual time,' Sigurd said. 'You know my wealth is more than equal to it.'

'I do hope so.' Ketil turned on his heel and strode off towards the hall.

Beyla made a move to join him, but Sigurd caught her arm and held her back. 'I have no idea what you are playing at,' he bit out, 'but you won't win. Drop it now and you may yet retain something for your son. Push me and you will have nothing. Your husband was a traitor and died a traitor's death.'

Beyla jerked her arm from him. Her eyes flashed cold fire. He wondered that he had ever thought her fascinating. Unlike Liddy, there was something reptilian and cold about her. 'I am not playing at anything. You should never have killed my husband in cold blood. But perhaps you thought you and I could be together again as we once were.' She tapped her finger against her mouth. 'Yes, that is why you sent your man to me. I see it now and you wish to claim my son as yours. Thorbin confessed his fear to you. A marriage will give us all that we dreamed of long ago...when we made my son.'

'I have no plans to marry you,' Sigurd stated between gritted teeth, struggling to control his temper. He had to hope that Beyla had some feeling for her son and would see the sense of not pursuing her claim of blood money. 'What we shared ended a long time ago and it ended badly. It suited you to proclaim Thorbin as your son's father. That is how it will remain. I don't want you to be here on a false assumption.'

Her lips became a thin white line. 'Then I hope you have lots of gold as I intend to take it.'

'I owe you no blood price.'

'Thorbin was a great warrior. The rumours

against him were all slander and lies. If he had been given the chance, he would have disproved them. We shall never know because someone killed him before he had a chance, against direct orders, I understand.' She jerked her head towards the hall. 'Enjoy the feast, Sigurd. It will be the last one you have.'

Sigurd clung on to his temper, just. He refused to give her the satisfaction. 'We both know what Thorbin was like. He answered a challenge and paid the price.'

'I will not have my son left destitute.' Her face falsely softened. 'Sigmund could be our son, Sigurd.'

'I understood he was Thorbin's acknowledged heir.'

Beyla gave a tiny shrug. 'We never had other children and Thorbin had no other children. I like to think of him as yours. I do have regrets, Sigurd, lots of them.'

Beyla clapped her hands and a youth of about seven came out. Sigurd's heart sank. Beyla was right. The boy did look like he had when he was that age, but that proved nothing. Thorbin and he had shared a father.

'He is a fine young man, I'm sure.'

'Now do you understand whom I fight for? Whom you seek to take everything away from?'

'You will not be happy.'

'Have I ever been happy?' Beyla answered with a sad smile. 'I am giving you the choice, Sigurd. You find the missing gold and demonstrate that my husband was the villain you claim, or we marry and you rule this place. Ketil will understand my reasoning. He knows of our past. You can have everything you ever wished for.'

Sigurd stared over Beyla's shoulder. Everything he wished for? How empty his life would be if he chose the so-called glittering future Beyla dangled in front of him. What he truly wished for had a pair of storm-tossed eyes and a butterfly on her chin. She had taught him that life was more than riches or honour, that living was about love and kindness. 'And if I choose neither option?'

Her face hardened into a mask of rage. 'I will destroy you. I did it once. I can do it again.'

Sigurd knew then who had been responsible for the final betrayal. It had not been Thorbin, but Beyla. 'Who left the food and arrows at the place where we used to meet? The truth.'

Her eyes widened. 'Thorbin. He couldn't bring himself to kill his brother. I wasn't brave enough to go against his mother, so I asked him to do it. You needed to be gone. That woman wanted you destroyed. But all of that is in the past, Sigurd.

You have no idea what having a wife like me can achieve.'

He stood very straight and made the perfect bow. 'Then, my lady, it is my duty to inform you that I would rather marry a viper than a woman like you.'

'If that is the way you want it.' Her eyes glittered. 'It will be war, then.'

'It is. To the victor, the spoils.'

Chapter Fifteen

'Awk, Liddy, I've no idea where to start. You are searching for something which isn't there. Will you nay give it up?'

Liddy surveyed the area just below the field they had used for cabbages last spring. There had to be a reason why Thorbin had travelled here. The group of oaks to the right of the field did look like the sacred grove. 'It will be here. Where is it that you saw the disturbed dirt?'

'The only thing you will discover is a sore back,' Malcolm muttered, leaning on the spade he had retrieved.

'But this is where you saw Thorbin and the woman. Thorbin departed and the woman didn't. He will have killed her so that her spirit will guard his treasure.'

'Yes, it was a full moon, the one before Easter. I was a bit late because I had been…well…there is no need for you to know what I had been doing over at the ale house.'

'I have a healthy imagination, Malcolm.'

Malcolm wrinkled his nose. 'Just so you don't go proclaiming to all and sundry.'

Liddy laughed. It felt good to have her brother back. 'Silent as the grave, me.'

Malcolm frowned. 'That is not in the least bit funny. If he killed someone here, her ghost will walk this place.'

'I need to know what you remember from that ale-fuddled night. Where precisely was that woman?'

'It was dark. I saw nothing beyond them going into this grove.' Malcolm threw down the spade in disgust. 'Why is this important? What one Northman did with his woman is nought to do with us.'

'Because it might save Sigurd.' Liddy regarded the great oak. 'I love him. I feel alive when I am with him. Your memories of that night may provide a way to save him. Why did you look at this field in the first place?'

Malcolm screwed up his eyes. 'A shriek like an owl caused me to look over and I saw the pair. He was dragging her. She fought against him, but I recognised him and decided to stay away. I'd seen him in the area several times. I also didn't stick around to see where they went. The next morning, I was hunting and went into the oak grove. The earth was disturbed. That is all I know.'

Grim determination filled Liddy. She could clearly see the sacred grove with its bodies. The configuration of oaks was nearly similar. 'He killed that woman to protect something and then buried it. We try digging in the middle of that grove.'

Malcolm screwed up his face. 'Are you sure? It is not where I saw the disturbed dirt. That was more under the largest oak. Or at least I think it was. My head was a bit fuzzy, you know.'

'I know precisely how hazy your memory can be and if I was going to bury something, I'd start in the middle.'

'What do you want me to do?'

'Dig, brother dear, dig.'

Sigurd sat in his room with Coll's head on his knee. Returning Coll at least gave him an excuse to contact Liddy and see if she would forgive him for sending her away. He should be able to clear his name, provided that Ketil was prepared to listen, rather than having his mind poisoned by Beyla's lies. He might lose the jaarldom, but they could have a good life together.

Coll gave him a hard look.

'I know, boy, I miss her as well and I should never have allowed her to go.'

Hring entered without bothering to knock. Coll gave a low growl, but didn't move from Sigurd's side.

'I thought you should know there is a guard outside your chamber.'

'I am hardly likely to flee.' Sigurd scratched Coll behind the ears. 'Is there something you wanted to say to me, Hring?'

'I wanted to apologise. I thought you exaggerated about Lady Beyla. Then I witnessed her performance today. I had understood she hated Thorbin.' Hring scratched his head. 'But she saved her real bile for you.'

'No, she only hates the idea of being poor and without power.' Sigurd concentrated on Coll, who licked his hand. 'Once, long ago, I thought she was different, but power consumes her.'

'That woman has wrapped Ketil around her little finger. I believe she has him convinced that Thorbin had nothing to do with the envoy's disappearance and only sent him back after he was discovered murdered by Ivar the Boneless's henchmen.'

'If so, where was the tribute?'

'You haven't found any gold. Perhaps her tale

about the ship being attacked by Ivar the Bone-less is the truth.'

'I doubt it.'

'Without some sort of proof, Sigurd, she will see you destroyed.' Hring shook his head.

'Ketil might listen. He can inspect the captured longboat. That bounty will enrich his coffers.'

'I will have to speak bluntly. You need a wealthy wife and unfortunately that is not your Eilidith.' Hring tugged at his collar. 'You could marry my daughter, Ragnhild. She needs a man to take her in hand. She has been allowed to run wild for far too long. And her dowry would be suffi-cient to provide the missing tribute. I am willing to stand proxy.'

Sigurd stilled. Hring had proved to be a true friend, but his offer held no appeal. Once he might have taken it, but not now, not when he had tasted what true love could be like.

'You are offering me your daughter—why?'

'Because I have seen the measure of you as a man. I would be proud to call you a son.'

Coll gave a warning growl and Hring took two steps backwards.

'The only woman I want for my wife is Liddy,' Sigurd declared. 'I regret I must decline your offer. Allow me to do this my way.'

'You are putting love above your career and your life? I never thought I'd see the day.'

'I will prevail because I am innocent.'

'My back aches something fierce,' Malcolm complained, standing up from the hole he'd been digging under the oak tree.

It was the fourth sample hole they had dug. Liddy had dug the first three before handing Malcolm the shovel and telling him to dig where he actually thought he saw the disturbed dirt.

'Just dig. It has to be here. I can feel it in my bones.' Liddy hugged her aching arms about her waist. It had to be here. Malcolm's vague memory had to be more than ale-fuelled ramblings. Thorbin putting him in prison proved it.

'Let me have a rest.'

'You rest after we have exhausted all possibilities. Do you think it will go any easier for this island and our family if Sigurd isn't here?'

Malcolm lent on his shovel. 'You really care about him.'

Liddy put her nose in the air. 'My feelings for Sigurd matter for nothing in this. It is about what is best for everyone. My duty, as our father would call it.'

'Forgive me, Liddy, but I'd rather you were doing this because you cared about Sigurd.'

'Why?'

'Because anyone can see he makes you happy. It would mean you were putting yourself first for once.'

'He made me happy, but it is over now. He left me with Aedan.'

'You enjoy lying to yourself. Anyone with half an eye can see you are well matched. It is why Fa sold you to him in the first place.'

'What? Fa sold me because…' Liddy stared at him.

'Because he thought you had roses in your cheeks and a smile on your lips. The old sparkle had returned to your eye. He confessed as much to me when I returned from trying to buy you with Aedan's gold.'

'He tried to matchmake by selling me?' Liddy put her hands on her hips. Right now she wasn't sure if she wanted to murder her father or kiss him. His selling of her had enabled her to rediscover life. 'It is not what I would call fatherly devotion.'

'All I know is that you shouldn't let it go lightly. Your dog likes him.'

A great longing swept through Liddy. More than anything, she wanted to see if Sigurd would listen to her declaration of love. She had let him go without confessing her feelings for him. If she didn't find the treasure, she'd go to him. She'd find a way of making him understand that she cared about him. 'Preaching to me will not find the treasure. Dig.'

Malcolm leant on the shovel. 'I am only saying you need to consider things from other people's perspectives.'

'You can talk and dig at the same time.'

Malcolm lifted a few more shovels of dirt. 'Do you even know what you are looking for?'

'I have a fair idea.' Liddy peered in the hole. It was the same as the other ones. Malcolm was right—her quest was hopeless. She was going to have to go empty-handed where she should have gone in the first place. She could at least give an account of why Sigurd had fought Thorbin. 'What's that muddy thing? It isn't a stone or another root.'

'What's what?' Malcolm wrinkled his nose. 'All I know is that suddenly it doesn't smell great around here.'

'It is a bit of cloth. Get out of the hole, Malcolm, and let me see better.'

Malcolm gagged. 'There is a body attached to that cloth. But there is something else beneath it.'

Liddy peered into the hole. A shimmer of gold was mixed in with a deep red pattern. Shona's shawl. She had been sacrificed.

'Dig the body out.'

'Eilidith.'

'We don't have much time. Just try not to breathe. And we can arrange for the body to be properly buried. If it is who I think it is, she was unlawfully killed. I will take the shawl as there will be people who recognise it. Ketil needs to see the proof.'

She grabbed a shovel and started to help. Working steadily, they were able to move the body fairly quickly. Liddy whispered several prayers as she did so.

Under the strangled woman lay a small iron-bound chest and a single gold piece.

'What are we going to do with it?'

'I am taking the shawl and the chest to Sigurd.'

'To the finder, the gold!' Malcolm's eyes gleamed as he grabbed the piece of gold. 'Do you think there is more? We could open it here and perhaps a little bit could go…astray.'

'And give Beyla the opportunity to say that we stole some of her inheritance? Not likely. This island has already lost enough. You think that Ketil Flatnose will just turn around and walk away? If he believes this Beyla, then we will all suffer.'

Malcolm sighed. 'I suppose you are right.'

'I know I am right. Come on.' All tiredness vanished. Then she halted. 'We will never get there in time if we travel over land. It will have to be by sea.'

'Do you want me to take it? My boat is moored quite near here.' Malcolm stood a little straighter. 'I won't let you down, Sister.'

'I'm the better sailor. Always have been. I will pilot the boat.' Liddy started to lift the heavy trunk while Malcolm stared at her open-mouthed. 'Now what?'

'But I thought you were cursed…and forbidden from going to sea.'

'That was one of Brandon's lies. We are going by sea and we are going to prevail. Sigurd is worth it.'

Sigurd stood in the great hall. Ketil and his bodyguard were on the raised dais. Beyla stood near Ketil, dressed in luxurious furs and with a queer triumphant smile on her face. She was striking in a cold reptilian way. He had no doubt that she thought she had won and vast riches would come her way. The man he'd been before might have been tempted, but he knew the value of a good woman and Beyla was only base metal.

'How do you answer to the charges?'

'Not guilty,' Sigurd replied. 'I challenged Thorbin in good faith and he lost his life. What I did, I did out in the open.'

'There are plenty who will swear that he had surrendered before you killed him,' Ketil said.

'A false surrender designed to lull me into dropping my sword. I had reason to believe he would attempt to prolong the fight.'

Ketil stroked his jaw. 'And yet you knew I wanted him to face charges of disloyalty. I wanted him alive.'

'Those charges were never proved,' Beyla said before Ketil had finished. 'My husband will be proved to be innocent.'

Ketil lowered his brow. 'Be silent, woman! Sometimes you jabber worse than a hungry seagull.'

Sigurd bowed his head to hide his smile. Obviously Ketil was not as enthralled with Beyla as she thought. The knowledge gave him hope. Her arrogance would prove her undoing. 'I acted with honour, my lord. I acted to prevent further harm to a woman whose only crime was that she believed in your justice.'

'Thorbin had threatened her? This woman?'

'He said that he would treat her the way he had treated my mother. I lost my temper as he knew I would do. I believe Thorbin wanted to die quickly by my hand, rather than face your punishment for the crimes he had committed.'

'He lies!' Beyla screamed.

'Alas for Lady Beyla—she was in the North and not on Islay at that time,' Sigurd said smoothly.

'I must agree with Sigurd Sigmundson,' Ketil proclaimed. 'Stop giving us your ill-considered opinions, Beyla Olafdottar.'

'Have you discovered where Thorbin hid the missing tribute?'

Sigurd bowed his head. 'I regret, no.'

'That is because there isn't any,' Beyla snapped. She curtsyed. 'As I told you, Lord Ketil, the problem lies elsewhere. Someone has blackened his name. Probably the islanders. There was one, Brandon mac Connall, the so-called king of the Loairn and laird of Kintra, who had repeatedly defied you and my husband. He and his men will be responsible for this.'

'It is just as well Lady Beyla is not a warrior,' Sigurd said. 'Brandon mac Connall perished in Ireland over a year ago, fighting the Dubh Linn Northmen. His brother, Aedan, recently returned from there. He helped me in my recent fight. He agreed the bulk of the spoils belonged to you.'

Ketil stroke his chin. 'A good warrior, Aedan mac Connall.'

Beyla pursed her lips as if she had eaten a rotten plum.

'Do you have enough to pay this year's tribute as well as the missing gold?' Ketil asked.

'There will be after the harvest,' Sigurd said.

'Aye, he will do it,' Hring said, giving him a significant look.

'Where have I heard that before?' Beyla commented, rolling her eyes. 'I wish you as much luck as my husband had. These islanders—'

'You must let me in!' Sigurd heard Liddy's voice outside. His heart gave a leap.

'There is a Gaelic female who demands entrance, my lord. She says that she has something of great importance, something with bearing on the case.'

'Your former slave? How touching.'

'Be quiet, woman!' Ketil thundered. 'Allow the woman in.'

Liddy came in, carrying a wrapped bundle. Behind her, her brother staggered with an iron-bound chest. At her nod, they placed both at Ketil's feet.

'And you are?' Ketil Flatnose raised a brow. 'Your intervention is most unusual.'

'Lady Eilidith, formerly of Cennell Fergusa. My father, Gilbreath mac Fergusa, swore his oath personally to you, Lord Ketil. You gave him a ring as a token of your friendship.'

'Ah, yes, I remember. A good man, your father.'

'What are you doing here, Liddy? You were supposed to be somewhere safe,' Sigurd asked in a furious undertone.

Liddy tried to ignore Sigurd's glower and concentrated on the Northman lord who was sitting, resplendent, on the throne. She had to do this properly. She had to bargain for Sigurd's life. 'We believe that this is Thorbin Sigmundson's treasure. My brother and I discovered the chest along with the woman who was murdered so that her spirit would guard it.'

'Shall we see what is in the chest? I do not recognise it as my lord Thorbin's,' the woman who stood next to Ketil said in a strident tone. From her bearing, Liddy guessed that this was the infamous Beyla. And she was as beautiful as the rumours had implied.

'We kept the chest's lock intact. I would not wish for any to say that anything was missing.' Silently Liddy prayed that she was right and that the chest did contain gold. The single gold piece Malcolm carried would only give credence to Beyla's lies.

Ketil motioned to one of his guards who struck off the lock with a resounding clang. When the lid was opened, the room shimmered in a golden glint. The entire chest was packed full of gold.

'But do we know who put it there?' Lady Beyla asked in an arched tone.

'We can't know for certain, but I have my suspicions.'

She nodded to Malcolm, who reached into the bag and withdrew the red-gold shawl. 'I believe this belonged to Thorbin's late mistress, Shona. She disappeared about the same time. We found a badly decomposed body of a woman with this wrapped around it.'

The entire room erupted in pandemonium. Several people called out that it was indeed Shona's shawl.

Ketil banged his fist down. 'Quiet! It would appear that this woman was unlawfully killed.'

Beyla's cheeks flushed. 'Of course I wasn't here, but no one can prove it was my husband who murdered her or buried that treasure chest.'

'No, you weren't there. You don't know what happened. Just as you did not know what actually happened when your husband met his end.'

'I know what happened that day,' Liddy said in a firm voice. 'Sigurd acted as my champion and when Thorbin threatened me, he killed him.'

'It seems to me that you have borne false witness, Lady Beyla,' Ketil said.

The woman blanched. 'I only acted how I saw fit. There were others who told me such things. I thought them to be true.'

Ketil inclined his head. 'I believe the life debt I owed your father is now settled. There will be no blood price for your husband as he was lawfully killed.'

Beyla gulped. 'Yes, my lord.'

'You may take your son and retire to your estate. Unless Sigurd wishes to pursue any claim against you.'

Sigurd shook his head. 'The lady has publicly acknowledged her mistake. It is enough, but the missing tribute must still be paid.'

'You have the gold in the chest,' Beyla spat.

'As Lady Beyla said, we do not know who put it there. Thorbin and his estate still owe Ketil the tribute.'

Ketil gave Sigurd an impressed look. 'You are wise beyond your years, Sigurd the Bold. It is an ideal solution. You may pay the missing tribute, Lady Beyla, and that will end the matter.'

Beyla gave a cold smile. 'Very well, on closer examination, I recognise that chest as belonging to my husband. The runes scratched into the iron are his. The amount should be taken from that.'

'Wait!' Sigurd shouted. 'The chest was buried and lost. It now has been found.'

Liddy stared at him in astonishment.

'To the finder,' Ketil answered. 'Of course. Forgive me, Lady Beyla, that chest no longer belongs to your husband. It belongs to the person who found it. Lady Beyla, you will have to find the missing gold from elsewhere.'

Beyla's face contorted with fury, but she appeared to have learnt her lesson and kept silent.

Ketil looked between Malcolm and Liddy. 'Who found it?'

'I did,' Liddy answered, perplexed. 'It was buried on my dower lands. After Malcolm told me the story of why he'd been arrested, I knew where to search for the gold.'

'Liddy did,' Malcolm confirmed a heartbeat too late. 'And she insisted we travel by boat to make it in time. I still say that she sails too close to the wind.'

'How say you, Sigurd Sigmundson?' Ketil asked.

'Then I say this horde belongs to Eilidith, formerly of Cennell Fergusa,' Sigurd declared. 'With a quarter belonging to her brother who helped. Of course they should pay a token of thanks to Ketil. Thorbin's estate should bear the cost of the missing tribute as it has not been proved how the tribute went missing and that should be paid as soon as possible.'

'Such is the wisdom I expect of my jaarls,' Ketil said. 'It is a fair solution. I approve.'

'My son will be left with nothing but a sword,' Beyla protested.

'Did I give you leave to speak?' Ketil thundered.

'Eilidith, you are one of the bravest women I have encountered. If all beautiful women displayed as much bravery as you do, the world would be a much better place. Sigurd Sigmundson, would that I were a decade younger, I would steal this woman from under your nose.'

'Are the charges against Sigurd Sigmundson dropped?' Liddy asked, meeting Ketil's gaze directly. Her mind reeled. She was entitled to most of the gold. In a blink of an eye she'd become a wealthy woman. And she could accept Ketil's compliment graciously, particularly as Lady Beyla appeared distinctly put out.

'Yes, and he is confirmed as the jaarl of these lands. I can't think of anyone better to rule for the wisdom he has shown today.' Ketil turned towards Sigurd. 'Will you rule these lands or do you wish to seek your fortune elsewhere?'

Sigurd bowed his head. 'I will abide by your wishes.'

'Good, it is about time someone did. I trust this year's tribute will arrive on time.'

Sigurd bowed low. 'I ask one further thing— allow me to be foster father to Thorbin's son. I promise to bring him up as an honourable warrior.'

'Why…why would you do that?' Beyla asked.

'Because—' Sigurd looked directly at Liddy rather than looking at Beyla '—he is my kin and

I will not leave my kin to starve or to suffer because of the actions his father took. Neither will I see him used as a counter in any game you choose to play, Lady Beyla.'

Ketil raised a brow. 'A truly generous offer. I will see that Lady Beyla accepts it.'

'I have always wanted what is best for my son,' Beyla said. 'I have no choice but to accept the offer.'

Saying that, Ketil went out of the hall with Beyla bleating at his heels about the unfairness of it all. The hall rapidly emptied after that until only Malcolm, Hring, Sigurd and Liddy were left.

'Liddy?' Malcolm cried. 'Shall we go? Fa isn't going to believe this. You are free with enough gold—'

'Come on, lad,' Hring said, pointedly taking Malcolm's arm and leading him away. 'We are not wanted here.'

An awkward silence descended once they had gone. Liddy wanted to run to Sigurd and confess her feelings, but the words stuck in her throat. All she could do was stare at him and think how close she had come to losing him.

'Did Malcolm speak the truth—you voluntarily went in a boat?'

'Not only in a boat, but I piloted it as Malcolm

tends to take the wrong tack,' Liddy confirmed, pressing her hands together.

He took a step closer. 'Why, Liddy?'

'Because I wanted to ensure justice was done. Because sometimes people are more important than fear.' She swallowed hard and hoped he'd understand. 'My share of the gold, it is yours. We made a deal.'

He stopped and tilted his head to one side. 'You came because of justice and duty? Because of the bargain we made? I have no need of your gold. Keep it.'

'I don't understand,' Liddy said to the floor. Her heart knocked against her chest. 'We made a bargain.'

Sigurd's face hardened. 'You are already free, Liddy. There is no need to buy your freedom. That gold only complicates things. It is yours to do what you will with.'

All the pretty speeches she had practised on the boat vanished from her mind. Had she totally mistaken everything? Had he truly been saying goodbye?

'I thought it was what you wanted.' She gestured about her. 'All this. I found the gold to give you your heart's desire.'

He crossed the room and gathered her hands within his. 'My heart's desire is something else.

My heart's desire cannot be bought with gold or lulled with empty promises. My heart's desire is true and honest and worth a thousand kingdoms. Her safety means more to me than life itself.'

'Your heart's desire is a person?' she breathed.

He lifted her chin so she looked directly into his eyes. 'Yes, and until I met you, I thought my heart was locked up tight for fear of losing it. Then you and that dog came into my life and I discovered that my heart had escaped and only wanted one thing—you. I love you, Eilidith. I'd offer you my heart, but you already hold it. You are all I want in the world and no amount of gold or riches would ever change that. I need you in my life. I should have told you this before I forced you to go with Aedan, but I wanted to keep you safe. I wanted to make sure I had something to offer you.'

Liddy looped her arms about Sigurd. 'And you are all I want. I don't care about the riches or the jaarldom, I care about you and being with you. You are the man I love.'

'Truly? You love me? The man who enslaved you?'

'The man who set me free.' Liddy stroked his cheek with her hand. 'I had thought my heart died with my children and I lived in a prison of my own making, a hell hole from which I was unwilling to escape, but you brought me back to life. You showed me that life had so much more to offer. Now I know hearts are not small things, but large with a capacity to grow. I love you, Sigurd, and I want to stay with you freely.'

'Good, then you will marry me as soon as possible. My mother was right—true love is worth waiting for and I have found mine.'

There was a sharp bark and Coll rushed into the room. He put his paws on both of them and nudged them together.

Liddy laughed. 'Coll thinks marriage to you is an excellent idea.'

'And you always trust Coll.'

'No, I trust my heart.'

He bent his head and captured her lips. And after that for a long while there was no need to say anything.

* * * * *

If you enjoyed this story,
you won't want to miss these
other great reads from Michelle Styles

PAYING THE VIKING'S PRICE
RETURN OF THE VIKING WARRIOR
SAVED BY THE VIKING WARRIOR
TAMING HIS VIKING WOMAN
SUMMER OF THE VIKING

Author's Historical Note

What do we know about the Vikings in Islay? Surprisingly little. Although many places on Islay in the Western Isles have Viking names, we don't know much about how the islands were conquered. We do know that they were part of the Viking empire which was ruled from the Isle of Man. Some archaeological evidence, including high-born Viking graves, has been found on Islay.

Ketil Flatnose, who appears in the opening part of the Laxdalea saga, is supposed to have conquered them, but as with most things from that shadowy era, there are discrepancies in timing. Some of the records refer to a Ketil the White who may or may not be the same Ketil.

The Laxdalea saga also references the experience of the Irish women taken as slaves and what could happen to their children. Eventually the island hopping would lead the Vikings to Iceland.

The Western Isles as well as Ireland proved a rich source of slaves.

We do know that there was rapidly a mixing of the two cultures. The word *galloway* refers to half-Gallic, half-Norse, and is a corruption of Gall-Gaedhil. And the great Scottish hero Somerled was actually half-Norse, supposedly with a Gallic father. His name comes from the Norse for summer warrior. As with most of the other conquerors of the island, the Vikings most likely did not leave, but became assimilated into the culture.

It is best to think of this empire as one dominated by the sea. People and goods travelled by the sea, rather than overland. Islay with its position between mainland Britain and Ireland was ideally placed to profit.

The question of whether Vikings practised human sacrifice is open for debate. There are several accounts from foreign observers that it happened, but how widespread it was is one of those great unknowns.

If you are interested in this time period, here are some non-fiction books I found useful when I was writing this book:

Ferguson, Robert, *The Hammer and the Cross A New History of the Vikings* (2010 Penguin Books, London)

Jesch, Judith, *Women in the Viking Age* (1991 The Boydell Press, Woodbridge, Suffolk)

Magnusson, Magnus KBE, *The Vikings* (2003 The History Press, Stroud, Gloucestershire)

Marsden, John, *Somerled and the Emergence of Gaelic Scotland* (2000 Tuckwell Press Ltd, Edinburgh)

Oliver, Neil, *Vikings a History* (2012 Weidenfeld & Nicolson)

Parker, Philip, *The Northmen's Fury: A History of the Viking World* (2014 Jonathan Cape, London)

Roesdahl, Else, *The Vikings*, Revised edition translated by Susan Margeson and Kirsten Williams (1998 Penguin Books, London)

Williams, Gareth, ed. *Vikings: Life and Legend* (2014 British Museum Press, London)

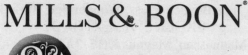

MILLS & BOON®

EXCLUSIVE EXTRACT

When Lady Sara Herriard's husband dies,
she decides it's time for her to live as she pleases.
She won't change for anyone—and certainly
not the infuriating Marquess of Cannock!

Read on for a sneak preview of
SURRENDER TO THE MARQUESS

The hoofbeats behind her were getting closer, much
closer. She risked a backwards glance and realised that
the only danger to her just at that moment was the
Marquess himself. He looked as though he wanted to
throttle her.

Sara twisted back round, wishing she was riding
astride and not wearing this so-fashionable habit with
its trailing skirts and broadcloth that slid on the saddle.
As she thought about sliding a buzzard flapped up out
of the long grass, a rabbit in its talons. The mare jinked,
stiff-legged, swerved back and Sara lost her stirrup, lost
her balance and went over Twilight's shoulder down to
meet the turf with a thud.

Instinctively she rolled, tucking herself up into a ball
as her great-uncle the Rajah's *syce* had taught her. The
clifftop was almost as hard as the sun-baked Indian plain,
she thought as she tumbled, arms around her head, braced
for the hooves of Lucian's horse.

There was the sound of furious, inventive, swearing,

then she came to a stop, untrampled, and lifted her head warily in time to see Lucian dismount from a rearing horse in a muscular, controlled slide.

'Sara!'

He was by her side and she closed her eyes strategically to postpone his anger and in sheer self-preservation. He had looked like a god just then and she could put no reliance on her own self-control. 'Mmm?' she managed.

'Are you hurt?'

Yes, was the honest answer. Her left shoulder hurt, her right wrist stung and her pride as a horsewoman was severely dented. 'No,' she said and opened her eyes.

'Excellent,' Lucian growled. 'Because I fully intend wringing your neck.'

'Why?' Indignant, Sara moved too quickly, found several other things that hurt and was hauled into an upright sitting position. 'Ow! What are you doing?'

'Checking.' His hands worked along her collarbone, wriggled her fingers and prodded her ribs. 'Move your feet. Let me see your eyes, your ears. What day of the week is it?'

'Thursday.'

'Correct.' Then he kissed her.

Don't miss
SURRENDER TO THE MARQUESS
by Louise Allen

Available March 2017
www.millsandboon.co.uk

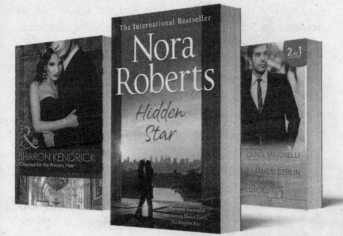

Join Britain's BIGGEST Romance Book Club

- **EXCLUSIVE offers every month**
- **FREE delivery dire to your door**
- **NEVER MISS a titl**
- **EARN Bonus Bool points**

Call Customer Services
0844 844 1358*

or visit
millsandboon.co.uk/subscriptio

BKCB3